FAR OUT

13 SCIENCE FICTION STORIES

BY

Damon Knight

SIMON AND SCHUSTER • NEW YORK

Acknowledgments

"Time Enough," published in Amazing Science Fiction Stories, copyright 1960 by Ziff-Davis Publishing Co.

"Thing of Beauty," published in Galaxy Magazine, copyright 1958 by Galaxy Publishing Corp.

"Idiot Stick," published in Star Science Fiction, copyright 1958 by Ballantine Books, Inc.

"Not with a Bang," published in The Magazine of Fantasy & Science Fiction, copyright 1949 by Mercury Press, Inc.

"To Serve Man," published in Galaxy Science Fiction, copyright 1950 by Galaxy Publishing Corp.

"Special Delivery," published in Galaxy Science Fiction, copyright 1953 by Galaxy Publishing Corp.

"You're Another," published in The Magazine of Fantasy & Science Fiction, copyright 1955 by Mercury Press, Inc.

"Babel II," published in Beyond Fantasy Fiction, copyright 1953 by Galaxy Publishing Corp.

"Cabin Boy," published in Galaxy Science Fiction, copyright 1951 by Galaxy Publishing Corp.

"The Last Word," published in Satellite Science Fiction, copyright 1956 by Renown Publications.

"The Enemy," published in Venture Science Fiction, copyright 1957 by Mercury Press, Inc.

"Extempore," published in Infinity Science Fiction, copyright 1956 by Royal Publications, Inc.

"Anachron," published in If Science Fiction, copyright 1953 by Quinn Publishing Co., Inc.

For Helen and the new one,
with love

CONTENTS

INTRODUCTION

This book is not science fiction.

I say this not because it is true,* but because such a statement is to-day's approved method, among publishers and critics, of persuading people to read imaginative fiction.

Time was when science fiction (hereafter to be known, for economy in typesetting, as s.f.) was—or was thought to be—hotly commercial. In the early 1950s every other publisher in New York was installing a line of s.f. books to parallel his mysteries and his westerns; and every cultural magazine was publishing critical articles on "S.F.: Hope or Menace of American Literature?" (That neither the publishers' editors nor the magazines' critics had read s.f. before last Tuesday was irrelevant.)

The Big Boom continued until the accounting offices discovered that it lacked one essential quality of a boom: it wasn't making money. Conclusion: the public doesn't want s.f. (and who said anything about the inevitable outcome of ignorant opportunistic publishing?).

By 1960 s.f., as a category, had all but vanished from American hard-cover publishing. (Paperbacks have been more persistent, and probably account today for more s.f. sales than magazines and hard-cover books together.) Only two major publishers admitted that they were publishing s.f.

But s.f. persists, in general uncategorized publishing, just as it always has since the days of Jules Verne and H. G. Wells. And the secret of its success is that you must never mention what it is.

The most distinguished s.f. novel of 1960—and probably of the past five years—was Walter M. Miller, Jr.'s A Canticle for Leibowitz. It is s.f. by any conceivable critical definition; it was first published in a s.f. magazine; it was enthusiastically acclaimed by s.f. readers. But it was

*It isn't.

subtitled *"a novel,"* and the jacket carried a statement by Pat Frank: *"One of the damnedest books I've ever read! It falls into no genre, certainly not science-fiction."*

The reviewers dutifully followed bellwether Frank; *"not s.f."* was the refrain of their rave reviews; and the book was a hit.

I do not know why it is considered the highest compliment to say that a book is not what the author thought he was writing. Some critics will even flatter a detective story by saying that it is *"not a detective story."* It is all a little like praising Gina Lollobrigida by saying *"clearly not a mammal."*

But I have learned the lesson. I very much want you to read this book, so:

This is not science fiction.

What is science fiction?

Well, I like Judith Merril's definition (in her recent The 5th Annual of the Year's Best S-F): *"trained wonderment—educated and disciplined imagination."*

And the foremost critic in the field has written: *"We live on a minute island of known things. Our undiminished wonder at the mystery that surrounds us is what makes us human. In science fiction we can approach that mystery, not in small, everyday symbols, but in the big ones of space and time."*

That same critic offers as an article of his credo: *"That science fiction is a field of literature worth taking seriously, and that ordinary critical standards can be meaningfully applied to it: e.g., originality, sincerity, style, construction, logic, coherence, sanity, garden-variety grammar."*

The fiction of Damon Knight, as you will shortly observe, meets all of these standards and a few others as well: It has that unpretentious ease and rightness which a reviewer calls, for lack of a more analytical term, readability. Though it deals always with ideas and often with technologies, it is miraculously clear even to the reader who has never before encountered s.f. When it uses tricks or gimmicks, they are inherent in the story; this collection contains two stories (I shall not say which) with dazzling surprise endings—and both stories are even better when you reread them knowing the twist. And there is, in addition, a delightful quality of urbanity which I find hard to pin down; Knight is surely one of the most civilized of s.f. writers.

The one man who might successfully analyze this happy but elusive quality is the critic quoted above, who is Damon Knight. Knight (who *used to be damon knight, but has recently been reincarnated in majuscules) is the only s.f. author—and quite possibly the only author—in history whose collected book reviews appeared in print* long before his collected stories . . . and are almost equally entertaining. He has also been an editor, and a distinguished one; and his critical-editorial-creative selves enjoy an astonishing symbiosis. More than once, when I was editing a magazine, I pondered over a Knight manuscript, trying to figure why a potentially excellent story did not quite come off— only to receive from the author an unprompted revision which answered every question and removed every doubt.*

If you know and like s.f., you are doubtless already in the thick of this volume, rereading old favorites and relishing a few that you've hitherto missed.

If you simply like fiction, go ahead to discover entertainments which, whatever their label, feature intelligence, wit, imagination and wonder.

And when you wish to commend the book to friends, remember: It is not sc**nc* f*ct**n.

ANTHONY BOUCHER

Berkeley, California

**In Search of Wonder*. Chicago: Advent, 1956; paperback, 1960.

TO SERVE MAN

The Kanamit were not very pretty, it's true. They looked something like pigs and something like people, and that is not an attractive combination. Seeing them for the first time shocked you; that was their handicap. When a thing with the countenance of a fiend comes from the stars and offers a gift, you are disinclined to accept.

I don't know what we expected interstellar visitors to look like— those who thought about it at all, that is. Angels, perhaps, or something too alien to be really awful. Maybe that's why we were all so horrified and repelled when they landed in their great ships and we saw what they really were like.

The Kanamit were short and very hairy—thick, bristly brown-gray hair all over their abominably plump bodies. Their noses were snoutlike and their eyes small, and they had thick hands of three fingers each. They wore green leather harness and green shorts, but I think the shorts were a concession to our notions of public decency. The garments were quite modishly cut, with slash pockets and half-belts in the back. The Kanamit had a sense of humor, anyhow.

There were three of them at this session of the U.N., and, Lord, I can't tell you how queer it looked to see them there in the middle of a solemn plenary session—three fat piglike creatures in green harness and shorts, sitting at the long table below the podium, surrounded by the packed arcs of delegates from every nation. They sat correctly upright, politely watching each speaker. Their flat ears drooped over the earphones. Later on, I believe, they learned every human language, but at this time they knew only French and English.

They seemed perfectly at ease—and that, along with their humor, was a thing that tended to make me like them. I was in the minority; I didn't think they were trying to put anything over.

The delegate from Argentina got up and said that his government was interested in the demonstration of a new cheap power source, which the Kanamit had made at the previous session, but that the Argentine government could not commit itself as to its future policy without a much more thorough examination.

It was what all the delegates were saying, but I had to pay particular attention to Señor Valdes, because he tended to sputter and his diction was bad. I got through the translation all right, with only one or two momentary hesitations, and then switched to the Polish-English line to hear how Gregori was doing with Janciewicz. Janciewicz was the cross Gregori had to bear, just as Valdes was mine.

Janciewicz repeated the previous remarks with a few ideological variations, and then the Secretary-General recognized the delegate from France, who introduced Dr. Denis Lévèque, the criminologist, and a great deal of complicated equipment was wheeled in.

Dr. Lévèque remarked that the question in many people's minds had been aptly expressed by the delegate from the U.S.S.R. at the preceding session, when he demanded, "What is the motive of the Kanamit? What is their purpose in offering us these unprecedented gifts, while asking nothing in return?"

The doctor then said, "At the request of several delegates and with the full consent of our guests, the Kanamit, my associates and I have made a series of tests upon the Kanamit with the equipment which you see before you. These tests will now be repeated."

A murmur ran through the chamber. There was a fusillade of flash-bulbs, and one of the TV cameras moved up to focus on the instrument board of the doctor's equipment. At the same time, the huge television screen behind the podium lighted up, and we saw the blank faces of two dials, each with its pointer resting at zero, and a strip of paper tape with a stylus point resting against it.

The doctor's assistants were fastening wires to the temples of one of the Kanamit, wrapping a canvas-covered rubber tube around his forearm, and taping something to the palm of his right hand.

In the screen, we saw the paper tape begin to move while the stylus traced a slow zigzag pattern along it. One of the needles began to jump rhythmically; the other flipped over and stayed there, wavering slightly.

"These are the standard instruments for testing the truth of a statement," said Dr. Lévèque. "Our first object, since the physiology of the Kanamit is unknown to us, was to determine whether or not they react to these tests as human beings do. We will now repeat one of the many experiments which were made in the endeavor to discover this."

He pointed to the first dial. "This instrument registers the subject's heartbeat. This shows the electrical conductivity of the skin in the palm of his hand, a measure of perspiration, which increases under stress. And this—" pointing to the tape-and-stylus device—"shows the pattern and intensity of the electrical waves emanating from his brain. It has been shown, with human subjects, that all these readings vary markedly depending upon whether the subject is speaking the truth."

He picked up two large pieces of cardboard, one red and one black. The red one was a square about three feet on a side; the black was a rectangle three and a half feet long. He addressed himself to the Kanama.

"Which of these is longer than the other?"

"The red," said the Kanama.

Both needles leaped wildly, and so did the line on the unrolling tape.

"I shall repeat the question," said the doctor. "Which of these is longer than the other?"

"The black," said the creature.

This time the instruments continued in their normal rhythm.

"How did you come to this planet?" asked the doctor.

"Walked," replied the Kanama.

Again the instruments responded, and there was a subdued ripple of laughter in the chamber.

"Once more," said the doctor. "How did you come to this planet?"

"In a spaceship," said the Kanama, and the instruments did not jump.

The doctor again faced the delegates. "Many such experiments were made," he said, "and my colleagues and myself are satisfied that the mechanisms are effective. Now—" he turned to the Kanama—"I shall ask our distinguished guest to reply to the question put at the last session by the delegate of the U.S.S.R.—namely, what is the motive of the Kanamit people in offering these great gifts to the people of Earth?"

The Kanama rose. Speaking this time in English, he said, "On my planet there is a saying, 'There are more riddles in a stone than in a philosopher's head.' The motives of intelligent beings, though they may at times appear obscure, are simple things compared to the complex workings of the natural universe. Therefore I hope that the people of Earth will understand, and believe, when I tell you that our mission upon your planet is simply this—to bring to you the peace and plenty which we ourselves enjoy, and which we have in the past brought to other races throughout the galaxy. When your world has no more

4

hunger, no more war, no more needless suffering, that will be our reward."

And the needles had not jumped once.

The delegate from the Ukraine jumped to his feet, asking to be recognized, but the time was up and the Secretary-General closed the session.

I met Gregori as we were leaving the chamber. His face was red with excitement. "Who promoted that circus?" he demanded.

"The tests looked genuine to me," I told him.

"A circus!" he said vehemently. "A second-rate farce! If they were genuine, Peter, why was debate stifled?"

"There'll be time for debate tomorrow, surely."

"Tomorrow the doctor and his instruments will be back in Paris. Plenty of things can happen before tomorrow. In the name of sanity, man, how can anybody trust a thing that looks as if it ate the baby?"

I was a little annoyed. I said, "Are you sure you're not more worried about their politics than their appearance?"

He said, "Bah," and went away.

The next day reports began to come in from government laboratories all over the world where the Kanamit's power source was being tested. They were wildly enthusiastic. I don't understand such things myself, but it seemed that those little metal boxes would give more electrical power than an atomic pile, for next to nothing and nearly forever. And it was said that they were so cheap to manufacture that everybody in the world could have one of his own. In the early afternoon there were reports that seventeen countries had already begun to set up factories to turn them out.

The next day the Kanamit turned up with plans and specimens of a gadget that would increase the fertility of any arable land by 60 to 100 per cent. It speeded the formation of nitrates in the soil, or something. There was nothing in the newscasts any more but stories about the Kanamit. The day after that, they dropped their bombshell.

"You now have potentially unlimited power and increased food supply," said one of them. He pointed with his three-fingered hand to an instrument that stood on the table before him. It was a box on a tripod, with a parabolic reflector on the front of it. "We offer you today a third gift which is at least as important as the first two."

He beckoned to the TV men to roll their cameras into closeup position. Then he picked up a large sheet of cardboard covered with drawings and English lettering. We saw it on the large screen above the podium; it was all clearly legible.

"We are informed that this broadcast is being relayed throughout your world," said the Kanama. "I wish that everyone who has equipment for taking photographs from television screens would use it now."

The Secretary-General leaned forward and asked a question sharply, but the Kanama ignored him.

"This device," he said, "generates a field in which no explosive, of whatever nature, can detonate."

There was an uncomprehending silence.

The Kanama said, "It cannot now be suppressed. If one nation has it, all must have it." When nobody seemed to understand, he explained bluntly, "There will be no more war."

That was the biggest news of the millennium, and it was perfectly true. It turned out that the explosions the Kanama was talking about included gasoline and Diesel explosions. They had simply made it impossible for anybody to mount or equip a modern army.

We could have gone back to bows and arrows, of course, but that wouldn't have satisfied the military. Besides, there wouldn't be any reason to make war. Every nation would soon have everything.

Nobody ever gave another thought to those lie-detector experiments, or asked the Kanamit what their politics were. Gregori was put out; he had nothing to prove his suspicions.

I quit my job with the U.N. a few months later, because I foresaw that it was going to die under me anyhow. U.N. business was booming at the time, but after a year or so there was going to be nothing for it to do. Every nation on Earth was well on the way to being completely self-supporting; they weren't going to need much arbitration.

I accepted a position as translator with the Kanamit Embassy, and it was there that I ran into Gregori again. I was glad to see him, but I couldn't imagine what he was doing there.

"I thought you were on the opposition," I said. "Don't tell me you're convinced the Kanamit are all right."

He looked rather shamefaced. "They're not what they look, anyhow," he said.

It was as much of a concession as he could decently make, and I invited him down to the embassy lounge for a drink. It was an intimate kind of place, and he grew confidential over the second daiquiri.

"They fascinate me," he said. "I hate them instinctively still—that hasn't changed—but I can evaluate it. You were right, obviously; they mean us nothing but good. But do you know—" he leaned across the table—"the question of the Soviet delegate was never answered."

I am afraid I snorted.

"No, really," he said. "They told us what they wanted to do—'to bring to you the peace and plenty which we ourselves enjoy.' But they didn't say *why*."

"Why do missionaries—"

"Missionaries be damned!" he said angrily. "Missionaries have a religious motive. If these creatures have a religion, they haven't once mentioned it. What's more, they didn't send a missionary group; they sent a diplomatic delegation—a group representing the will and policy of their whole people. Now just what have the Kanamit, as a people or a nation, got to gain from our welfare?"

I said, "Cultural—"

"Cultural cabbage soup! No, it's something less obvious than that, something obscure that belongs to their psychology and not to ours. But trust me, Peter, there is no such thing as a completely disinterested altruism. In one way or another, they have something to gain."

"And that's why you're here," I said. "To try to find out what it is."

"Correct. I wanted to get on one of the ten-year exchange groups to their home planet, but I couldn't; the quota was filled a week after they made the announcement. This is the next best thing. I'm studying their language, and you know that language reflects the basic assumptions of the people who use it. I've got a fair command of the spoken lingo already. It's not hard, really, and there are hints in it. Some of the idioms are quite similar to English. I'm sure I'll get the answer eventually."

"More power," I said, and we went back to work.

I saw Gregori frequently from then on, and he kept me posted about his progress. He was highly excited about a month after that first meeting; said he'd got hold of a book of the Kanamit's and was trying to puzzle it out. They wrote in ideographs, worse than Chinese, but he was determined to fathom it if it took him years. He wanted my help.

Well, I was interested in spite of myself, for I knew it would be a long job. We spent some evenings together, working with material from Kanamit bulletin boards and so forth, and with the extremely limited English-Kanamit dictionary they issued to the staff. My conscience bothered me about the stolen book, but gradually I became absorbed by the problem. Languages are my field, after all. I couldn't help being fascinated.

We got the title worked out in a few weeks. It was *How to Serve Man*, evidently a handbook they were giving out to new Kanamit members of the embassy staff. They had new ones in, all the time now, a shipload about once a month; they were opening all kinds of research laboratories, clinics and so on. If there was anybody on Earth besides Gregori who still distrusted those people, he must have been somewhere in the middle of Tibet.

It was astonishing to see the changes that had been wrought in less than a year. There were no more standing armies, no more shortages, no unemployment. When you picked up a newspaper you didn't see H-BOMB or SATELLITE leaping out at you; the news was always good. It was a hard thing to get used to. The Kanamit were working on human biochemistry, and it was known around the embassy that they were nearly ready to announce methods of making our race taller and stronger and healthier—practically a race of supermen—and they had a potential cure for heart disease and cancer.

I didn't see Gregori for a fortnight after we finished working out the title of the book; I was on a long-overdue vacation in Canada. When I got back, I was shocked by the change in his appearance.

"What on earth is wrong, Gregori?" I asked. "You look like the very devil."

"Come down to the lounge."

I went with him, and he gulped a stiff Scotch as if he needed it.

"Come on, man, what's the matter?" I urged.

"The Kanamit have put me on the passenger list for the next exchange ship," he said. "You, too, otherwise I wouldn't be talking to you."

"Well," I said, "but—"

"They're not altruists."

I tried to reason with him. I pointed out they'd made Earth a paradise compared to what it was before. He only shook his head.

Then I said, "Well, what about those lie-detector tests?"

"A farce," he replied, without heat. "I said so at the time, you fool. They told the truth, though, as far as it went."

"And the book?" I demanded, annoyed. "What about that—*How to Serve Man*? That wasn't put there for you to read. They *mean* it. How do you explain that?"

"I've read the first paragraph of that book," he said. "Why do you suppose I haven't slept for a week?"

I said, "Well?" and he smiled a curious, twisted smile.

"It's a cookbook," he said.

IDIOT STICK

The ship came down out of a blue sky to land in a New Jersey meadow. It sank squashily into the turf. It was about a mile long, colored an iridescent blue-green, like the shell of a beetle.

A door opened, and a thin, stick-bodied man came out to sniff the cool air. The sky overhead was full of fluffy cumulus clouds and criss-crossing con-trails. Across the river, the tall buildings of Greater New York were picturesquely gilded by the early sun.

A dun-colored Army copter came into view, circling the ship at a cautious distance. The thin man saw it, blinked at it without interest, and looked away.

The river was smooth and silvery in the sunlight. After a long time, the sound of bullhorns came blaring distantly across the marshes. Then there was a clanking and a roaring, and two Army tanks pulled into sight, followed by two more. They deployed to either side, and slewed around with their 90-mm. guns pointing at the ship.

The alien watched them calmly. More helicopters appeared, circling and hovering. After a while a gray-painted destroyer steamed slowly into view up the river.

More tanks arrived. There was a ring of them around the spaceship, rumbling and smelling of Diesel oil. Finally a staff car pulled up, and three perspiring general officers got out of it.

From his low platform the alien looked down with a patient expression. His voice carried clearly. "Good morning," he said. "This is a ship of the Galactic Federation. We come in peace. Your guns will not fire; please take them away. Now, then. I shall tell you what I am going to do. The Federation wishes to establish a cultural and educational organization upon your continent; and for your land and your co-operation, we will pay you generously. Here, catch these." He raised his arm, and a cloud of glittery objects came toward them.

One of the officers, white-faced, tugged at the pistol in his belt holster;

but the objects dropped harmlessly in and around the car. The senior officer picked one up. It was insubstantial to the touch, more like a soap bubble than anything else. Then it tingled suddenly in his palm. He sat down, glassy-eyed.

The other two shook him. "Frank! Frank!"

His eyes slowly cleared; he looked from one to the other. "Are you still here?" he said faintly, and then: "My God!"

"Frank, what was it? Did it knock you out?"

The senior officer looked down at the glittery thing in his hand. It felt now like nothing in particular—just a piece of plastic, perhaps. There was no more tingle. The zip was gone out of it.

"It was . . . happiness," he said.

The rest of the objects glittered and gleamed in the rank grass around the car. "Go on," called the alien encouragingly, "take all you want. Tell your superiors, tell your friends. Come one, come all! We bring happiness!"

Within half a day, the word was out. Work stopped in New York offices; by ferry and tube, people poured across the river. The governor flew in from Trenton and was closeted with the aliens for half an hour, after which he emerged with a dazed and disbelieving look on his face, wearing a shoulder bag full of the glittering little capsules.

The crowd, muddy to the knees, milled around the ship. Every hour the thin alien appeared and tossed out another handful of capsules. There were shouts and screams; the crowd clotted briefly where the capsules fell, then spread apart again like filings released from a magnet.

Dull, used-up capsules littered the grass. Everywhere you saw the dazed expression, the transported look of a man who had had one.

Some few of the capsules got carried home to wives and children. The word continued to spread. No one could describe the effect of the capsules satisfactorily. It lasted only a few seconds, yet seemed to take a long time. It left them satiated and shaken. It was not pleasure of any specific kind, they said; it was happiness, and they wanted more.

Expropriation measures passed the state and national legislatures with blinding speed. There was furious debate elsewhere, but nobody who had had one of the capsules was in any doubt that he was getting a bargain. And the kicker was "What else can we do?"

The aliens, it appeared, wanted five hundred acres of level ground to put up certain buildings and other structures. Their explanations to the press and public were infrequent and offhand in tone; some people found them unsatisfactory. When asked why the aliens had chosen a site so near heavily populated centers, rather than wasteland which would have been plentiful elsewhere, the spokesman replied (he was either the same stick-thin man who had appeared first, or one just like him), "But then who would build us our buildings?"

New York, it seemed, represented a source of native labor to the aliens.

The pay would be generous: three capsules a day a man.

When the aliens announced they were hiring, half the population of Greater New York tried to get over onto the Jersey flats. Three quarters of the population of Hoboken, Jersey City, Hackensack and Paterson was already there.

In the queues that eventually formed out of the confusion, the mayor of New York City was seen alongside an upstate senator and two visiting film stars.

Each person, as he reached the head of the line, was handed a light metal or plastic rod, five feet long, with a curved handle and a splayed tip. The lucky workers were then herded out onto the designated acreage. Some of it was marshland, some was a scraggly part of the New Jersey Parks System, some was improved land. The buildings on the site —a few homes, some factories and warehouses—had all been evacuated but not torn down. The workers with their rods were lined up at one edge of this territory, facing the opposite side.

"When the command 'Go' is heard," said the alien's voice clearly, "you will all proceed directly forward at a slow walking pace, swinging your sticks from side to side."

The voice stopped. Apparently that was going to be all.

In the middle of the line, young Ted Cooley looked at his neighbor, Eli Baker. They both worked in the same pharmaceuticals house and had come out together to try their luck. Cooley was twenty-five, blond and brawny; Baker, about the same age, was slight and dark. Their eyes met, and Baker shrugged, as if to say, Don't ask me.

It was a clear, cool day. The long line of men and women stood waiting in the sunlight.

"Go!" said the alien's voice.

The line began to move. Cooley stepped forward and waggled his stick hesitantly. There was no feeling of movement in the stick, but he saw a line of darkness spring out on the ground ahead of him. He paused instinctively, thinking that the stick must be squirting oil or some other liquid.

Up and down the line, other people were stopping, too. He looked more closely and saw that the ground was not wet at all. It was simply pressed down flat—dirt, stones, weeds, everything all at once—to form one hard, dark surface.

"Keep going," said the alien's voice.

Several people threw down their sticks and walked away. Others moved forward cautiously. Seeing that nothing happened to them when they stepped on the dark strip, Cooley moved forward also. The dark ground was solid and firm underfoot. As he moved forward, swinging the stick, the dark area spread; and, looking closely now, he could see the uneven ground leap downward and darken as the stick swept over it.

"Get in rhythm," called the voice. "Leave no space between one man's work and the next."

The line moved forward, a little raggedly at first, then faster as they got the hang of it. The dark, hard strip, running the whole length of the area, widened as they moved. It was as if everything under the business end of the stick were instantly compressed and smoothed down. Looking closely, you could see the traces of anything that had been there before, like the patterns in marbled linoleum: stones, sticks, grass and weeds.

"How the heck does it work?" said Baker, awed.

"Search me," said Cooley. In his hands, the tube felt light and empty, like the aluminum shaft of a tank vacuum cleaner. He didn't see how it could possibly have any mechanism inside. There were no controls; he hadn't turned anything on to make it operate.

A few yards ahead, there was a stone wall, overgrown with weeds. "What's going to happen when we come to that?" Baker asked, pointing.

"Search me." Cooley felt bewildered; he walked mechanically forward, swinging the stick.

The wall grew nearer. When they were within a few paces of it, a rabbit burst suddenly out of cover. It darted one way, then the other, hind legs pumping hard. Confused by the advancing line, it leaped for the space between Baker and Cooley.

"Look out!" shouted Cooley instinctively. Baker's swinging stick went directly over the rabbit.

Nothing happened. The rabbit kept on going. Cooley and a few others turned to watch it: it bounded away across the level strip and disappeared into the tall grass on the other side.

Baker and Cooley looked at each other. "Selective," said Cooley through dry lips. "Listen, if I—" He shortened his grip on the stick, moving the splayed end toward himself.

"Better not," said Baker nervously.

"Just to see—" Cooley slowly brought the stick nearer, slowly thrust the tip of one shoe under it.

Nothing happened. He moved the stick nearer. Bolder, he ran it over his leg, his other foot. Nothing. "Selective!" he repeated. "But how?"

The weeds were dried vegetable fiber. The stick compressed them without hesitation, stamped them down flat like everything else. His trousers were dried vegetable fiber, part of them, anyhow—cotton. His socks, his shoelaces—how did the stick know the difference?

They kept on going. When they came to the stone wall, Cooley waved his stick at it. A section of the wall slumped, as if a giant had taken a bite out of it. He waved it again. The rest of the wall fell.

Somebody laughed hysterically. The line was advancing. The wall was just a lighter stripe in the smooth floor over which they walked.

The sun crept higher. Behind the line of men and women stretched a level, gleaming floor. "Listen," said Cooley nervously to Baker, "how bad do you want those happiness gadgets?"

Baker looked at him curiously. "I don't know. What do you mean?"

Cooley moistened his lips. "I'm thinking. We get the gadgets, we use them up—"

"Or sell them," Baker interrupted.

"Or sell them, but then, either way, they're gone. Suppose we walked off with *these*." He hefted his stick. "If we could find out what makes it do what it does—"

"Are you kidding?" said Baker. His dark face was flushed; beads of sweat stood out on his forehead. He waved his stick. "You know what this is? A shovel. An idiot stick."

"How's that?" said Cooley.

"A shovel," Baker told him patiently, "is a stick with some dirt on one end and an idiot on the other. Old joke. Didn't you ever do any common labor?"

"No," said Cooley.

"Well, you're doing some now. This thing that looks so wonderful to us—that's just a shovel, to them. An idiot stick. And we're the idiots."

1

"I don't like that," said Cooley.

"Who likes it?" Baker demanded. "But there isn't a thing you can do about it. Do your work, take your pay, and that's all. Don't kid yourself we can ever get the bulge on them; we haven't got what it takes."

Cooley thought hard about it, and he was one of the fifty-odd people who walked off the site with Galactic tools that day. The Galactics made no complaint. When daylight failed, they called in the first crew and sent another out under floating lights. The work went on, around the clock. The tools were stolen at a steady rate; the Galactics handed out more indifferently.

The site became level and smooth; the surface was glassy-hard, almost too slick to walk on. The next thing the aliens did was to set up a tall pole on a tripod in the middle of the site. Most of the floating lights went out and drifted away. In the dusk, a network of fluorescent lines appeared on the glassy surface. It looked like the ground plan for a huge building. Some of the pale lines went a little askew because of minor irregularities in the surface, but the Galactics did not seem to mind. They called in part of the crew and made some adjustment in each man's stick. A narrow tab, something like the clip in an automatic, came out of the butt; a different one went in.

So equipped, the reduced crew was sent back onto the site and scattered along the diagram, one man every two hundred yards or so. They were instructed to walk backward along the lines, drawing their sticks after them.

There was some confusion. The tools now worked only on contact, and instead of flattening the surface down, they made it bulge up, like suddenly rising dough, to form a foot-high ridge. The ridge was pale in color and felt porous and hard to the touch, like styrene foam.

A few men were called in and had still another set of control tabs put into their sticks. Wherever somebody had jumped, or twitched, and made a ridge where it didn't belong, these men wiped it out like wiping chalk with a wet sponge: the expanded material shrank again and became part of the dark surface.

Meanwhile, the rest of the crew, finishing the first set of lines, was walking along beside them, making the ridges twice as wide. They repeated this process until each ridge was nearly a yard across. Then they stepped up on top of the ridges and began again, making a second foot-high bulge on top of the first.

The building was going up. It was irregularly shaped, a little like an arrowhead, with an outer shell composed of many small compartments. The interior was left unpartitioned, a single area more than half a mile across.

When the shell was up ten feet, the aliens had connecting doorways cut between all the small chambers. A stick, looking no different from the others, was tossed into each chamber from the wall above. Where it landed, clear liquid immediately began to gush. The liquid rose, covered the stick, and kept on rising. It rose until it reached the level of the walls, and then stopped. A few minutes later, it was cold to the touch. In half an hour, it was frozen solid.

The control tabs were changed again, and a crew began walking across the frozen surface, forming another layer of the hard, dark, glassy substance. Afterward, more doorways were cut in the outer shell, and the liquid drained off toward the river. The sticks that had been dropped into the chambers were recovered. Each had left a slight irregularity in the floor, which was smoothed out.

The second story went up in the same way. Walking backward along the high walls, a good many people fell off. Others quit. The aliens hired more, and the construction went on.

Hardly anybody except a few high government officials got to see the inside of the alien spaceship; but the Galactics themselves became familiar sights in the towns and cities of the eastern seaboard. They walked the streets in inquisitive, faintly supercilious pairs, looking at everything, occasionally stopping to aim little fist-size machines which might or might not have been cameras.

Some of them fraternized with the populace, asking many earnest questions about local laws and customs. Some bought vast quantities of potatoes, playing cards, Cadillacs, junk jewelry, carpets, confetti, nylons and other goods, paying, as usual, with the happiness capsules. They ate local foods with interest and drank heroically without getting drunk, or even tipsy. Skin-tight clothes cut in imitation of the Galactics' bottle-green uniform began to appear on the market. There were Galactic dolls and Galactic spaceship toys.

Legislatures everywhere were relaxed and amiable. Wherever the Galactics had trouble, or sensed it coming, they smoothed the way with more of the happiness capsules. Prices were beginning to be marked not only in "$" and "¢," but in "Hc," for "Hapcap." Business was booming.

In the laboratories of the Bureau of Standards in Washington there was a concerted program—one of many—to discover the secrets of the Galactic all-purpose tool. Specimens had been measured, X-rayed and cut apart. The material, whatever it was, seemed to have been formed in one piece. It was light, chemically inert and fairly strong. The hollow inside was irregularly curved, according to no discernible principle.

There were only two parts—the tool proper and the control tab which fitted into a slot in the handle. With the tab in, the tool functioned. It did work, while the dials of every test instrument calmly reported that no energy was being released. With the tab out, nothing happened at all.

The tabs for various functions could be distinguished by color; otherwise, in shape and dimensions, they seemed identical.

The first—and last—breakthrough came when the tabs were examined by X-ray microscopy. The substance, which had seemed amorphous, was found to have a crystalline structure, permanently stressed in patterns which differed consistently between tabs that produced different functions.

By an elaborate series of test heatings, compressions and deformations, Dr. Crawford Reed succeeded in altering the stress pattern of a type "A" tab to approximately that of a type "C" tab.

When the tab was inserted in a tool, the laboratory went up in an explosion that demolished buildings within a radius of three city blocks.

The explosion was recorded by instruments in the giant spaceship. When he saw the record, the bored officer on duty smiled.

One of the aliens, who said his name was Pendrath go Pendrath, showed up frequently in the pleasant little town of Riverdale, New Jersey. He poked his nose into church bazaars, Little League baseball games, soda fountains, summer camps, chamber of commerce meetings. At first he gathered crowds wherever he went; then the natives, and even the tourists, got used to him.

Three nights after the rough shell of the building was finished, a young *Star-Ledger* reporter named Al Jenkins found him in the back of a bar, maudlin drunk.

Pendrath looked up as Jenkins slid into the booth next to him. "Ah, my friend," he said blurrily, "how I regret your poor planet."

"You don't like our planet?" said Jenkins.

"No, it is a nice little planet. Extremely picturesque. Pardon me."

Pendrath sipped from the glass he was holding. He blinked, and straightened up slightly.

"You must understand, that is Galactic progress," he said. "It cannot be helped. We all must go someday."

Jenkins looked at him critically. "You've been having quite a few of those, haven't you?" he said. "I thought you people were immune to alcohol, or something."

"No, it is the aps—as—aspirin," said the alien. He produced a small bottle, and solemnly shook a tablet out into his palm. "Your liquors gave me a headache, and so I took an apsirin—aspirin—and your aspirin is wonderful." He looked lugubrious. "To think, no more aspirin. No more church bazaar. No more baseball."

"Why, what's going to happen to them?"

Pendrath spread his fingers and made an expressive fizzing noise with his mouth. "Blooie," he said.

Jenkins said incredulously, "You're going to blow up the world?"

The alien nodded sadly. "Soon our building will be finished. Then we will put in the big machines, and drill, drill." He made twisting motions downward with one hand. "We will drill to the core. Then we will drop the transformer and close up the shaft. Then we will go away. Then your poor little planet will go—" he made the fizzing noise again—"Blooie."

Jenkins' fists were clenched. "But why? Why would you do a thing like that?"

"For dust," Pendrath explained. "Your little planet will all be dust. No big pieces left—nothing bigger than this." He pinched his thumb and forefinger together, squinting, to show how tiny. "We are making defenses for the Galaxy. This sector is too open. We will make a little screen of dust here. If there is dust, a ship cannot go very fast. The dust slows it down. Some places, there is already dust. Other places, we will make it. It is the only way to protect ourselves from invasion."

"Invasion by whom?"

Pendrath shrugged. "Who can tell? We have to look ahead."

Jenkins' hands began to shake. He took a dog-eared notebook out of his pocket, thumbing it open automatically; he looked at it and put it back. His hands didn't want to do anything but make fists. He said thickly, "You lousy—" and swung a left to Pendrath's beaky face.

The blow never landed. His fist slowed down and stopped; strain as hard as he would, he couldn't push it any farther.

"No, no," said Pendrath, smiling sadly. "No use. I regret very much."

Jenkins' heart was thumping. "Why us?" he burst out angrily. "If you had to have dust, why couldn't you take one of the other planets? Jupiter, Venus—any of them—why pick the one we live on?"

Pendrath blinked at him. "But on your other planets no one lives," he said. "Who, then, would do the work for us?" He popped another tablet into his mouth. "And besides," he said, "remember that this dust will make a blanket around your sun. It will make the planets very cold. You see, I have thought of all these things. And then suppose we went to some other sun, and did not come here at all. It would be just the same. You would make big spaceships, and we would have to come and finish you anyway. This way, it will be very quick—you will not feel a thing."

Jenkins had lost his hat. He fumbled on the floor for it. "We'll stop you," he said, red-faced over the tabletop. "You'll be sorry you ever opened your mouth to me, mister. I'll spread this from here to Belfast."

"You are going to tell?" the alien asked, in dull surprise.

"You bet your sweet life I'm going to tell!"

Pendrath nodded owlishly. "It does not matter now. The work is nearly done. You cannot stop us, my poor friend."

The story broke the following day, when the installation of the complex system of girders and braces in the interior of the building had already been finished. A hatch in the side of the ship was open, and under the aliens' direction, crews were carrying out a steady stream of machine parts to be assembled inside the building.

There were a thousand and one pieces of different sizes and shapes: gigantic torus sections, tubes, cylinders, globes; twisted pipes, jigsaw-puzzle pieces. The material was not metal, but the same light substance the tools were made of.

Some of the tools were serving as grip-sticks: they clung like magnets to the machine parts, and to nothing else. Some, applied to massive pieces of equipment, made them extraordinarily slippery, so that it was easy to slide them across the site and into the building. Others were used in assembling: drawn along the join between two pieces, they made the two flow together into one.

The story did not reach the day shift at all. The second and third shifts turned up a little under strength; the aliens hired enough people from the crowd of curiosity-seekers to make up the difference.

At his regular press conference, the alien spokesman, Mr. Revash go Ren, said, "Mr. Jenkins' story is a malicious fabrication. The machines you mention will provide pleasant heating, air conditioning, Galactic standard gravitation, and other necessary services for the clerical workers in our offices. We are accustomed to have many conveniences of this kind, and that is why we cannot live or work in buildings suitable for you."

Hersch of the *Times* demanded, "Why does that take a half-mile area, when your office space is only a thin ring around the outside of the building?"

Revash smiled. "Why do you take a whole cellar to heat your buildings?" he asked. "One of your savages would say that a fire of sticks and a hole in the ceiling are sufficient."

Hersch had no answer to that; nevertheless, belief in the story spread. By the end of the week, half a dozen newspapers were thumping the drum for a crusade. A Congressional investigating committee was appointed. More workers quit. When the labor supply slackened, the aliens doubled the pay, and got more applicants than there were jobs. Riots broke out on the Jersey side of the tubes. There were picket lines, fulminations from the pulpit, attempts at sabotage. The work went on just the same.

"The whole problem is psychological," said Baker. "We know what kind of people they are—it sticks out all over them—they're decadent. That's their weak point; that's where we've got to hit them. They've got the perfect machines, but they don't know how to use them. Not only that, they don't want to; it would soil their lily-white hands. So they come here, and they get us to do their dirty work, even though it means an extra risk."

"That doesn't sound so decadent to me," said Cooley argumentatively. It was past midnight, and they were still sitting in Baker's living room over a case of beer, hashing it all out. Cooley's face was flushed, and his voice a little loud. "Take an archaeological expedition, say—I don't know, maybe to Mesopotamia or somewhere. Do they drag along a lot of pick and shovel men? They do not; they take the shovels, maybe, but they hire native labor on the spot. That isn't decadence, that's efficiency."

"All right, but if we had to, we could get out there and pick up a shovel. They can't. It just wouldn't occur to them. They're overrefined, Ted; they've got to the point where the machines *have* to be perfect, or they couldn't stay alive. That's dangerous; that's where we've got to hit them."

"I don't see it. Wars are won with weapons."

"So what are we supposed to do, hit them with atom bombs that don't go off, or guns that don't shoot?"

Cooley put down his stein and reached for the tool that lay on the floor. It had rolled the last time he put it down. He said, "Damn," and reached farther. He picked it up, the same "idiot stick" he had stolen from the Galactic site the first day. "I'm betting on this," he said. "You know and I know they're working on it, day and night. I'm betting they'll crack it. *This* is a weapon, boy—a Galactic weapon. If we just get that—"

"Go ahead, wish for the moon," said Baker bitterly. "What you're talking about happens to be impossible. We can change the stress patterns in the control tabs, yes. We can even duplicate the formative conditions, probably, and get as many tabs as you want with the same pattern. But it's all empirical, Ted, just blind chance. We don't know *why* such and such a stress pattern makes the tool do a certain thing, and until we know that, all we can do is vary it at random."

"So?"

"So there are millions of wrong patterns for every right one. There's the patterns that make things explode, like in Washington; there're the ones that boil the experimenter alive or freeze him solid, or bury him in a big lump of solid lead. There're the radioactive ones, the corrosive ones—and for every wrong guess, we lose at least one man."

"Remote control?" said Cooley.

"First figure out what makes the tools operate when somebody's holding them, and stop when they let go."

Cooley drank, frowning.

"And remember," said Baker, "there's just about one choice that would do us any good against the Galactics. One pattern, out of millions. No. It won't be technology that licks them; it'll be guts."

He was right; but he was wrong.

Al Jenkins was in the *Star-Ledger* city room, gloomily reading a wire story about denunciations of the aliens issued by governors of eight states. "What good is that?" he said, tossing it back onto the city editor's desk. "Look at it."

Through the window, they could see the top of the alien building shining in the distance. Tiny figures were crawling over the domed roof. The aliens had inflated a hemispherical membrane, and now the workers were going over it with the tools, forming a solid layer.

The dome was almost finished. Work on the interior of the building had stopped two days before.

"He knew what he was talking about," said Jenkins. "We couldn't stop them. We had three weeks to do it in, but we just couldn't get together that fast."

Cigarette ash was spilling down the front of his shirt. He scrubbed at it absently, turned, and walked out of the office. The editor watched him go without saying anything.

One morning in July, two months after the aliens' landing, a ragged mob armed with Galactic tools appeared near the spaceship. Similar mobs had formed several times during the last few nights. When a native grew desperate, he lost what little intelligence he had.

The officer in charge, standing in the open doorway, looked them over disdainfully as they approached. There was no need for any defensive measures; they would try to club him with the tools, fail, and go away.

The native in the lead, a big, burly male, raised his tool like a pitchfork. The Galactic watched him with amusement. The next instant, he was dead, turned into bloody mush on the floor of the airlock.

The mob poured into the ship. Inside, the green-lit hallways were as dim and vast as a cathedral. Bored Galactics looked out of doorways. Their bland expressions changed to gapes of horror. Some ran; some hid. The tools cut them down.

The long corridors echoed to the rattle of running feet, to shouts of excitement and triumph, screams of dismay. The mob swept into every room; it was over in fifteen minutes.

The victors stopped, panting and sweaty, looking around them with the beginnings of wonder. The high-ceilinged rooms were hung with gleaming gold-and-green tapestries; the desks were carved crystal. Music breathed from somewhere, soothing and quiet.

A tray of food was steaming on a table. A transparent chart had been pulled out of a wall. Under each was a pulpy red smear, a puddle of disorganized tissue.

Baker and Cooley looked up and recognized each other. "Guts," said Baker wryly.

"Technology," said Cooley. "They underrated us; so did you." He raised the tool he held, careful not to touch the butt. "Ten thousand tries, I hear—and ten thousand dead men. All right, have it your way. I call that guts, too." He lifted his head, staring off into the distance, trying to imagine the hundreds of research stations, hidden in remote areas, with their daily, ghastly toll of human life. "Ten thousand," he said.

Baker was shaking with reaction. "We were lucky; it might have been a million. . . ." He tried to laugh. "Have to find a new name for this now—no more idiot stick."

Cooley glanced at the floor. "It depends," he said grimly, "which end of the stick the idiot's on."

THING OF BEAUTY

There was a time slip in Southern California at about one in the afternoon. Mr. Gordon Fish thought it was an earthquake. He woke up confused and sullen from his midday nap, blinking fiercely, as pink as a spanked baby's behind, with his sandy-yellow beard and eyebrows bristling. He got off the sofa and listened. No screams, no rumble of falling buildings, so probably it was all right.

He heard a knock.

Squinting uneasily, Fish went to the door. He had left his glasses on the table, but never mind; it might be a client, or even an investigator from the city. In which case . . . He opened the door.

A slender man in purple was standing there. He was small, hardly an inch taller than Gordon Fish. He said, "Three twenty-two and a half Platt Terrace?" His face was an oval blurr; he seemed to be wearing some kind of tight uniform, like a bellboy's—but purple?

"That's right, three twenty-two and a half, this is it," said Fish, straining to make out the fellow's salmon-colored face. He caught sight of some other people standing behind him, and a shadowy bulk, like a big box of some kind. "I don't know if you—"

"All right, fezh, bring it in," said the man, turning to speak over his shoulder. "Bung, did we have a time finding you," he said to Fish, and pushed his way into the living room. Behind him, other men in tight purple clothing came staggering under the weight of boxes, first a big one, then two smaller ones, then a *really* big one, then a clutter of smaller boxes.

"Listen, wait, there must be some mistake," said Fish, dancing out of the way. "I didn't order—"

The first man in purple looked at some papers in his hand. "Three twenty-two and a *half* Platt *Terrace?*" he said. His voice sounded slurred and angry, as if he were half drunk or had just waked up, like Fish himself.

Fish was unreasonably irritated. "I tell you I didn't order anything! I don't care if— You walk in here, into a man's home, just like— Listen! You get that out of there!" Infuriated, he rushed at two of the men who were setting down one of the smaller boxes on the sofa.

"This is the address," said the first man in a bored voice. He shoved some papers into Fish's hand. "You don't want 'em, send 'em back. We just deliver 'em." The purple men began to move toward the door.

The spokesman went out last. "Bung, are *you* a dvich!" he said, and closed the door.

Raging, Fish fumbled for his glasses. They ought to be right *there*, but the movers had upset everything. He went to the door anyway, twitching with anger. Dammit, if he could just find his glasses he'd *report* them, but . . . He opened the door. The purple-uniformed men, a little knot of them, were standing in the courtyard looking bewildered. One of them turned a salmon-colored dot of a face. "Hey, which way is . . ." Something. It sounded like "enchmire."

There was a tremor, and Fish lurched against the door frame. It felt like an earth shock, a heavy one, but when he looked up the palm trees in the street were not swaying, and the buildings were solid and firm. But the purple men were gone.

Swearing frantically to himself, Fish went back into the living room and slammed the door behind him. The biggest box was in his way. He kicked it, and a slat fell out. He kicked it again, grunting with angry satisfaction. The whole side fell down with a clatter, revealing a black-enameled panel. Fish kicked that, and bruised his toe.

"Hm," said Fish, looking at the sleek black finish of whatever it was. "Hah." It looked like money. Peering, he ran his finger along the metal. Cool and smooth. Why, it might be almost anything. Industrial machinery, worth thousands of dollars to the right party. With rising excitement, Fish ran to the table, found his glasses pushed into some magazines, and ran back, fitting the glasses over his mean little eyes.

He pulled some more slats aside. The box fell away, disclosing an oddly shaped hunk of metal with knobs, dials and switches in the top. An engraved white plate read: "TECKNING MASKIN," and then some numbers. It sounded ominous and important. Heart beating, Fish rubbed his fingers over the knurled knobs and the gleaming switch handles. There was a faint click. He had accidentally moved one switch, he saw, from "Av" to "På." The dials were lighting up, and a set of long hooked arms, like claws, were slowly drifting out over the flat empty space in the middle.

Hastily, Fish turned the switch back to "Av." The lights went out; the arms, looking disappointed, he thought, drifted back into their enclosures.

Well, it *worked*, whatever it was, which was funny, because come to think of it he hadn't plugged it in anywhere. Fish stared at the machine uneasily, rubbing his podgy hands together. Batteries? In a machine that size? And those funny dials, the peculiar *expression* the whole thing had, and "Teckning Maskin"—not even English. There it sat, all eight or nine pieces of it, filling up his living room—one crate, he saw with a pang, blocked off his view of the TV. Suppose it was all some kind of *joke?*

The instant he thought of it, he saw the whole thing in a flash. The crates sitting here, and then in a few days the bill would come in the mail—maybe they wouldn't even take the things away until he'd paid the shipping—and all the time, the joker would be laughing himself sick. Laughing, whoever it was that had ordered the machines in Fish's name—some old enemy, or it could even be someone he thought of as a *friend.*

With tears of rage in his eyes, he rushed to the door again, flung it open and stood panting, staring around the courtyard. But there was nobody there. He slammed the door and stood looking helplessly at the crates. If they would fight *fair!* How was he going to watch *Dragnet*, and, good heaven, where was he going to talk to clients—in the *kitchen?*

"Oh!" said Fish, and he kicked another crate hard. Slats gave, and something fell out, a little yellow booklet. Fish glimpsed more black-enameled machinery inside. He bent wildly to pick up the booklet and tried to tear it across, but it hurt his hands. He threw it across the room, shouting, "Well, then!" He danced from one crate to another, kicking. Slats littered the floor. Gleaming machines stood up from the mess, some with dials, some without. Fish stopped, out of breath, and stared at them with a new bewilderment.

A trick—no, it couldn't be. Big industrial machines like that—it wasn't like ordering something from a department store. But then what? A mistake. Fish sat down on the arm of a chair and frowned, scrubbing his beard with his fingers. In the first place, now, he hadn't *signed* anything. Even if they came back tomorrow, if he could manage to get rid of say one piece, he could always claim there had been *eight* instead of *nine.* Or suppose he even got rid of all of it, discreetly of course, then when they came back he could simply deny the whole thing. Say he never heard of any machinery. Fish's nerves began to twitch. He jumped up, looked around, sat down again. Speed, speed, that was the thing. Get it over with. But what kind of machinery *was* it?

Fish frowned, squirmed, got up and sat down. Finally he went to the phone, looked up a number and dialed. He smoothed down his vest, cleared his throat musically. "Ben? This is Gordon Fish, Ben. . . . Just fine. Now, Ben—" his voice dropped confidentially—"I happent to have a client who wants to dispose of a Teckning Maskin. Eight— What? Teckning Maskin. It's machinery, Ben. T-E-C-K-N-I-N-G— No? Well, that's the name they gave me. I have it written down right here. You never— Well, that's funny. Probably some mistake. I tell you, Ben, I'll check back and see. Yes, thanks a lot. Thanks, Ben, bye-bye."

He hung up, chewing his whiskers in vexation. If Ben Abrams had never·*heard* of it, then there couldn't be any market for it, not in *this* part of the country anyhow. . . . Something funny. He was beginning to have a hunch about this thing now. Something . . . He prowled around the machines, looking at them this way and that. Here was another engraved white plate; it said "TECKNING MASKIN," and under that "BANK 1," and then two columns of numbers and words: "3 Folk, 4 Djur, 5 Byggnader," and so on, a lot more. Crazy words; it didn't even look like any language he'd ever *heard* of. And then those maniacs in the purple uniforms . . . Wait a minute! Fish snapped his fingers, stopped, and stood in a pose of thought. Now what was it that fellow had said just as he was leaving? It had made him mad, Fish remembered —something like, "Boy, are you a dvich." Made him mad as a hornet; it *sounded* insulting, but what did it *mean*?

And then that kind of earthquake just before they got here—woke him up out of a sound sleep, left him feeling all funny. And then another one after they left—only *not* an earthquake, because he remembered distinctly that the palm trees didn't even tremble.

Fish ran his finger delicately over the shining curved edge of the nearest machine. His heart was thumping; his tongue came out to lick his lips. He had a feeling—no, he really *knew*—nobody would be coming back for the machines.

They were his. Yes, and there was money in them, somewhere; he could smell it. But how? What did they *do*?

He opened all the crates carefully. In one of them, instead of a machine, there was a metal box full of creamy-thick sheets of paper. They were big rectangular sheets, and they looked as if one would just about fit onto the flat center space on the biggest machine. Fish tried one, and it did.

Well, what could go wrong? Fish rubbed his fingers nervously, then turned the switch on. The dials lighted and the hooked arms drifted out, as before, but nothing else happened. Fish leaned nearer again and looked at the other controls. There was a pointer and a series of marks labeled "Av," "Bank 1," "Bank 2," and so on down to "Bank 9." He moved the pointer cautiously to "Bank 1." The arms moved a little, slowly, and stopped.

What else? Three red buttons marked "Utplåna," "Torka" and "Avslå." He pressed one down, but nothing happened. Then a series of white ones, like on an adding machine, all numbered. He pressed one down at random, then another, and was about to press a third when he leaped back in alarm. The hooked arms were moving, rapidly and purposefully. Where they passed over the paper, thin dark-gray lines were growing.

Fish leaned closer, his mouth open and his eyes bulging. The little points under the ends of the arms were riding smoothly over the paper, leaving graceful lines behind them. The arms moved, contracted on their little pivots and springs, swept this way and that, lifted slightly, dropped again and moved on. Why, the machine was drawing—drawing a picture while he watched! There was a face forming under the arm over on the right, then a neck and shoulder—kind of a sappy-looking man, it was, like a Greek statue. Then over here on the left, at the same time, another arm was drawing a bull's head, with some kind of flowers between the horns. Now the man's body—he was wearing one of those Greek togas or whatever you call them—and the back of the bull curving around up on top. And now the man's arm, and the bull's tail, and now the other arm, and the bull's hind legs.

There it was. A picture of a man throwing flowers at this bull, who was kind of leaping and looking at the man over his shoulder. The arms of the machine stopped moving, and then pulled back out of sight. The lights went out, and the switch clicked by itself back to "På."

Fish took the paper and looked it over, excited but a little disappointed. He didn't know anything about *art*, of course, but he knew this was no good—all flat looking and kind of simple, like a kid would draw. And that bull—whoever saw a bull dancing like that? With flowers between its horns? Still, if the machine would draw this, maybe it would draw something better; he couldn't quite see the angle. Where would you sell drawings, even good ones? But it was there, somewhere. Exhibit the machine, like in a fair of science and industry? No, his mind hurriedly buried the thought—too exposed, too many questions. Heavens, if Vera found out he was still alive, or if the police in Scranton . . .

Drawings. A machine that made drawings. Fish looked at it, all eight lumpy black-enameled massive pieces of it scattered around his living room. It seemed like a lot of machinery just to make *drawings*. He admitted it: he was disappointed. He had expected, well, metal stampings or something like that, something real. Crash, bang, the big metal jaw comes down, and tink, the bright shaped piece falls out into the basket. There was machinery for you; but this . . .

Fish sat back and pondered, twitching the paper disapprovingly between his fingers. Things were always letting him down like this. Really, his best line was marriage. He had been married five times, and always made a little profit out of it. He smoothed the vest down over his suety front. Between times, he turned to whatever was handy—marital counseling some years, or gave life readings if he could get enough clients, or naturopathy. It all depended. But somehow every time it looked as if he had a real gold mine, it slipped out from under his hand. He reddened with discomfort as he thought of the one winter he had been forced to go to work in a *shoe store*. . . . Having this house had softened him up, too, he had been getting lazy—just a client or two a week for life readings. He ought to be getting busy, working up new contacts before his money ran out.

The thought of poverty made him ravenously hungry, as it always did. He kneaded his stomach. Time for lunch. He got his jacket hurriedly, and, as an afterthought, rolled up the drawing—it would not fold—and tucked it under his arm.

He drove to the barbecue place three blocks down the boulevard where he had been eating a lot of his meals lately, to save funds. The counterman was a young fellow named Dave, lean and pale, with a lock of straight dark hair falling over his forehead. Fish had got into friendly conversation with him and knew he was going to art school nights, over in Pasadena. Fish had tried to get him over for a life reading, but the youngster had said frankly that he "didn't believe in it" in such an honest and friendly way that Fish bore him no ill will.

"Bowl o' chile, Dave," he said cheerfully, hoisting himself up on a stool with the rolled drawing precariously on his lap. His feet dangled; the paper was squeezed tight between his vest and the counter.

"Hello, Doc. Coming up." Fish hunched forward over the bowl, loosening his collar. The one other customer paid and left.

"Say, Dave," said Fish indistinctly, munching, "like to get your opinion of something. Unh." He managed to get the rolled paper free and opened it on the counter. "What do you think—is it any good?"

"Say," said Dave, coming nearer. "Where'd you get *that?*"

"Mm. Nephew of mine," Fish answered readily. "He wants me to advise him, you know, if he should go on with it, because—"

"Go on with it! Well, say. Where's he been studying, anyhow?"

"Oh, just by himself, you know—back home." Fish took another mouthful. "Ver' bright boy, you understand, but—"

"Well, if he learned to draw like that all by himself, why he must be a world-beater."

Fish forgot to chew. "You really mean it?"

"Why, sure. Listen, are you sure he drew this himself, Doc?"

"Oh, certainly." Fish waved the imputation of dishonesty away. "Ver' honest boy, I know'm well. No, 'f he tells me he drew it, why—" he swallowed—"he drew it. But now don't fool me, is it—do you really think it's as *good*—"

"Well, I tell you the truth, when I first saw it, I thought Picasso. You know, his classical period. Of course I see now it's different, but, my gosh, it's good. I mean, if you want *my* opinion, why—"

Fish was nodding to indicate that this only confirmed his own diagnosis. "M-hm. M-hm. Well, I'm glad to hear you say it, son. You know, being a relative of the boy, I thought— Of course, I'm very impressed. Very impressed. I thought of Pricasso, too, same as you. Of course, now from the money end of it—" he wagged his head dolefully —"you know and I know . . ."

Dave scratched his head under the white cap. "Oh, well, he ought to be able to get commissions, all right. I mean, if I had a line like that—" He traced in air the outline of the man's lifted arm.

"Now, when you say *commissions*," Fish said, squirming with eagerness.

"Oh, well, you know, for portraits, or industrial designs or, you know, whatever he wants to go in for." Dave shook his head in admiration, staring at the drawing. "If this was only in color."

"How's that, Dave?"

"Why, I was just thinking—see, there's a competition up in San Gabriel for a civic center mural. Ten-thousand-dollar prize. Now I don't know, it might not win, but why don't you have him render this in color and send it in?"

"Color," said Fish blankly. The machine wouldn't color anything, he was sure. He could get a box of water color paints, but . . . "Well, now, the fact is," he said, hastily revolving ideas, "you know, the boy is laid up. Hurt his hand—oh, not serious," he said reassuringly (Dave's mouth had fallen into an O of sympathy), "but won't be able to draw any more pictures for a while. It's a shame, he could use the money, you know, for doctor bills." He chewed and swallowed. "Tell you, this is just a wild idea, now, but why couldn't you color it up and send it in, Dave? Course if it doesn't win, I couldn't pay you, but—"

"Well, gee, I don't know how he'd like that, Doc. I mean, suppose he'd have something else in mind, like some other color scheme altogether. You know, I wouldn't like to—"

"I'll take full responsibility," said Fish firmly. "Don't you worry about that, and if we win, why I'll see that you're paid handsomely for your work, Dave. Now there, how's that?"

"Well, sure, then, Doc. I mean, sure," said Dave, nodding and blushing. "I'll do it tonight and tomorrow, and get it right off in the mail. Okay? Then—oh, uh, one thing, what's your nephew's name?"

"George Wilmington," said Fish at random. He pushed the cleaned chile bowl away. "And, uh, Dave, I believe I'll have an order of ribs, with French fries on the side."

Fish went home with a vastly increased respect for the machine. The civic center competition, he was positive, was in the bag. Ten thousand dollars! For one drawing! Why, there was millions in it! He closed and locked the front door carefully behind him, and pulled down the Venetian blinds to darken the gloomy little living room still further. He turned on the lights. There the machine still was, all eight gleaming pieces of it, scattered around on the floor, the furniture, everywhere. He moved excitedly from one piece to another, caressing the slick black surfaces with his palm. All that expensive machinery—all his!

Might as well put it through its paces again, just to see. Fish got another sheet of creamy paper from the stack, put it in position, and turned the switch to "Pả." He watched with pleasure as the dials lighted, the hooked arms drifted out and began to move. Lines grew on the paper: first some wavy ones at the top—could be anything. And farther down, a pair of long, up-curved lines, kind of like handlebars. It was like a puzzle, trying to figure out what it was going to be.

Under the wavy lines, which Fish now perceived to be hair, the pointer drew eyes and a nose. Meanwhile the other one was gliding around the outline of what, it became clear in a moment, was a bull's head. Now here came the rest of the girl's face, and her arm and one leg—not bad, but kind of beefy—and now the bull's legs, sticking out all different ways, and then, whoops, it wasn't a bull: there was the whatyoumaycallum with the teats swinging; it was a cow. So, a girl riding on a cow, with flowers between its horns like before.

Fish looked at the drawing in disappointment. People and cows—was that all the thing could *do*?

He scrubbed his beard in vexation. Why, for heaven's sake, suppose somebody wanted a picture of something *besides* bulls and people? It was ridiculous—eight big pieces of machinery . . .

Wait a minute. "Don't go off half cocked, Gordon," he told himself aloud. That was what Florence, his second, always used to say, except she always called him "Fishy." He winced with discomfort at the memory. Well, anyway, he noticed now that the same buttons he had pressed down before were still down. That must have something to do with it. Struck by another thought, he trotted over and looked at the machine marked "Bank 1." Now this list here, number 3 was "Folk," and number 4 was "Djur." Those were the numbers he had pressed on the big machine, so . . . maybe "folk" meant *people*, and "djur," why, that might be some crazy word for *bulls*. Then if he pressed a different set of buttons, why, the machine would have to draw something else.

In fifteen minutes he verified that this was the case. Pressing down the first two buttons, "Land" and "Planta," gave him drawings of outdoor scenes, just hills and trees. "Folk" was people, and "Djur" seemed to be animals; now he got goats or dogs instead of bulls. "Byggnader" was buildings. Then it got more complicated.

A button marked "Arbete" gave him pictures of people at work; one labeled "Kärlek" produced scenes of couples kissing—all in the kind of Greek-looking clothes—and the landscapes and buildings were sort of vague and dreamy. Then there was a whole row of buttons under the heading "Plats," and another headed "Tid," that seemed to control the time and place of the pictures. For instance, when he pressed "Egyptisk" and "Gammal," along with "Folk," "Byggnader" and, on a hunch, the word he had decided meant *religion*, he got a picture of some priests in Egyptian headdresses bowing in front of a big statue of Horus. Now *there* was something!

The next day he nailed up the crates again, leaving the tops loose so that he could remove them whenever he wanted to use the machines. In the process, he came across the little yellow booklet he had thrown away. There were diagrams in it, some of which made sense and some didn't, but the printing was all in the same unfamiliar language. Fish put the booklet away in a bureau drawer, under an untidy heap of clothes, and forgot about it. Grunting and sweating, he managed to push the smaller crates into corners and rearranged the furniture so there was room to put the big one against the wall. It still looked terrible, but at least he could get around, and have clients in, and he could see the TV again.

Every day he ate lunch at the barbecue place, or at least stopped in, and every day, when Dave saw him come in, he shook his head. Then all afternoon he would sit with a glass of beer, or maybe a plate of nuts or fudge, watching the machine draw. He used up all the paper in the stack and started turning them over to use the other sides.

But where was the money coming from? After some thought, Fish built a simple magic-writing box, and used it with his Egyptian drawings—he had a dozen, all of different gods, but after the first one the machine didn't draw any priests—to show clients what they had been up to in previous incarnations. He began to get a little more business, and once or twice his instinct told him he could raise the fee on account of the drawings, but that was only pocket money. He knew there was *millions* in it, he could almost taste it, but where?

Once it occurred to him that maybe he could take out a patent on the machine and sell it. Trouble with that was, he didn't have any idea how the thing worked. It seemed like the little machines must have pictures inside, or pieces of pictures, and the big machine put them together—how? Fuming with impatience, Fish took the big crate apart again, moved furniture out of the way, and fumbled at the smooth black side of the machine to see if there was any way of opening it up.

After a moment his fingers found two shallow depressions in the metal; he pushed experimentally, then pressed upward, and the side plate of the machine came off in his hands.

It weighed almost nothing. Fish put it aside, staring doubtfully into the interior of the machine. It was all dark in there, nothing but a few very tiny specks of light, like mica dust hanging motionless. No wires, no nothing. Fish got a sheet of paper and put it in position, and turned the machine on. Then he squatted down. The tiny specks of light seemed to be moving, circling slowly around one another in time to the motion of the drawing arms. It was darker in there, and looked farther away, somehow, than it had any right to.

Holding the front of the machine, Fish touched another shallow depression and, without really meaning to, he pushed upward. The whole front of the machine fell off, and the other side with it.

He sprawled backward frantically to get out of the way, but the top of the machine didn't fall. It stayed there, rock-steady, although there was nothing holding it up but the back panel.

And underneath, nothing. No framework, just the thick darkness, with the little stars going slowly around as the machine drew.

Fish hastily picked up the front and side panels and put them back. They slid easily and perfectly into place, and fitted so closely that he couldn't see any line between them.

After that, he put the crate back together and never tried to look inside the machine again.

Dave hurried around the end of the counter to him. "Doc! Where have you been?" He was drying his hands on his apron and grinning nervously, with a sort of pole-axed expression around his eyes. A customer around the other side of the counter looked up, then went on chewing with his mouth open.

"Well, I had quite a lot of things to do," Fish began automatically. Then he began to feel excited. "Say! You don't mean—"

Dave fished a long white envelope out of his back pocket. "Came yesterday! Look here!" The envelope crackled in his nervous fingers. He pulled out a folded letter, and Fish seized it. Dave looked over his shoulder, breathing heavily, as he read.

DEAR MR. WILMINGTON:

It is my very great pleasure to inform you that your design has been awarded the First Prize in the San Gabriel Civic Center Mural Competition. In the opinion of the judges, the classic simplicity of your entry, together with its technical mastery, made it far superior to anything else submitted.

Enclosed please find our check for three thousand dollars ($3,000.00). . . .

"Where?" cried Fish, looking up.

"Right here," said Dave, with a grin that looked painful. He held up a salmon-colored strip of paper. The red-printed lettering read: "EXACTLY 3,000.⁰⁰ DOLLARS*****."

Fish hugged Dave, who hugged him back, and then looked at the letter again.

. . . the remainder to be paid when the design is executed to the satisfaction of the Committee. . . .

"Executed?" said Fish, with a sinking feeling. "What's that mean? Dave, what's he mean here, where he says—"

"When he paints the mural on the wall. Gee, Doc, I just can't tell you—"

"Who?"

"Your nephew. George Wilmington. See, when he paints the mural—"

"Oh," said Fish. "Oh. Well, you see, Dave, the fact *is*—"

Dave's long face grew solemn. "Oh, gosh, I never thought. You mean he's not well enough to draw yet?"

Fish shook his head mournfully. "No, sir. It's a terrible shame, Dave, but—" He folded the check absently and slipped it into his pocket.

"I thought you said, I mean, it wasn't serious or anything. . . ."

Fish continued to shake his head. "Turned out, there was more to it than they thought. It looks like now, they just don't know when he'll ever be able to draw again."

"Oh, Doc," said Dave, stricken.

"That's the way it is. These things—the doctors don't know as much about 'em as they'd like you to think, Dave." Fish went on staring fiercely at the letter, barely listening to the sound of his own voice. *To be paid when the design is executed . . .*

"Look here," he said, interrupting Dave's murmurs of commiseration. "It don't say *who* has to execute it, now does it? Notice right there? Says 'when the design is executed.'"

"How about a glassa water over here?" called the customer.

"Coming right up, sir. Look, Doc, I think you got an idea." He retired sidewise toward the counter, still talking. "You know, anybody could scale that up and do the actual painting—any competent artist, I mean. Gee, I'd do it myself, I mean if George didn't care. And if it was all right with the committee, why, you know, it would be an opportunity for me." He gave the customer his water, mopped the counter blindly and came back.

Fish leaned over the counter, beard in hand, frowning. "Wilmington" was just a name. Dave could take the part, just as well as not, and it would be a lot better in one way, because then Fish himself could stay out of sight. But, whoops, if they did that, then Dave would *be* Wilmington, and he might want to take off on his own. . . .

"Well, Dave," he said, "are you a *good* artist?"

Dave looked embarrassed. "Gee, Doc, you put me on the spot, but, well, anyway, they liked how I rendered the design, didn't they? See,

I used a color scheme of deep aqua and a kind of buff, with accents of rose, you know, to make it cheerful? And, gee, if I did it on the paper, I could do it on a wall."

"Sold!" said Fish heartily, and clapped Dave on the shoulder. "George don't know it yet, but he just got himself an assistant!"

A slim female figure popped up at him suddenly from beside a potted palm. "Mr. Wilmington? If I could just have a moment . . ."

Fish paused, one hand going to his chin in the old gesture, although he had shaved off the beard over a year ago. He felt exposed without it, and his features tended to twitch when he was startled like this. "Why, yes, uh, miss . . ."

"My name is Norma Johnson. You don't know me, but I have some drawings here . . ."

She was carrying a big black portfolio fastened with tapes. Fish sat down beside her and looked at the drawings. They looked all right to him, but skimpy, like the kind of thing he turned out mostly himself. What he *liked* was pictures with some meat to them, like Norman Rockwell, but the one time he had set the machine to draw something like that, his agent—the first one, Connolly, that crook!—had told him there was no market for "genre stuff."

The girl's fingers were trembling. She was very neat and pale, with black hair and big expressive eyes. She turned over the last drawing. "Are they any good?" she asked.

"Well, now, there's a good deal of spirit there," said Fish comfortably. "And a very fine sense of design."

"Could I ever be successful at it?"

"Well . . ."

"See, the thing is," she said rapidly, "my Aunt Marie wants me to stay here in Santa Monica and come out next season. But I don't want to. So she agreed, if you said I had real talent, that she would send me abroad to study. But if you didn't, I'd give up."

Fish looked at her intently. Her fingernails were short but looked cared for. She was wearing a simple white blouse and a little blue jacket and skirt; there was a whiff of woodsy perfume. Fish smelled money.

He said, "Well, my dear, let me put it this way. Now you could go to Europe and spend a lot of money—ten thousand, twenty thousand dollars." She watched him without blinking. "Fifty thousand," said Fish delicately. "But what would be the point of it? Those fellows over there don't know as much as they'd like you to think."

She fumbled blindly for her purse and gloves. "I see." She started to get up.

Fish put a pudgy hand on her arm. "Now what *I* would suggest," he said, "why don't you come and study with me for a year instead?"

Her pale face lengthened. "Oh, Mr. Wilmington, *would* you?"

"Well, anybody with as much talent as these drawings"— Fish patted the portfolio on her knee—"why, we have to do something, because—"

She stood up excitedly. "Will you come tell that to Aunt Marie?"

Fish smoothed down the front of his pink shirt. "Why, gladly, my dear, gladly."

"She's right here in the lounge."

Fish followed her and met Aunt Marie, who was a handsome woman of about fifty, plump but beautifully tailored in brown linen. They agreed that Norma would take a studio near Mr. Wilmington's home in Santa Monica, and that Mr. Wilmington would look in several times a week and give her the full benefit of his great experience, in return for ten thousand dollars per annum. It was, as Fish pointed out to them, less than half the amount he usually got now for major commissions; but, never mind, every little bit helped. Murals, institutional advertising, textile designs, private sales to collectors—my God, how it was rolling in!

The only thing that really worried him was the machine itself. He kept it now in a locked inner room of the house he was renting—twenty rooms, furnished, terrific view of the Pacific Ocean, lots of room for parties—and up to a point he could work it like a kiddy car. One time or another, he had figured out and memorized every one of the dozens of labeled buttons on the "Bank" machines, and just by combining the right ones, he could get any kind of a drawing he wanted. For instance, that commission for stained glass for a church—"Religion," "People," "Palestine," "Ancient," and there you were.

The trouble was, the machine wouldn't draw the same thing twice in a row. On that church window job, he got one picture of Christ and then couldn't get another, no matter how long he tried, so he had to fill out with saints and martyrs. The church put up a beef, too. Then sometimes at night, for his own amusement, he used to put the machine through its paces—for instance, set it for "Historical figures" and "Romantisk," which seemed to be the machine's name for the present era, and then push the button marked "Overdriva," and watch the famous faces come out with big cartoony noses, and teeth like picket fences.

Or he would set it for "Love," and then various interesting times and places—ancient Rome gave him some spicy ones, and Samoa was even better.

But every time he did this, the machine turned out fewer drawings; and finally it wouldn't do any more like that at all.

Was there some kind of a censor built into the thing? Did it *disapprove* of him?

He kept thinking of the funny way those men in purple uniforms had delivered the thing. They had the right address, but the wrong . . . time? Whatever it was, he knew the machine wasn't intended for him. But who was it meant for? What was a "dvich"?

There were eight pieces—six banks, the master machine, and one which he had discovered would enlarge any detail of a drawing to almost full size. He could handle all that. He could manage the controls that governed the complexity or simplicity of a drawing, gave it more or less depth, changed its style and mood. The only buttons he wasn't sure of were the three red ones marked "Utplåna," "Torka," and "Avslå." None of them seemed to *do* anything. He had tried all three both ways, and they didn't seem to make any difference. In the end he left them the way they had been: "Torka" down, the other two up, for lack of any better idea. But big and red like that, they must be important.

He found them mentioned in the booklet, too: "*Utplåna en teckning, press knappen 'Utplåna.' Avlägsna ett mönster från en bank efter användning, press knappen 'Torka.' Avslå en teckning innan slutsatsen, press knappen 'Avslå.'* "

Press knappen, press knappen, that must be "push button." But *when*? And that business about "mönster," that made him a little nervous. He had been pretty lucky so far, figuring out how to work the whole machine without any accidents. Suppose there was still something that could go wrong—suppose the booklet was a *warning*?

He prowled restlessly around the empty house—empty, and untidy, because he wouldn't have any servants in the place. You never knew who was going to spy on you. A woman came in two days a week to clean the place up—all but the locked room—and once in a while he'd bring a couple of girls up for a party, but he always threw them out the next morning. He was busy, all right, seeing a lot of people, traveling around, but he'd had to drop all his old friends when he decided to become Wilmington, and he didn't dare make any new ones for fear of giving himself away. Besides, everybody was out for something. The fact was, dammit, he wasn't *happy*. What the hell good was all the money he was making, all the things he'd bought, if they didn't make him happy? Anyhow, pretty soon now that oil stock would start paying off—the salesman had assured him that the drillers were down within a few hundred feet of oil right now—and then he'd be a millionaire; he could retire—move to Florida or someplace.

He paused in front of his desk in the library. The booklet was still there, lying open. The thing was, even suppose that was some language anybody had ever heard of, who would he dare show it to? Who could he trust?

An idea occurred to him, and he leaned over, staring at the yellow pages with their incomprehensible text. After all, he could already figure out some of the words; he didn't have to show anybody the whole book, or even a whole sentence. . . . Then there was that information business that came with his de luxe set of the Encyclopaedia Britannica—he ought to have it right here somewhere. Fish hunted in the file drawers and finally came up with a folder and a sheet of gummed yellow stamps.

Grunting, he sat down at the desk, and after much cigar-chewing, scribbling and crossing out, he typed the following:

DEAR SIRS:
Kindly inform me as to what language the enclosed words are, and also what they mean. Kindly give this matter your best attention, as I am in a hurry.

On a separate sheet he wrote all the doubtful words from the paragraph about the red buttons, cannily mixing them up so no one could guess what order they came in. Feeling a little foolish, he carefully drew in all the tiny circles and dots. Then he addressed an envelope, stuck one of the yellow stamps to his letter, and mailed the thing off before he could regret it.

"My rhetorical question is," said Fish craftily to the young physicist, shouting over the hum of cocktail-party conversation, "purely in interest of science, could you make a machine that would draw?" He beamed over his glasses at the horn-rimmed blur of the young man's face. He had had three martinis, and whew! he was floating. But fully in command of his senses, of course.

"Well, draw what? If you mean charts and graphs, sure, or something like a pantograph, to enlarge—"

"No, no. Draw *beau'ful* pictures." The last word sprayed a little. Fish rocked forward and back again. "Purely rhetorical question." He put his glass down with precision on a passing tray and took another one, which spilled icy liquid down his wrist. He gulped to save it.

"Oh. Well, in that case, no. I would say not. I assume you mean it would originate the drawings, not just put out what was programmed into it. Well, that would mean, in the first place, you'd have to have an incredibly big memory bank. Say if you wanted the machine to draw a horse, it would have to know what a horse looks like from every angle and in every position. Then it would have to select the best one out of say ten or twenty billion—and then draw it in proportion with whatever else is in the drawing, and so on. Then, for God's sake, if you wanted *beauty*, too, I suppose it would have to consider the relation of every part to every other part, on some kind of esthetic principle. *I* wouldn't know how to go about it."

Fish, thick-fingered, probed for his olive. "Say it's impossible, hey?" he asked.

"Well, with present techniques, anyhow. I guess we'll be staying out of the art business for another century or two." The blur smiled and lifted its highball glass.

"Ah," said Fish, putting a hand on the young man's lapel to support himself and keep the other from moving out of the corner. "Now, suppose you had machine like that. Now, suppose that machine kept forgetting things. What would be the reason for that?"

"Forgetting things?"

"What I said." With a disastrous sense that he was talking too much, Fish was about to go on, but a sudden hand on his arm forestalled him. It was one of the bright young men—beautiful suit, beautiful teeth, beautiful handkerchief in pocket. "Mr. Wilmington, I just wanted to say, what an absolutely marvelous piece of work that new mural is. One enormous foot. I don't know what the significance is, but the draftsmanship is marvelous. We must get you on *File Seven* some afternoon and have you explain it."

"Never go on television," said Fish, frowning. He had been fending off invitations like this one for almost a year.

"Oh, too bad. Nice to have met you. Oh, by the way, somebody asked me to tell you there's a phone call for you over there." He waved his arm and drifted away.

Fish excused himself and set an adventurous course across the room. The phone was lying on one of the side tables giving him a black look. He picked it up jauntily. "Hello-o."

"Dr. Fish?"

Fish's heart began to knock. He put the martini glass down. "Who's that?" he demanded blankly.

"This is Dave Kinney, Doc."

Fish felt a wave of relief. "Oh, Dave. I thought you were in Boston. Or, I suppose you *are*, but the connection—"

"I'm right here in Santa Monica. Look, Doc, something's come up that—"

"What? what're you doing here? Now I hope you haven't quit school, because—"

"This is summer vacation, Doc. Look, the fact is, I'm here in Norma Johnson's studio."

Fish stood with the sweaty black phone in his hand and said nothing. Silence hummed in the wires.

"Doc? Mrs. Prentice is here too. We've been kind of talking things over, and we think you ought to come over and explain a few things."

Fish swallowed, with difficulty.

"Doc, you hear me? I think you ought to come over. *They're* talking about calling the police, but I wanted to give you a chance first, so—"

"I'll be right over," said Fish hoarsely. He hung up the phone and stood bemused, with his hand to his flushed forehead. Oh, Lord, three—no, four—martinis and this had to happen! He felt dizzy. Everybody seemed to be standing at a slight angle on the Kelly-green carpet, all the bright young men in glossy summer jackets and the pastel women in cocktail dresses with bright, phony smiles on their faces. What did they care if all he could get out of the machine any more was parts of bodies? His last one a big clenched fist, and now a foot, and don't you think the committee didn't beef. They beefed plenty but they had to take it, because they had already announced the commission. Now this morning his agent had called up. Some church group in Indiana, they wanted sample sketches. So it was all going down the drain while he watched, and now this. Dave, good God, you'd think at least he would stay stuck off in Boston, and how the *hell* did he ever run into Norma?

One of the newspaper reporters turned away from the free lunch and planted himself in Fish's path as he lurched toward the door. "Oh,

Mr. Wilmington, what would you say was the real significance of that foot?"

"Gow my way," said Fish, staggering around him.

He took a cab home, told the driver to wait, ducked in for a quick shower and a cup of black coffee, and came out again, shaky but not as drunk as before. Those God-damn cocktails . . . He never used to get like this when he just drank beer. Things were better back on Platt Terrace; how did he ever get mixed up in this crazy art game anyway?

His stomach felt hollow. He hadn't eaten any lunch, he remembered. Well, too late now. He braced himself and rang the bell.

Dave opened the door. Fish greeted him with cries of pleasure, shaking his limp hand. "Dave, boy! Good to see you! How long has it been, anyway?" Without waiting for a reply, he bustled on into the room. It was a gray, windowless place that always made him nervous; instead of a roof there was one big slanting skylight, high overhead; the light filtered down cool and colorless through the translucent panes. There was an easel in one corner and some drawings pinned up on the otherwise bare walls. Down at the far end, Norma and her aunt were sitting on the red-padded bench. "Norma, how are you, honey? And Mrs. Prentice—now this is a real pleasure!"

That wasn't hard to say—she really did look good in that new dark-blue suit. He could tell he was projecting the old charm, and he thought he saw her eyes glint with pleasure. But it was only for an instant, and then her expression hardened. "What's this I hear about your not even coming to see Norma?" she demanded.

Fish registered deep surprise. "Why . . . why, Norma, didn't you explain to your aunt? Excuse me a minute." He darted over to the drawings on the wall. "Well. Now these are really excellent, Norma; there's a good deal of improvement here. The symmetry, you see, and the dyamic *flow*—"

Norma said, "Those are three months old." She was wearing a man's shirt and dungarees, and looked as if she might have been crying recently, but her face was carefully made up.

"Well, honey, I wanted to come back, even after what you said. I did come around, twice, you know, but you didn't answer your bell."

"That's not so."

"Well, I suppose you might have been out," said Fish cheerfully. He turned to Mrs. Prentice. "Norma was upset, you know." His voice dropped. "About a month after we started, she told me to get out and not come back."

Dave had drifted back across the room. He sat down beside Norma without comment.

"The idea of taking the poor child's money for *nothing*," said Mrs. Prentice vehemently. "Why didn't you give it back?"

Fish pulled up a folding chair and sat down close to her. "Mrs. Prentice," he said quietly, "I didn't want Norma to make a mistake. I told her, now, if you'll live up to your agreement and study with me for a year, I said, and then if you're not satisfied, why, I'll gladly refund every cent."

"You weren't doing me any *good*," said Norma, with a hysterical note in her voice.

Fish gave her a look of sorrowful patience.

"He'd just come in, and look at my work, and say something like, 'This has a good feeling,' or 'The symmetry is good,' or some *meaningless* thing like that. I was getting so nervous I couldn't even *draw*. That's when I wrote you, Aunt Marie, but you were in Europe. My golly, I had to do something, didn't I?" Her hands were clenched white in her lap. "There, dear," Mrs. Prentice murmured, and gave her arm a little squeeze.

"I've been going to day classes at the Art Center," Norma said between her teeth. "It was all I could *afford*."

Mrs. Prentice's eyes sparkled with indignation. "Mr. Wilmington, I don't think we have to discuss this much longer. I want you to return the money I paid you. I think it's disgraceful, a well-known artist like you, *stooping*—"

"Mrs. Prentice," said Fish, pitching his voice lower again, "if it wasn't for my faith in Norma's great future as an artist, why I would hand you over ev-ry cent. But as it is she would be making a great mistake, so I suggest again—"

"Doc," said Dave rudely, "you give her back that money pretty damn quick." He leaned forward to speak to the older woman. "You want to know what his real name is, it's Fish. Anyhow, it was when I met him. This whole thing is just a joke. Why, he's no artist. The real George Wilmington is his nephew; he's an invalid out in Wisconsin. Doc here has just been fronting for him, because he's too sick to stand the publicity and all. Now, that's the truth. Or as much of it as I know."

Fish said sorrowfully, "Dave, is this the thanks I get for putting you through art school?"

"You got me the scholarship, but it didn't cost you anything. I found that out from the director. I guess you just wanted to put me out of the way so I wouldn't talk too much. Hell, Doc, that was all right. But when I met Norma here, over at your place yesterday—"

"What? When was that?"

"About ten o'clock." Fish winced; he had been in bed with a bad head and hadn't answered the bell; if he'd only known! "You weren't home, so we got to talking, and—well, pretending to be your nephew, that's one thing, but when you promise to teach somebody when you can't even draw a line yourself!"

Fish raised a hand. "Now, Dave, there's a thing or two you don't know. You say my real name is Fish. Now did you ever see my birth certificate, or did you know anybody that knew me as a child? How do you know my name is Fish?"

"Well, you *told* me."

"That's right, Dave, I did. And you say the real George Wilmington is an invalid out in Wisconsin. You ever see him, Dave? You ever been in Wisconsin?"

"Well, no, but—"

"Neither have I. No, Dave—" he lowered his voice solemnly—"every single thing I told you about that was just a lie. And I admit it." Now here was the place for a tear. Fish turned his mind to the creditors, the trouble with the machine, the oil stock salesman who had gone south with his money, the lawyers who were robbing him blind trying to get it back, the ungratefulness of everybody. A warm trickle crept out onto his cheek and, lowering his head, he knuckled it away.

"Well, what?" said Dave, bewildered.

Fish said with an effort. "I had reasons. Certain reasons. You know, it's . . . it's hard for me to talk about 'em. Mrs. Prentice, I wonder if I could just see you alone for a minute."

She was leaning forward a little, looking at him with concern. It never failed—a woman like that couldn't stand to see a man cry.

"Well, it's certainly all right with *me*," said Norma, getting up. She walked away, and Dave followed her. After a moment the door closed behind them.

Fish blew his nose, dabbed unobtrusively at his eyes, straightened up bravely and put his handkerchief away. "Mrs. Prentice, I don't s'pose you know that I'm a widower." Her eyes widened a little. "It's true, I lost my dear wife. I don't usually talk about it, as a matter of fact, but somehow—I don't know if you've been bereaved yourself, Mrs. Prentice."

She said nervously, "Didn't Norma tell you? I'm a widow, Mr. Wilmington."

"No!" said Fish. "Isn't that strange? I felt something—you know, a *vibration*. Well, Mrs. Prentice—can I call you Marie?—you know, after my loss—" time for another tear now; once started, they came easily— "I just went to pieces. I don't excuse myself, I didn't want to live. I couldn't touch a pencil for a year. And even to this day I can't draw a line if there's anybody watching me. Now—there's the reason for this whole mixup. That business about my nephew and all, that was just a story I made up to make things a little easier. That's what I *thought*. I don't know, I'm so clumsy where it takes a little tact. I'm just like a bull in a china closet, Marie. And that's the whole story." He sat back, blew his nose vigorously again.

Mrs. Prentice's eyes were moist, but her handsome face had a wary expression. "I honestly don't know what to think, Mr. Wilmington. You say you can't draw in public—"

"Call me George. You see, it's what the psychologists call a trauma."

"Well, how would this be? I'll step outside for a few minutes, and you draw a picture. Now, I think that would be—"

Fish was shaking his head sadly. "It's worse than I told you. I can't draw *anywhere* except in one room in my house—I've got it fixed up with her picture, and some mementos." He gulped hard, but decided against a third tear. "I'm sorry, I'd do it for you if I could, but . . ."

She sat quietly in thought for a moment. "Then let's say this. You go home, Mr. Wilmington, and draw something—a sketch of me, my face, from memory. I believe any competent artist could do that?"

Fish hesitated, not liking to say no.

"Now, you see, that will settle it. You couldn't get a snapshot of me and send it off to Wisconsin—there wouldn't be time. I'll give you, oh, half an hour."

"Half an—"

"That should be enough, shouldn't it? So that when I come to call on you, in half an hour from now, if you have a sketch of me—a likeness —why then I'll know that you're telling the truth. If not . . ."

Boxed in, Fish made the best of it. He got to his feet with a confident smile. "Well, now, that's fair enough. One thing, I know I could never forget *your* face. And I want to tell you how relieved I am that we had this little talk, incidentally, and—well, I better go and get that drawing started. I'll expect you in half an hour, Marie!" He paused at the door.

"I'll be there . . . George," she said.

Grunting and twitching, Fish stormed into the house banging doors behind him. Place was a mess—sofa cushions and newspapers all over the living room—but, never mind, she might marry him to clean up his house. Thing was—he unlocked the private room, feverishly swept the cover off the big machine, and began pushing buttons on one of the banks—thing was, get that sketch made. One chance in a hundred. But better than no chance at all. He switched on the machine, watched in helpless impatience while the arms drifted out and hung motionless.

A face—and a likeness! Only hope he had was to put it together from bits and pieces. Nothing left now that would work in the whole machine but some useless items, mechanical drawings and architecture, and a few scraps of anatomy. Let there be enough for one more face! And let it be something like Marie's face!

The machine clicked suddenly and began to trace a line. Fish stood over it in hand-wringing anxiety, watching how the combined motion of the two revolving pivots translated the straight push of the arm into a subtle line. Pretty thing to watch, even if he never could like what it made. Now here it came curving around; now the arm was lifting, going back. A nose! It was drawing a nose!

It was a kind of Greek nose, shapely but thick, not much like Marie's fine curved nose, but, never mind, he could talk her into it—give him the raw material, he could always sell. Let there be *any* kind of a female face, so long as it wasn't ugly. Come on, now, an eye!

But the arms stopped and hung motionless again. The machine hummed quietly, the dials were lighted; nothing happened.

Eaten by impatience, Fish looked at his watch, clapped his palm over it, peeked, swore, and wandered rapidly out of the room. Sometimes lately the machine would just sit like that for minutes at a time, as if it were trying and trying to work, but somehow not succeeding, and then, *click*, off it would go again. He hurried back, looked—still nothing —and went back, pacing the empty rooms, looking for something to do.

For the first time he noticed there was some mail in the basket under the letter drop. Mostly bills. He threw them behind the living-room sofa, but one was a long, bulky brown envelope with "Encyclopaedia Britannica Library Research Service" in the corner.

It had been so long ago, it took him a moment to remember. A couple of weeks after he sent in his letter, there had been a polite printed postcard acknowledging it, then nothing for months. Somewhere along the line he had decided he wasn't going to get an answer.

There wasn't any such language. . . . Well, let's see. He picked the end of the envelope open.

His restless eye was caught by the dining-room clock. Look at the time! Clutching the envelope forgetfully, he rushed into the private room again. The machine was still sitting motionless, humming, lighted. There was nothing on the paper but a noble nose.

Fish pounded on the side of the big machine, with no result except to his fist, and then on the bank that was in use. Nothing. He turned away, noticed he was still holding the envelope, and irritably plucked out the papers inside.

There was a stiff orange folder, stapled at the top. When he lifted the cover, there was a single sheet of paper inside. At the top, the Britannica letterhead, and "V. A. Sternback, Director." Then, in the middle, "SWEDISH WORDS."

His eye ran down the list, startled. There were all the words he had copied off, and opposite each one a word in English. *Teckning* . . . drawing. *Mönster* . . . pattern. *Utplåna* . . . to erase. *Användning* . . . application, use.

Fish looked up. Then that was why nothing had happened when he pressed the *Utplåna* button—he'd always tried it before the machine made a drawing, never while there was a finished one on the board. Now why hadn't he thought of that? Yes, and here was *Avslå* . . . to reject. And *slutsatsen* . . . completion. "To reject a drawing before completion, press . . ." He'd never done that, either.

What about the middle button? *Torka* . . . to wipe. To wipe? Let's see, there was another word—*Avlägsna*, that was it. Sometimes the phrase "*Avlägsna ett mönster*" would be running through his head when he was half awake, like a whispered warning. . . . Here it was. *Avlägsna* . . . to remove.

His hands were shaking. "To remove a pattern from bank after use, press button 'Wipe.'" He let the folder fall. All this time, not knowing, he'd been systematically using up the precious patterns in the machine, throwing them away one by one, until now there was nothing left—just eight big hunks of useless machinery, made for somebody somewhere who spoke Swedish. . . .

The machine clicked softly and the other arm began to move. It traced a graceful upright line, some distance in front of the nose. It looped over and came back down again, then up. . . .

Somewhere distant, the doorbell rang imperiously.

Fish stared, mesmerized, at the paper. The moving point traced another graceful open loop, then another, like a squeezed-together roller coaster. Then another one, moving inexorably and without hurry: now there were four. Without pausing, it extended the last line downward and then brought it across. The line met the tip of the nose and curved back.

The four open loops were fingers. The fifth one was a thumb.

The machine, humming quietly, withdrew its arms into their recesses. After a moment the lights went dark and the hum stopped. Outside, the doorbell rang again, and went on ringing.

THE ENEMY

The spaceship lay on a rockball in the middle of the sky. There was a brilliance in Draco; it was the sun, four billion miles away. In the silence, the stars did not blink or waver: they burned, cold and afar. Polaris blazed overhead. The Milky Way hung like a frozen rainbow above the horizon.

In the yellow circle of the airlock, two figures appeared, both women, with pale, harsh faces behind the visors of their helmets. They carried a folding metal disk a hundred yards away and set it up on three tall insulators. They went back to the ship, moving lightly on tiptoe, like dancers, and came out again with a bulky collection of objects wrapped in a transparent membrane.

They sealed the membrane to the disk and inflated it by means of a hose from the ship. The objects inside were household articles: a hammock on a metal frame, a lamp, a radio transceiver. They entered the membrane through its flexible valve and set the furniture in order. Then, carefully, they brought in three last items—three tanks of growing green things, each in its protective bubble.

They unloaded a spidery vehicle with six enormous puffed wheels and left it standing on three insulators of its own.

The work was done. The two women stood facing each other beside the bubble house. The elder said, "If your finds are good, stay here till I return in ten months. If not, leave the equipment and return in the escape shell."

They both glanced upward, where a faint spark was moving against the field of stars. The parent ship had left it in orbit before landing. If needed, it could be called down to land automatically by radio; otherwise, there was no need to waste the fuel.

"Understood," said the younger one. Her name was Zael; she was fifteen, and this was her first time away from the space city alone. Isar, her mother, went to the ship and entered it without another glance.

48

The lock door closed; the spark overhead was drifting down toward the horizon. A short burst of flame raised the parent ship; it drifted, rising and turning as it went. Then the torch blazed out again, and in a few moments the ship was only a brighter star.

Zael turned off her suit light and stood in the darkness under the enormous half-globe of the sky. It was the only sky she knew; like her mother's mother before her, she was space-born. Centuries ago, driven out of the fat green worlds, her people had grown austere, like the arid fields of stars they roamed among. In the five great space cities, and on Pluto, Titan, Mimas, Eros and a thousand lesser worlds, they struggled for existence. They were few; life was hard and short; it was no novelty for a fifteen-year-old child to be left alone to mine a planetoid.

The ship was a dim spark, climbing up the long slant toward the ecliptic. Up there, Isar and her daughters had deliveries to make and cargoes to take on at Pluto. Gron, their city, had sent them down this long detour to make a survey. The planetoid was now approaching the sun, on its eccentric cometary orbit, for the first time in twenty thousand years. Once here, it would be folly not to surface-mine the planetoid for whatever it might be worth. One child could do that, and survey the planetoid as well.

Alone, Zael turned impassively to the six-wheeled crawler. She might have rested awhile in the bubble house, but she had some hours of suit time left, and there was no need to waste it. She lifted herself easily against the slight gravity into the cab; turned on the lights and started the motor.

The spidery vehicle crawled ahead on its six individually sprung wheels. The terrain was astonishingly broken; giant spires and craters alternated with ravines and with fissures, some of them forty feet wide and thousands of feet deep. The planetoid's orbit passed near the sun, according to the astronomers, perhaps nearer than the orbit of Venus. Even now, the temperature of the rocks was a few degrees above absolute zero. This was a cold beyond anything Zael had ever experienced. She could feel it drawing at her feet through the long insulator spikes of her boot soles. The molecules of every stone were slowed to stillness; the whole world was one frozen yawn of hunger.

But once it had been a hot world. The record was here. At every perihelion passage, the rocks must have split, again and again, to make this nightmare of tumbled stone.

The surface gravitation was only one tenth G, almost like free-fall; the light, puffy-wheeled vehicle crawled easily up slopes within a few degrees of the vertical. Where it could not climb, it went around. Narrow fissures were bridged by the crawler's extensible legs; when she came to larger ones, Zael fired a harpoon which soared across the gap and embedded itself on the other side. The crawler edged forward, toppled and swung at the end of its cable; but while the slight gravity drew it toward the far side of the fissure, the crawler's winch motor was reeling in the cable. It arrived with a faint jar at the opposite side and, without pausing, inched up and over.

Sitting erect behind her instruments, Zael was charting the mineral deposits she passed over. It was a satisfaction to her to find they were rich enough to repay surface mining. The cities could make almost anything out of anything, but they needed a primary source: they had to have metals.

Methodically, she spiraled outward from the bubble house, charting a region no more than thirty miles in diameter. In the unpressurized crawler, it was not feasible to take in a larger area.

Laboring alone, hour after hour under the unchanging sky, she identified the richest lodes, marked them and established routes. Between times, she ate and slept in the bubble house, tended her necessary plants, serviced her equipment. Out of her armor, she was slender and spare, quick in her movements, with the harsh, thin-lipped comeliness of her people.

When her chart was made, she rode out again. At each marked spot, she dropped two widely separated poles. Self-embedding, each pair generated a current which ionized the metals or metallic salts and would slowly deposit pure metal around the cathode. Eventually the concentration would be such that the metal could be sawed out in blocks for convenient loading.

Only then did she turn her attention to the traces of shaped metal that clung here and there to the rocks. They were fragments, for the most part, such as were commonly found on cold satellites like Mimas and Titan, and occasionally on stony asteroids. It was not a matter of any importance; it simply meant that the planetoid had been inhabited or colonized at one time by the same pre-human civilization that had left its traces throughout the solar system.

But she had been sent to see whatever was to be seen. Her real work was almost done; she conscientiously examined the traces, photographed some, took others for specimens. She beamed regular radio reports to Gron; sometimes, five days later, there would be a curt acknowledgment waiting for her in the printer; sometimes not. Regularly she made the rounds of the poles, testing the concentration of metal. She was ready to replace any faulty poles she might find, but the occasion did not arise; Gron equipment seldom failed.

The planetoid hung in its millennial arc. The sky imperceptibly turned around it. The moving spark that was the escape shell traced its path, again and again. Zael grew restless and took the crawler on wider explorations. Deep in the cold crannies of the mountains, she found some metal constructions that were not mere fragments but complete works—dwellings or machines. The dwellings, if they were that, were made for some creature smaller than man; the doorways were ovals not more than a foot across. She dutifully radioed this information back to Gron and received the usual acknowledgment.

Then, one day the printer came to life out of season. The message read: I AM COMING. ISAR.

The ship would be three months slower than the message. Zael kept her calendar, rode her rounds, her starlit face impassive. Above her the escape shell, unneeded now, made its monotonous passage over and over. Zael was tracing the remnants of a complex of surface structures that had miraculously survived, some half buried, others naked to the stars. She found where they led, in a crater only forty miles from her base, a week before the ship was due.

In the crater was a heavily reinforced globe of metal, dented and scarred, but not smashed. As Zael's light shone steadily on it, a sudden puff of vapor went out; the globe seemed to haze over briefly. Zael peered, interested: the minute warmth of the light beam must have thawed some film of frozen gas.

Then it happened again, and this time she could see distinctly: the jet escaped from a thin, dark seam that had not been there before.

The seam widened as she watched. The globe was splitting. In the narrow gap between the two halves, something moved. Startled, Zael threw the crawler into reverse. The cab lights dipped as the crawler retreated up-slope. In the dimness outside the light beams, she saw the globe expanding still more. There was an ambiguous motion between the barely visible halves of the globe, and she wished she had not taken the light away.

The crawler was tilting sidewise up a steep, broken slab of rock. Zael turned downward, still backing at a sharp angle. The light swung away from the globe altogether, then came back to it as she leveled out.

The two halves of the globe had separated completely. In the middle, something jerked as the light struck it. She could see nothing but a thick, gleaming coil of metal. While she hesitated, there was new motion between the halves of the globe. Something gleamed briefly; there was a short ground shock, and then something struck the cab a hard, resonant blow. The lights whirled bewilderingly and went out.

In the darkness, the cab was tipping. Zael clutched at the controls, but she was too slow. The crawler went over on its back.

Zael felt herself being flung out of the cab. As she rolled over, ears ringing, her first and sharpest impression was of the cold that struck through her armor at gauntlet and knee. She scrambled up quickly to a kneeling position, supporting herself on the brushlike spiked soles of her boots.

Even the brief contact had made her fingers smart with cold. She searched automatically for the crawler, which meant safety and warmth. She saw it smashed on the mountainside. Even so, her instinct drew her toward it, but she had hardly taken a first step before the wrecked machine leaped again and rolled another dozen yards down the slope.

She turned now, for the first time fully realizing that something down there was shooting at the crawler. Then she saw a glimmering shape that writhed up toward the wrecked machine. Her helmet light was not turned on; she crouched still and felt two grinding, metallic shocks transmitted through the rock.

The moving thing appeared again on the other side of the crawler, vanished inside, and after a long time came out again. Zael caught a glimpse of a narrow head upraised, and two red eyes gleaming. The head dropped; the sinuous form glided down into a ravine, coming toward her. Her only thought was to get away. She scrambled up in the dark, circled a spire. She saw the gleaming head upraised farther down, among a tangle of boulders, and went at a headlong, dangerous run across the slope to the wrecked crawler.

The control board was ruined, levers bent off or flattened down, dials smashed. She straightened to look at the engine and transmission, but saw at once that it was no use; the heavy drive shaft was bent out of true. The crawler would never run again without shop repairs.

Down in the bowl, she caught sight of the silvery shape casting along the edge of a fissure. Keeping it in view, she examined her suit and instruments all over. As far as she could tell, the suit was tight, her oxygen tanks and recirculation system undamaged.

She was thinking coldly and clearly as she looked at the split globe, gaping empty under the stars. The thing must have been coiled in there, inert, for thousands of years. Perhaps there had been a light-sensitive device in the globe, designed to open it when the planetoid approached the sun again. But her light had broken the globe prematurely; the thing inside was awake before its time. What was it, and what would it do, now that it was alive again?

Whatever happened, her first duty was to warn the ship. She turned on the broadcast transmitter in her suit; its range was small, but now that the ship was so near, there was a chance.

She waited long minutes, but no answer came. From where she stood, the sun was not visible; one of the high crags must be blocking her transmission.

The loss of the crawler had been a disaster. She was alone and afoot, forty miles across an impassable terrain from the bubble house. Her chances of survival now, she knew, were very small.

Still, to save herself now, without finding out more about the thing, would be less than her duty. Zael looked doubtfully down at the empty globe in the starlight. The way between was broken and dangerous; she would have to go slowly, for fear of attracting the thing if she used a light.

She started down nevertheless, picking her way carefully among the tumbled stones. Several times she leaped fissures too long to by-pass. When she was halfway down the slope, she saw movement, and froze. The thing writhed into view over a broken ridge—she saw the triangular head again, and a waving ruff of tentacles—and then disappeared inside the open globe.

Zael moved cautiously nearer, circling to get a view directly into the gap. After a few moments the thing emerged again, curiously stiff and thick-looking. On a level place outside the globe, it separated into two parts, and she saw now that one was the thing itself, the other a rigid metal framework, narrow and perhaps ten feet long. The thing retreated inside the globe again. When it came out, it was burdened with a bulbous mechanism which it fitted on somehow to one end of the framework. It continued working for some time, using the tentacle-like jointed members that sprouted from just behind its head. Then it returned to the globe, and this time came out with two large cubical objects. These it began to attach to the opposite end of the framework, connecting them by a series of tubes to the bulbous mechanism.

For the first time, the suspicion entered her mind that the thing was building a spacecraft. Nothing could look less like a conventional ship, to be sure: there was no hull, nothing but a narrow shaft on which the thing could lie, the bulbous object which might be an engine, and the two big containers for reaction mass. Abruptly, she was certain. She had no Geiger with her—it was back in the crawler—but she felt sure there must be radioactives in the bulbous mechanism—a micropile, unshielded, for a spaceship without a hull! It would kill any living creature that rode on it—but what creature of flesh and blood could survive for twenty thousand years on this airless planetoid, at close to absolute zero?

She stood gravely still. Like all her people, she had seen the evidences of an eons-old war among the cold planetoids. Some thought the war had ended with the deliberate destruction of the fourth planet, the one which had formerly occupied the place of the asteroids. A bitter war, that one must have been; and now Zael thought she could understand why. If one side had been humanlike, and the other like this thing, then neither could rest until it had wiped out the other. And if this thing were now to escape, and perhaps breed more of its kind . . .

Zael inched forward, making her way from stone to stone, moving only when the thing was out of sight. The alien had finished attaching several small ambiguous objects to the front of the frame. It went back inside the globe. To Zael, the structure looked almost complete. It did not seem possible to encumber it any more and still leave space for the rider.

Her heart was thudding. She left her concealment and went forward in a clumsy tiptoe pace that was faster than leaping. When she was almost in reach of the framework, the thing came out of the open globe. It glided toward her, enormous in the starlight, with its metal head rearing high.

Out of pure instinct she hit the light switch. The helmet beams flared: she had an instant's glimpse of skeletal metal ribs and gleaming jaws. Then the thing was thrashing away from her into the darkness. For a moment more she was stunned. She thought, it can't stand light! And she scrambled forward desperately into the globe.

The thing was coiled there, hiding. When the light struck it, it hurled itself out the other side. Zael pursued again, and caught it once more on the far side of the low ridge. It dived into a ravine and was gone.

She turned back. The framework lay on the rock where it had been left. Zael picked it up tentatively. It had more mass than she had expected, but she was able to swing it at arm's length until it gained a respectable speed. She dashed it against the nearest stone; the impact numbed her fingers. The framework leaped free, slid to rest on the stone. The two containers were detached: the bulbous mechanism was bent away from the frame. She picked it up again, and again swung it hard against the rock. The frame bent and buckled; small pieces came loose. She swung it again, and again, until the frame broke and the bulbous part came free.

The alien thing was not in sight. Zael carried the pieces of the framework to the nearest fissure and dropped them in. In her helmet beams, they drifted silently down and were gone.

She returned to the globe. The creature was still nowhere to be seen. She examined the interior: it was full of oddly shaped partitions and of machines, most too large to be moved, some that were detached and portable. She could not with certainty identify any of them as weapons. To be safe, she took all the movable objects and dropped them after the framework.

She had done all she could, and perhaps more than was prudent. Her task now was to survive—to get back to the bubble house, call the escape shell down, and get away.

She turned back up the slope, past the wrecked crawler, retracing her route until she came to the crater wall.

The crags loomed over her, hundreds of feet above her head, and so sheer that when she tried to climb them, even her momentum would not keep her upright; she began to topple back and had to dance her way slowly down again to firmer footing.

She made the full circuit of the crater before she was convinced: there was no way out.

She was sweating under the armor: a bad beginning. The ragged tops of the mountains seemed to bend forward, peering down at her mockingly. She stood still to calm herself, took a salt pill and a sip of water from the dispenser in her helmet. The indicators showed that she had less than five hours of air left. It was little enough. She had to get out.

She chose what seemed to be the easiest slope within reach. She went up it with a rush. When her momentum began to fail, she used her hands. The cold bit through her gauntlets like needles of fire. The slightest contact was painful; to grasp firmly became an agony. She was within yards of the top when her fingers began to grow numb. She clawed upward furiously, but her fingers refused to grip; her hands slid uselessly away from the rock.

She was falling. She toppled slowly down the slope she had climbed with so much pain; caught herself with an effort and came to rest, shaken and trembling, at the bottom.

Cold despair settled at her heart. She was young; she had no taste for death, even for a quick and clean one. To die slowly, gasping for air in a foul suit, or bleeding out her warmth against the stone, would be horrible.

Out across the crater floor, she saw a dim movement in the starlight. It was the alien thing; what could it be doing, now that she had destroyed its means of escape? The thought came to her slowly that perhaps it could not get out of the crater, either. After a moment, hesitantly, she went down the slope toward it.

Halfway down, she remembered to turn off her suit lights so as not to drive it away. The crater floor was crisscrossed with innumerable fissures. As she came nearer, she saw that the split sphere was surrounded by them on all sides. Down at one end of this long, irregular island of rock, the alien was throwing itself back and forth.

It turned to face her as she leaped the last gap. She could see its red eyes gleaming in the darkness, and the circle of thin, jointed arms that formed a collar behind its head. As she approached, the head reared higher, and the jaws gaped.

The sight of the thing, so near, filled her with a cold loathing she had never experienced before. It was not only that the creature was metal, and alive; it was some radiance of evil that seemed to reach her directly from the thing, as if to say, I am the death of all you love.

The blind, red eyes stared with implacable hatred. How could she make it understand?

The body of the thing was sinuous and strong; its jointed arms could grasp and hold. It was made for climbing, but not for jumping.

Abruptly, her loathing for the alien was more than she could master. She turned and jumped the chasm again. On the far side, she looked back. The alien was swaying high, with more than half its length raised from the rock. She saw now that there was another cluster of gripping members at its tail. The thing glided forward to the very edge of the fissure and swayed upright again, jaws agape, eyes glaring.

They had nothing in common but hatred—and fear. Staring across at the alien, Zael realized that it must be as afraid as she. Metal though it was, it could not live forever without warmth. She had broken its machines, and now, like her, it was trapped. But how could she make it understand?

She moved a few yards away along the edge of the fissure, and then jumped again, back to the alien's side. It watched her alertly. The thing was intelligent; it must be. It must know that she was not native to the planetoid, and therefore that she must have a ship, or some means of escape.

She spread her arms. The alien's circle of limbs widened in response: but was that a gesture of invitation or of menace? Suppressing her fear and repugnance, she walked nearer. The tall shape swayed above her in the starlight. She saw now that the segments of the alien's body were metal rings that slid smoothly upon one another. Each ring was slightly open at the bottom, and inside she could glimpse some mechanism.

Such a thing could never have evolved on any world; it must have been made, for some unguessable purpose. The long, supple body was built for pursuit and capture; the jaws were for killing. Only a depth of hatred beyond her comprehension could have conceived this horror and let it loose in the world of the living.

She forced herself to move a step nearer. She pointed to herself, then back to the crater wall. She turned and leaped across the fissure, recovered herself and leaped back.

It seemed to her that the alien's attitude, as it stared at her, was an almost human parody of wariness and doubt. She pointed to herself, and to the alien; again, she turned and leaped across the chasm, then leaped back. She pointed to herself and to the alien, and then gestured across the fissure, a wide, slow motion of one arm. She waited.

After a long time the alien moved slowly forward. She retreated, as slowly, until she was at the edge of the fissure. Trembling, she held out her arm. Slowly the great head dipped; the circle of grasping members waved forward to wrap themselves around her sleeve. The red eyes stared blindly into hers from a few inches away.

She turned and kicked off strongly. She tried to allow for the alien's mass, but the unaccustomed drag on her arm tipped her backward in midair. They landed together with a grating jar. Awkwardly, Zael scrambled up, away from the cold that searched through her armor. The alien was swaying erect, near—too near.

By instinct again, she hit the light switch. The thing writhed away in silvery coils.

Zael was trembling with reaction. Her heart pounded at her throat. With an effort, she turned off the light again. The thing rose into view, waiting for her, a dozen yards away.

When she moved, it moved, keeping its distance. When they reached the next fissure, she stood still until it again approached and laid its grasping members on her arm.

On the far side, they separated once more. In this way, they traversed four of the islands of rock before they came to the crater wall.

The alien thrust its body slowly up along the steep incline. At full stretch, the gripping arms found a hold; the tail swung free. The long body looped gracefully up; the tail members found another hold above the alien's head.

It paused there, looking down at her. Zael spread her arms; she pantomimed climbing, then stepped back, shaking her head. She held out her arms again.

The alien hesitated. After a long moment, the head members gripped again; the tail swung down. Zael braced herself as the alien slid nearer. The smooth, shining head loomed over her. In that frozen moment, Zael found herself thinking that to the alien, the universe might be like a photographic negative: all the evil things good, the good things evil. It gave her a queer sense of exhilaration to realize when they met, the alien too might be embracing darkness.

Then the head glided past her shoulder; the heavy coils looped around her body with a faint scraping sound. The thing was cold, but not with the numbing super-cold of the rocks. As the coils tightened, she felt the chill, constrictive strength of the great body. Then she was being lifted off her feet. The steep wall tilted and swung at a crazy angle.

A faintness sapped her strength as she lay in the metal coils. The stars swung around her head; they steadied and burned still. The alien had set her down at the top of the crater wall.

The cold coils slowly slipped away. Shaken and stunned, Zael followed the alien down the broken, tilted land. The touch still burned in her flesh. It was like a meaning that lay so heavily and coldly inside her that she had to puzzle to make it out. It was like a ring that, having been worn so long, still seems to be there after it has been removed.

Down in the tumbled vastness of the valley, the alien's head was upraised, waiting for her. Humbly she went down to it, where it lay at the edge of a fissure. This time, instead of clutching her arm, the heavy mass coiled itself around her.

She leaped. At the other side, slowly, almost reluctantly, the supple body slid down and away from her. When they came to a high place, again the alien took her in its cold embrace and swung her up, weightlessly, like a woman in a dream.

The sun was in the sky, low over the horizon. Zael put her hand to the radio switch, hesitated, and let her hand fall away. What could she tell them? How could she make them understand?

Time slipped away. When they passed one of her mining areas, where the cold purple light flickered from the rocks, she knew they were on the right path. She steered by that, and by the sun. At each fissure, the alien coiled itself around her shoulders; at each steep ascent, it cradled her about the waist and lifted her in long, free arcs to the top.

When, standing on a height, she saw the bubble house, she realized with a shock that she had lost account of time. She looked at the indicators. There was half an hour of air left.

The knowledge brought to wakefulness some part of her mind which had been submerged and asleep. She knew that the other had seen the bubble house too; there was a new tension in its manner, a new fixity in the way it stared ahead. She tried to recall the topography that lay between this spot and the house. She had been over it dozens of times, but always in the crawler. It was very different now. The high ridges that had been only momentary obstacles before were now impassable. The whole aspect of the country was changed; she could not be certain even of her landmarks any longer.

They were passing the last of the mining areas. The cold purple light rolled across the rocks. Just beyond this point, Zael recalled, there should be a wide fissure; the alien, a few yards distant, was not looking her way. Bending forward, she broke into a stiff-toed run. The fissure was there; she reached the edge, and jumped.

On the far side, she turned to look. The alien was writhing back and forth at the edge of the fissure, its collar of limbs extended in fury, its red eyes blazing. After a moment, its motion slowed and stopped. They stared at each other across the gap of silence; then Zael turned away.

The indicators gave her fifteen minutes more. She set off at a brisk pace and soon found herself descending into a deep ravine she recognized. All around her were the landmarks of the route she was accustomed to take in the crawler. Ahead and to the right, where stars gleamed in a gap, must be the place where a broken fall of rock formed a natural stairway to the top of the ravine. But as she neared the place, something made her uneasy. The far wall of the ravine was too sheer and too tall.

.She stood beneath the gap at last, and there was no stairway.

She must have mistaken the spot. There was nothing for it but to cast along the ravine until she came to the right place. After a moment's indecision, she set off hurriedly to the left.

At every step, the ravine promised to become familiar. Surely, she could not have gone so far wrong in so short a time! The dots of light from her helmet beams danced ahead of her mockingly elusive. Abruptly, she realized that she was lost.

There were seven minutes of air left.

The thought came to her that the alien must still be where she had left it, trapped on one of the islands of rock. If she went straight back to it, now, without hesitating a second, there might still be time.

With an involuntary groan of protest, she turned back. Her movements were hurried and unsure; once she stumbled, and caught herself barely in time to prevent a bad fall. Yet she dared not slow down or stop for a moment. Inside the helmet, her breath was labored; the familiar reek of the recirculated air seemed to have grown stuffier and more foul.

She looked at the indicators: five minutes.

Topping a rise, she saw a liquid glint of metal moving down among the purple fires. She leaped the last fissure and came to a wary halt. The alien was approaching her slowly. The great metal head was expressionless, the jaws closed; the ruff of grasping members was almost still; only now and then, one of the jointed limbs twitched abruptly. There was a grim, waiting stillness about it that she found disquieting, but she had no time for caution.

Hurriedly, with abrupt gestures, she tried to pantomime her need. She held out her arms. The alien glided forward slowly, and slowly wrapped its coils around her.

She scarcely felt the leap, or the landing. The alien glided beside her: close, this time, near enough to touch. Down into the starlit half-darkness of the ravine they went, Zael treading uncertainly because she could not use her helmet lights. They paused at the foot of the precipice. The alien turned to look at her for a moment.

Zael's ears were ringing. The great head swayed toward her and passed by. The metal arms gripped the rock; the great body swung up, over her head. She looked up to see it looping diagonally across the face of the rock; it glimmered briefly against the stars and then was gone.

Zael stared after it in incredulous horror. It had happened too quickly; she did not understand how she could have been so stupid. She had not even tried to grasp the coils as they passed!

The indicators were blurred; the needles hung near the zero mark. Staggering a little, she set off down the ravine to the right. She had perhaps a minute or two of air left, and then five or six minutes of slow asphyxiation. She might still find the stair; she was not dead yet.

The ravine wall, instead of sinking to an easier level, rose in spires and pinnacles. Zael stopped, cold and sodden with weariness. The silent peaks rose high against the stars. There was no help there, nor in all the dead, vampirish world around her.

Something leaped out of the stone at her feet. Startled, she drew back. The thing was spinning away under the stars. As she watched, another fragment of rock burst into view, and then another. This time she saw it fall, strike the stone and rebound.

She jerked her head back. Halfway down the rock face, swinging easily from hold to hold, came the alien. A cloud of rock fragments, dislodged by its passage, floated slowly down and rebounded about her head. The alien slid the last few yards and came to rest beside her.

Her head was swimming. She felt the heavy coils wind themselves around her; felt herself lifted and carried. The coils were too tight; she could not get her breath. When she was released, the pressure did not relax.

Reeling, she went forward toward the bubble house, where it winked and beckoned from the low horizon. Her throat was afire. Beside her, the alien went like quicksilver among the rocks.

Once she fell—an appalling, slow, helpless fall into the bruising cold—and the alien's heavy coils helped her up.

They came to a fissure. Zael stood tottering on the lip of it, dimly understanding now why the alien had come back for her. It was tit for tat; and now she was too bemused to play that game again. The alien's grasping members were on her sleeve.

Up there, somewhere in Draco, Isar's ship was on the way. Zael fumbled for the radio switch. Her voice came hoarse and strange: "Mother . . ."

The heavy body was winding itself around her shoulders. Breathing hurt her chest, and her vision was dim. Gathering her strength, she jumped.

On the far side, she moved with a blurred slowness. She could see the bubble-house light winking prismatically at the end of an avenue of mist, and she knew that she had to get to it. She was not sure why; perhaps it had something to do with the silvery being that glided beside her.

The hum of a carrier wave suddenly filled her earphones. "Zael, is that you?"

She heard the words, but their meaning slipped away. The bubble house was near now; she could see the flexible valve of its doorway.

She had the idea that the silver thing must not be allowed to go inside, or it might breed there, and then there would be a plague of metal creatures running everywhere.

She turned clumsily to prevent it but lost her balance and fell against the side of the bubble. The great, silvery head was looming over her. She saw the jaws open and a pair of gleaming fangs slide into view. The head dipped delicately, the jaws seized her thigh, and the fangs went in, once. Without haste, the thing coiled itself away, out of her range of vision.

A coldness was spreading outward from her thigh. She saw two thin jets of vapor escaping from the armor where it was pierced. She turned her head; the alien creature was just disappearing through the flexible valve into the bubble. Inside, she could see it coursing back and forth, avoiding the one tiny light. It nosed at the hammock, the lamp, then the radio transceiver. Remembering, Zael said plaintively, "Mother?"

As if in answer, the carrier hum came again, and the voice said, "Zael, what is it?"

She tried to respond, but her thick tongue could not find the words. She felt weak and cold, but not at all afraid. Fumbling in her kit, she found the adhesive paste and smeared it over the punctures. The paste bubbled for a moment, then hardened. Something slow and languorous was spreading from the icy hurt in her thigh. As she turned again, she saw that the alien was still curved over the radio transceiver. Even from here, she could see the bright red knob of the escape shell signaler. As she watched, one of the alien's limbs grasped it and pushed it down.

She glanced up. After a moment the crawling orange spark in the sky seemed to pause and then grow slowly larger. The light burned to a bright star, then to a golden flare.

The escape shell came down on the rocky plain a hundred yards away. The torch winked out. Dazzled, she saw the dark shape of the alien come gliding down out of the bubble house.

It stopped, and for a moment the cruel head was poised, looking down at her. Then it flowed on.

The airlock door was a circle of yellow light. The alien seemed to hesitate before it; then it moved on and disappeared inside. The door closed. After a few moments the torch blazed again, and the shell rose on a pillar of fire.

Zael lay cradled against the bubble's resilient curve. Dimly the thought was in her mind that inside the bubble, a few feet away, were air and warmth. Whatever venom the alien had deposited in her flesh, perhaps it would not kill her for a long time. Her mother's ship was coming. She had a chance to live.

But the escape shell was still rising on its long golden plume; and she had eyes for nothing but that terrible beauty ascending into the night.

NOT WITH A BANG

Ten months after the last plane passed over, Rolf Smith knew beyond doubt that only one other human being had survived. Her name was Louise Oliver, and he was sitting opposite her in a department-store café in Salt Lake City. They were eating canned Vienna sausages and drinking coffee.

Sunlight struck through a broken pane like a judgment. Inside and outside, there was no sound; only a stifling rumor of absence. The clatter of dishware in the kitchen, the heavy rumble of streetcars: never again. There was sunlight; and silence; and the watery, astonished eyes of Louise Oliver.

He leaned forward, trying to capture the attention of those fishlike eyes for a second. "Darling," he said, "I respect your views, naturally. But I've got to make you see that they're impractical."

She looked at him with faint surprise, then away again. Her head shook slightly. *No. No, Rolf, I will not live with you in sin.*

Smith thought of the women of France, of Russia, of Mexico, of the South Seas. He had spent three months in the ruined studios of a radio station in Rochester, listening to the voices until they stopped. There had been a large colony in Sweden, including an English cabinet minister. They reported that Europe was gone. Simply gone; there was not an acre that had not been swept clean by radioactive dust. They had two planes and enough fuel to take them anywhere on the Continent; but there was nowhere to go. Three of them had the plague; then eleven; then all.

There was a bomber pilot who had fallen near a government radio station in Palestine. He did not last long, because he had broken some bones in the crash; but he had seen the vacant waters where the Pacific Islands should have been. It was his guess that the Arctic ice fields had been bombed.

There were no reports from Washington, from New York, from

London, Paris, Moscow, Chungking, Sydney. You could not tell who had been destroyed by disease, who by the dust, who by bombs.

Smith himself had been a laboratory assistant in a team that was trying to find an antibiotic for the plague. His superiors had found one that worked sometimes, but it was a little too late. When he left, Smith took along with him all there was of it—forty ampoules, enough to last him for years.

Louise had been a nurse in a genteel hospital near Denver. According to her, something rather odd had happened to the hospital as she was approaching it the morning of the attack. She was quite calm when she said this, but a vague look came into her eyes and her shattered expression seemed to slip a little more. Smith did not press her for an explanation.

Like himself, she had found a radio station which still functioned, and when Smith discovered that she had not contracted the plague, he agreed to meet her. She was, apparently, naturally immune. There must have been others, a few at least; but the bombs and the dust had not spared them.

It seemed very awkward to Louise that not one Protestant minister was left alive.

The trouble was, she really meant it. It had taken Smith a long time to believe it, but it was true. She would not sleep in the same hotel with him, either; she expected, and received, the utmost courtesy and decorum. Smith had learned his lesson. He walked on the outside of the rubble-heaped sidewalks; he opened doors for her, when there were still doors; he held her chair; he refrained from swearing. He courted her.

Louise was forty or thereabouts, at least five years older than Smith. He often wondered how old she thought she was. The shock of seeing whatever it was that had happened to the hospital, the patients she had cared for, had sent her mind scuttling back to her childhood. She tacitly admitted that everyone else in the world was dead, but she seemed to regard it as something one did not mention.

A hundred times in the last three weeks, Smith had felt an almost irresistible impulse to break her thin neck and go his own way. But there was no help for it; she was the only woman in the world, and he needed her. If she died, or left him, he died. Old bitch! he thought to himself furiously, and carefully kept the thought from showing on his face.

"Louise, honey," he told her gently, "I want to spare your feelings as much as I can. You know that."

"Yes, Rolf," she said, staring at him with the face of a hypnotized chicken.

Smith forced himself to go on. "We've got to face the facts, unpleasant as they may be. Honey, we're the only man and the only woman there are. We're like Adam and Eve in the Garden of Eden."

Louise's face took on a slightly disgusted expression. She was obviously thinking of fig leaves.

"Think of the generations unborn," Smith told her, with a tremor in his voice. Think about me for once. Maybe you're good for another ten years, maybe not. Shuddering, he thought of the second stage of the disease—the helpless rigidity, striking without warning. He'd had one such attack already, and Louise had helped him out of it. Without her, he would have stayed like that till he died, the hypodermic that would save him within inches of his rigid hand. He thought desperately, If I'm lucky, I'll get at least two kids out of you before you croak. Then I'll be safe.

He went on, "God didn't mean for the human race to end like this. He spared us, you and me, to—" he paused; how could he say it without offending her? "parents" wouldn't do—too suggestive "—to carry on the torch of life," he ended. There. That was sticky enough.

Louise was staring vaguely over his shoulder. Her eyelids blinked regularly, and her mouth made little rabbitlike motions in the same rhythm.

Smith looked down at his wasted thighs under the tabletop. I'm not strong enough to force her, he thought. Christ, if I were strong enough!

He felt the futile rage again, and stifled it. He had to keep his head, because this might be his last chance. Louise had been talking lately, in the cloudy language she used about everything, of going up in the mountains to pray for guidance. She had not said "alone," but it was easy enough to see that she pictured it that way. He had to argue her around before her resolve stiffened. He concentrated furiously and tried once more.

The pattern of words went by like a distant rumbling. Louise heard a phrase here and there; each of them fathered chains of thought, binding her reverie tighter. "Our duty to humanity . . ." Mama had often said—that was in the old house on Waterbury Street, of course, before Mama had taken sick—she had said, "Child, your duty is to be clean, polite, and God-fearing. Pretty doesn't matter. There's plenty of plain women that have got themselves good, Christian husbands."

Husbands . . . To have and to hold . . . Orange blossoms, and the bridesmaids; the organ music. Through the haze, she saw Rolf's lean, wolfish face. Of course, he was the only one she'd ever get; *she* knew that well enough. Gracious, when a girl was past twenty-five, she had to take what she could get.

But I sometimes wonder if he's really a nice man, she thought.

". . . in the eyes of God . . ." She remembered the stained-glass windows in the old First Episcopalian Church, and how she always thought God was looking at her through that brilliant transparency. Perhaps He was still looking at her, though it seemed sometimes that He had forgotten. Well, of course she realized that marriage customs changed, and if you couldn't have a regular minister . . . But it was really a shame, an outrage almost, that if she were actually going to marry this man, she couldn't have all those nice things. . . . There wouldn't even be any wedding presents. Not even that. But of course Rolf would give her anything she wanted. She saw his face again, noticed the narrow black eyes staring at her with ferocious purpose, the thin mouth that jerked in a slow, regular tic, the hairy lobes of the ears below the tangle of black hair.

He oughtn't to let his hair grow so long, she thought. It isn't quite decent. Well, she could change all that. If she did marry him, she'd certainly make him change his ways. It was no more than her duty.

He was talking now about a farm he'd seen outside town—a good big house and a barn. There was no stock, he said, but they could get some later. And they'd plant things, and have their own food to eat, not go to restaurants all the time.

She felt a touch on her hand, lying pale before her on the table. Rolf's brown, stubby fingers, black-haired above and below the knuckles, were touching hers. He had stopped talking for a moment, but now he was speaking again, still more urgently. She drew her hand away.

He was saying, ". . . and you'll have the finest wedding dress you ever saw, with a bouquet. Everything you want, Louise, everything . . ."

A wedding dress! And flowers, even if there couldn't be any minister! Well, why hadn't the fool said so before?

Rolf stopped halfway through a sentence, aware that Louise had said quite clearly, "Yes, Rolf, I will marry you if you wish."

Stunned, he wanted her to repeat it but dared not ask, "What did you say?" for fear of getting some fantastic answer, or none at all. He breathed deeply. He said, "Today, Louise?"

She said, "Well, *today* . . . I don't know quite . . . Of course, if you think you can make all the arrangements in time, but it does seem . . ."

Triumph surged through Smith's body. He had the advantage now, and he'd ride it. "Say you will, dear," he urged her. "Say yes, and make me the happiest man . . ."

Even then, his tongue balked at the rest of it; but it didn't matter. She nodded submissively. "Whatever you think best, Rolf."

He rose, and she allowed him to kiss her pale, sapless cheek. "We'll leave right away," he said. "If you'll excuse me for just a minute, dear?"

He waited for her "Of course" and then left, making footprints in the furred carpet of dust down toward the end of the room. Just a few more hours he'd have to speak to her like that, and then, in her eyes, she'd be committed to him forever. Afterward, he could do with her as he liked—beat her when he pleased, submit her to any proof of his scorn and revulsion, use her. Then it would not be too bad, being the last man on earth—not bad at all. She might even have a daughter. . . .

He found the washroom door and entered. He took a step inside, and froze, balanced by a trick of motion, upright but helpless. Panic struck at his throat as he tried to turn his head and failed; tried to scream, and failed. Behind him, he was aware of a tiny click as the door, cushioned by the hydraulic check, shut forever. It was not locked; but its other side bore the warning MEN.

BABEL II

From the front he looked a little like Happy Hooligan, if you remember that far back. From the side, where you got a better view of that silver-white crest, he looked more like a cross between George Arliss and a cockatoo.

He stood just under four feet tall, big head, crest and all. He had a wrinkled violet-gray skin, curious S-whorled ears, and a Tweedledum tummy; he was dressed in an electric-blue jacket and small-clothes of some crinkly material that glittered when he moved, with jackboots on his stubby legs and a white-metal disk, a quarter as big as he was, slung by a baldrick from one narrow shoulder.

Lloyd Cavanaugh saw the apparition first, at eleven o'clock on a Wednesday morning in May, in the living room of his studio apartment on East 50th Street in Manhattan. It stepped into view, seemingly, from behind the drawing table at the far end of the room.

Which was nonsense. The drawing table, with its top horizontal and the breakfast dishes still on it, was shoved back against the closed drapes of the window. On the right, between the table and the record cabinet, there was about six inches clearance; on the left, between the table and the keg he kept his ink and brushes on, even less.

Cavanaugh, a bad-tempered young man with a long morose face casually connected to a knobby, loose-jointed body, scowled across the pool of brilliance on the model table and said, "What the hell?" He switched off the floods and turned on the room lights.

Suddenly illuminated, the Holligan-thing blazed at him like a Christmas tree ornament. Its eyes blinked rapidly; then the long upper lip curled up in an astonishing crescent-shaped bucktoothed smile. It made a sound like "*Khakh-ptui!*" and nodded its head several times.

Cavanaugh's first thought was for the Hasselblad. He picked it up, tripod and all, carried it crabwise backward to safety behind the armchair, then crossed the room and took a poker out of the fireplace rack. Gripping this weapon, he advanced on the Hooligan.

The thing came to meet him, grinning and nodding. When they were two strides apart it stopped, bowed jerkily, and lifted the white disk at the end of the baldrick, holding it at the top, with one of the flat sides toward Cavanaugh.

A picture formed in the disk.

In stereo and full color, it showed a ten-inch Cavanaugh bending over something on a tripod. The hands moved swiftly, fitting pieces together; then the figure stepped back and stared with evident approval at an oblong box shape at the top of the tripod, with a chromed cylinder projecting from the front of it. The Hasselblad.

Cavanaugh lowered the poker. Jaw unhinged, he stared at the disk, which was now blank, then at the Hooligan's violet face and the silvery growth above it, which was neither hair nor feathers, but something in between. . . . "How did you do that?" he demanded.

"Szu szat," said the Hooligan alertly. He jiggled the disk at Cavanaugh, pointed to his head, then to the disk, then to Cavanaugh's head, then to the disk again. Then he held the thing out at arm's length, cocking his head to one side.

Cavanaugh took the disk gingerly. Gooseflesh was prickling along his arms. "You want to know if I made the camera?" he said tentatively. "Is that it?"

"Szat it," said the Hooligan. He bowed again, nodded twice, and opened his eyes very wide.

Cavanaugh reflected. Staring at the disk, he imagined an enormous machine with a great many drive belts and moving parts, all whirling furiously. There it was, a little blurred, but not bad. He put a hopper on one side of it, made a man walk up and pour in a bucketful of scrap metal, and then showed a stream of cameras coming out the other side.

The Hooligan, who had been peering intently at the other side of the disk, straightened up and took the disk back with another bow. Then he whirled around rapidly three times, holding his nose with one hand and making violent gestures with the other.

Cavanaugh fell back a step, gripping his poker more firmly.

The Hooligan darted past him, moving so fast his legs twinkled, and fetched up with his chin on the edge of the model table, staring at the setup in the middle of the tabletop.

"Hey!" said Cavanaugh angrily, and followed him. The Hooligan turned and held out the disk again. Another picture formed: Cavanaugh bending over the table, this time, putting tiny fingers together and arranging them in front of a painted backdrop.

. . . Which was substantially what had happened. Cavanaugh was, by profession, a comic-book artist. He was indifferent to the work itself; it was automatic; it paid him well; but it had ruined him as a draftsman. He couldn't draw, paint or etch for fun any more. So he had taken up photography—specifically, tabletop photography.

He built his models out of clay and papier-mâché and wire and beads and bits of wood and a thousand other things; he painted or dyed them, composed them, lighted them—and then, with the Hasselblad and a special, very expensive shallow-focus lens, he photographed them. The results, after the first year, had begun to be surprising.

The setup on the table now was a deceptively simple one. Background and middle distance were a tangle of fir and mountain laurel, scaled half an inch to a foot. In the foreground were three figures grouped around the remains of a campfire. They were not human; they were attenuated, gray, hairless creatures with big mild eyes, dressed in oddly cut hiking clothes.

Two, with their backs to a block of crumbling masonry half sunken in the ground, were leaning together over a sheet of paper unrolled from a metal cylinder. The third was seated on a stone, nearer the camera, with a shank of meat in its hand. The shape of the half-gnawed bones was disturbingly familiar; and when you looked more closely you would begin to wonder if those projections at the end could be fingers, all but concealed by the eater's hand. As a matter of fact, they were; but no matter how long you looked at the photograph you would never be quite sure.

The Hooligan was thrusting the disk at him again, grinning and winking and teetering on his heels. Cavanaugh, suppressing annoyance in favor of curiosity, accepted it and ran through the same sequence the Hooligan had shown him.

"That's right," he said. "I made it. So what?"

"Szo khvat!" The Hooligan's hand made a gesture, too swift to follow, and suddenly contained what looked like a large fruit, like a purple pear with warts. Seeing Cavanaugh's uncomprehending expression, he put it back wherever it had come from and produced a wadded mass of translucent pink threads. Cavanaugh scowled irritably. "Look—" he began.

The Hooligan tried again. This time he came up with a brilliant, faceted white stone about the size of a cherry.

Cavanaugh felt his eyes bulging. If that was a diamond . . .

"Khoi-ptoo!" said the Hooligan emphatically. He pointed to the stone and to Cavanaugh, then to himself and the model setup. His meaning was clear: he wanted to trade.

It was a diamond, all right; at least, it scribed a neat line in the glass of an empty beer bottle. It was also brilliant, pure white and, so far as Cavanaugh could tell, flawless. He put it on his postage scale; it weighed a little less than an ounce. Say twenty grams, and a carat was two hundred milligrams. . . . It worked out to a preposterous one hundred carats, a little less than the Hope diamond in its prime.

He stared at the thing suspiciously. There *had* to be a catch in it, but with the best will in the world he couldn't see any. The models were a means to an end; once he was finished with them, they simply took up room. So what could he lose?

The Hooligan was gazing at him, owl-eyed. Cavanaugh picked up the disk and gave him his answer: a series of pictures that showed Cavanaugh photographing the models, processing the film, and then ceremoniously accepting the diamond and handing the models over.

The Hooligan bowed repeatedly, capered, stood briefly on his hands, and patted Cavanaugh's sleeve, grinning. Taking this for consent, Cavanaugh put the Hasselblad back in place, turned on the floods, and began where he had left off. He took half a dozen color shots, then reloaded with black-and-white film and took half a dozen more.

The Hooligan watched everything with quivering attention. He followed Cavanaugh into the darkroom and goggled over the edge of the workbench while Cavanaugh developed the black-and-white film, fixed it, washed and dried it, cut it apart and printed it.

And as soon as the first print came out of the frame, the Hooligan made urgent gestures and held out another diamond, about half the size of the first. He wanted the prints, too!

Sweating, Cavanaugh dug into his files and brought up color prints and transparencies of his other work: the Hansel and Gretel series, Cavor and the Grand Lunar, *Walpurgisnacht*, Gulliver extinguishing the palace fire in Lilliput, the Head of the N.I.C.E. The Hooligan bought them all. As each bargain was struck, he picked up his purchase and put it away wherever it was that he got the diamonds. Cavanaugh watched him closely, but couldn't figure out where they went.

For that matter, where had the Hooligan come from?

Assured that Cavanaugh had no more pictures, the Hooligan was darting around the room, peering into corners, bending to look into bookshelves, standing on tiptoe to see what was on the mantelpiece. He pointed at a five-inch wooden figurine, a squatting, hatchet-faced man-shape with its arms crossed, elbows on knees—an Ifugao carving that Cavanaugh had brought home from the Philippines. In the disk, a copy of the Goldberg machine Cavanaugh had used, to explain cameras, appeared for an instant. The Hooligan cocked his head at him.

"No," said Cavanaugh. "Handmade." He took the disk and gave the Hooligan a view of a brown-skinned man gouging splinters out of a block of mahogany. Then, for kicks, he made the man shrink to a dot on an island on a globe that slowly turned, with Asia and Australia vanishing around one limb while the Americas rolled into sight from the other. He made a red dot for New York, and pointed at himself.

"Khrrrzt," said the Hooligan thoughtfully. He turned away from the Ifugao and pointed to a bright diamond-patterned rug that hung on the wall over the couch. "Khand-mate?"

Cavanaugh, who had just made up his mind to give up the Ifugao for another diamond, was nonplused. "Wait a minute," he said, and made another moving picture in the disk: himself handing over the Ifugao for the standard emolument.

The Hooligan leaped back, ears flapping, crest aquiver. Recovering somewhat, he advanced again and showed Cavanaugh a revised version: the Hooligan receiving a wood carving from, and handing a diamond to, the brown-skinned man Cavanaugh had pictured as its creator.

"Khand-mate?" he said again, pointing to the rug.

Somewhat sourly, Cavanaugh showed him the rug being woven by a straw-hatted Mexican. Still more sourly, he answered the Hooligan's pictographed "Where?" with a map of Mexico; and more sourly still, he identified and located the artists responsible for a Swedish silver pitcher, a Malay kris, an Indian brass hubble-bubble, and a pair of loafers hand-cobbled in Greenwich Village.

The Hooligan, it appeared, bought only at the source.

At any rate, if he wasn't going to get any more diamonds, he could get some information. Cavanaugh took the disk and projected a view of the Hooligan popping into sight and moving forward across the room. Then he ran it backward and looked inquiringly at the Hooligan.

For answer, he got a picture of a twilit depthless space where crested little creatures like the Hooligan walked among tall fungoid growths that looked like tiers of doughnuts on a stick. Another planet? Cavanaugh touched the disk and made the viewpoint tilt upward; the Hooligan obligingly filled in more of the featureless violet haze. No sun, no moon, no stars.

Cavanaugh tried again: a picture of himself, standing on the globe of the earth and peering at the night sky. Suddenly a tiny Hooligan-figure appeared, uncomfortably perched on a star.

The Hooligan countered with a picture that left Cavanaugh more confused than before. There were two globes, swinging in emptiness. One was solid-looking, and standing on it was a tiny man-shape; the other was violet mist, with the tubby, crested figure of a Hooligan inside it. The two spheres revolved very slowly around each other, coming a little nearer with each circuit, while the solid globe flickered light-dark, light-dark. Eventually they touched, clung, and the Hooligan-figure darted across. The solid globe flickered once more, the Hooligan shot back to the misty one, and the spheres separated, moving very gradually apart as they circled.

Cavanaugh gave up.

The Hooligan, after waiting a moment to be sure that Cavanaugh had no more questions, made his deepest bow to date and conjured up a final diamond: a beauty, larger than all but one or two that Cavanaugh already had.

Picture of Cavanaugh accepting the diamond and handing over something blurred: *What for?*

Picture of the Hooligan rejecting the blur: *For nothing.* Picture of the Hooligan patting Cavanaugh's sleeve: *For friendship.*

Feeling ashamed of himself, Cavanaugh got a bottle of May wine and two glasses out of the bookshelf. He explained to the Hooligan, via the disk, what the stuff was and—sketchily—what it was supposed to do to you.

This was a mistake.

The Hooligan, beaming enormously between sips, drank the wine with every sign of enjoyment. Then, with an impressive flourish, he put a smallish green and white doodad on the table. It had a green crystalline base with a slender knob-tipped metal shaft sprouting upright from the center of it. That was all.

Feeling abnormally open-minded and expectant, Cavanaugh studied the Hooligan's pictograph explanation. The gadget, apparently, was the Hooligan equivalent of alcoholic beverages. (Picture of Cavanaugh and the Hooligan, with enormous smiles on their faces, while colored lights flashed on and off inside their transparent skulls.) He nodded when the little man glanced at him for permission. With one thick finger, the Hooligan carefully tapped the doodad's projecting knob. Knob and shaft vibrated rapidly.

Cavanaugh had the odd sensation that someone was stirring his brains with a swizzle stick. It tickled. It was invigorating. It was delightful. "Ha!" he said.

"Kho!" said the Hooligan, grinning happily. He picked up the doodad, and put it away—Cavanaugh *almost* saw where it went—and stood up. Cavanaugh accompanied him to the door. He patted Cavanaugh's sleeve; Cavanaugh pumped his hand. Then, cheerfully bouncing three steps at a time, he disappeared down the stairwell.

From the window, a few minutes later, Cavanaugh saw him riding by—atop a Second Avenue bus.

II

The euphoric feeling diminished after a few minutes, leaving Cavanaugh in a relaxed but bewildered state of mind. To reassure himself, he emptied his bulging trousers pockets onto the table. Diamonds— solid, cool, sharp-edged, glowingly beautiful. He counted them; there were twenty-seven, ranging from over a hundred carats to about thirty; worth, altogether—how much?

Steady, he warned himself. There may be a catch in it yet. The thing to do was to get downtown to an appraiser's and find out. Conveniently, he knew where there was one—in the French Building, across the hall from Patriotic Comics. He picked out two of the stones, a big one and a little one, and zipped them into the inner compartment of his wallet. Jittering a little with excitement, he dumped the rest into a paper bag and hid them under the kitchen sink.

A yellow cab was cruising down the avenue. Cavanaugh hailed it and got in. "Forty-fifth and Fifth," he said.

"Boo?" said the driver, twisting to look at him.

Cavanaugh glowered. "Forty-fifth Street," he said distinctly, "and Fifth Avenue. Let's go."

"Zawss," said the driver, pushing his cap up, "owuh kelg trace wooj'l, fook. Bnog nood ig ye nolik?"

Cavanaugh got out of the cab. "Pokuth *chowig'w!*" said the driver, and zoomed away, grinding his gears.

Jaw unhinged, Cavanaugh stared after him. He felt his ears getting hot. "Why didn't I get his license number?" he said aloud. "Why didn't I stay upstairs where it was safe? Why do I live in this idiotic goddamn city?"

He stepped back onto the sidewalk. "Lowly, badny?" said a voice in his ear.

Cavanaugh whirled. It was an urchin with a newspaper in his hand, a stack of them under his arm. "Will you kindly mind your own business?" Cavanaugh said. He turned, took two steps toward the corner, then froze, faced around again, and marched back.

It was as he had thought: the headline of the paper in the boy's hand read, MOTN LNIUL IMAP QYFRAT.

The name of the paper, which otherwise looked like the *News*, was *Pionu Vajl*.

The newsboy was backing away from him, with a wary look in his eyes.

"Wait," said Cavanaugh hastily. He clutched in his pocket for change, found none, and got a bill out of his wallet with trembling fingers. He thrust it at the child. "I'll take a paper."

The boy took the bill, glanced at it, threw it on the pavement at Cavanaugh's feet, and ran like sixty.

Cavanaugh picked up the bill. In each corner of it was a large figure 4. Over the familiar engraving of G. Washington were the words FRA EVOFAP LFIFAL YK IQATOZI. Under it, the legend read, YVA PYNNIT.

He clutched his collar, which was throttling him. That vibrating gadget— But that couldn't be it; it was the world that was scrambled, not Cavanaugh. And *that* was impossible, because . . .

A dirty little man in a derby rushed at him, grabbing for his lapels. "Poz'k," he gabbled, "fend gihekn, fend gihekn? Fwuz eeb l' mwukd sahtz'kn?"

Cavanaugh pushed him away and retreated.

The little man burst into tears. "FWUH!" he wailed. "Fwuh vekn r' NAHP shaoo?"

Cavanaugh stopped thinking. Out of the corner of his eye, he saw that a crosstown bus had just pulled up down at the end of the block. He ran for it.

The red-faced driver was half out of his seat, bellowing gibberish at a fat woman who was shrieking back at him, brandishing a dangerous parasol. Beyond them the narrow aisle was packed full of bewildered faces, annoyed faces, shouting faces. The air bristled with dislocated consonants.

Farther down, somebody shrieked and hammered on the rear door. Cursing, the driver turned around to open it. The fat woman seized this opportunity to clout him on the head, and when the resulting melee was over, Cavanaugh found himself halfway down the bus, well wedged in, without having paid his fare.

The bus moved. Hysterical passengers got off at every stop, but the ones that crowded on were in no better shape. Nobody, Cavanaugh realized numbly, could understand anybody; nobody could read anything written.

The din was increasing; Cavanaugh could hear the driver's bellowing voice getting steadily hoarser and weaker. Up ahead, horns were blowing furiously. Concentrating with the greatest difficulty, he managed: *How far?* That was the crucial point—had whatever it was happened simultaneously all over New York . . . or all over the world? Or, horrid thought, was it a sort of infection that he was carrying with him?

He had to find out.

The traffic got thicker. At Sixth Avenue the bus, which had been moving by inches, stopped altogether and the doors slammed open. Peering forward, Cavanaugh saw the driver climb down, hurl his uniform cap to the street and disappear, shoulders hunched, into the crowd.

Cavanaugh got out and walked west into bedlam. Auto horns were howling, sirens shrieking; there was a fight every fifteen yards and a cop for every tenth fight. After a while it became obvious that he would never get to Broadway; he battled his way back to Sixth and turned south.

The loudspeaker over a record store was blaring a song Cavanaugh knew and detested; but instead of the all-too-familiar words, the raucous female voice was chanting:

"Kee-*ee* tho-*iv* i-*if* zegmlit *Podn mawgeth ooooguaatch* . . ."

It sounded just as good.

The street sign directly ahead of him read, 13FR. LF. Even the *numbers* were cockeyed.

Cavanaugh's head hurt. He went into a bar.

It was well patronized. Nobody in a white coat was in evidence, but about a third of the customers were behind the bar, serving the rest— a bottle at a time.

Cavanaugh elbowed his way into the first tier and hesitated between two bottles labeled respectively CIF 05 and ZITLFIOTL. Neither sounded particularly appetizing, but the amber liquid in each looked to be what he needed. He settled for the Zitlfiotl. After his second swallow, feeling more alert, he scanned the backbar and located a radio.

It was, he found when he reached it, already turned on, but nothing was coming out but a power hum. He twiddled with the knobs. At the right of the dial—which was eccentrically numbered from 77 to 408—he picked up an orchestra playing *Pictures at an Exhibition*; otherwise, nothing.

That, he decided, settled it. WQXR, with an all-music program, was on the air; the others were off. That meant that speech was coming out double-talk, not only in New York and New Jersey broadcasts, but in network programs from the West Coast. Or—wait a minute—even if a radio performer in Hollywood were able to speak straight English, wouldn't it be nonsense to an engineer in Manhattan?

This led him by easy stages to the next problem. Selecting an unfrequented table in the rear, and carrying his Zitlfiotl with him, he seated himself with circumspection and carefully laid out on the table the following important articles:

A partially used envelope.

A fountain pen.

A one-dollar bill.

His social-security card.

A salvaged newspaper.

Now, the question was, did any order remain in the patterns of human speech, or was all reduced to utter chaos? Scientific method, encouraged by Zitlfiotl, would discover the answer.

As a preliminary gambit, he wrote the letters of the alphabet, in a severely vertical line, on the unused surface of the envelope.

Next, after reflection, he copied down the text of the one-dollar bill. Thusly:

FRA EVOFAP LFIFAL YK IQATOZI YVA PYNNIT

Under each line, letter by letter, he added what *ought* to be the text of the one-dollar bill.

This gave him fifteen letters, which he wrote down in their proper places opposite the already established letters of the alphabet. Following the identical procedure with the *Pionu Vajl*, or *Daily News*, and, with his own signature, which appeared on the card as *Nnyup Ziciviemr*, gave him four letters more, with the result:

A E	H	O I	V N
B	I A	P D	W
C V	J W	Q M	X
D	K F	R H	Y O
E U	L S	S	Z C
F T	M G	T R	
G	N L	U Y	

Now came the supreme test. He copied down the V*ajl*'s puzzling headline and transliterated it according to his findings:

MOTN LNIUL

GIRL SLAYS

IMAP QYFRAT

AGED MOTHER

A triumphant success. He could now communicate.

The point is, he told himself lucidly, when I think I am saying "Listen to me," in actuality I am saying "Nolfav fy qa," and this is why nobody understands anyone else. And therefore, if I were to think I am saying "Nolfav fy qa," I would actually be saying "Listen to me." And in this way will we build the Revolution.

But it didn't work.

Some time later he found himself in a disused classroom with an unruly student body consisting of three men with spectacles and beards and a woman with hair in her eyes; he was attempting to teach them by means of blackboard exercises a new alphabet which began E, blank, V, blank, U, T, blank. The blanks, he explained, were most important.

At a later period he was standing on the first landing of the left-hand staircase in the lobby of the Forty-second Street Branch of the New York Public Library shouting to an assembled crowd, over and over, "Myp-piqvap opoyfl! Myp-piqvap opoyfl!"

And at a still later time he woke up, cold sober, leaning on the imitation-marble-topped table in a partially wrecked cafeteria. Sunlight was slanting through the plate glass onto the wall to his left; it must be either late afternoon or early morning.

Cavanaugh groaned. He had gone into that bar, he remembered, because his head hurt: about like taking a mickey fin for nausea.

And as for the rest of it—before *and* after . . . how much of that had he imagined?

He raised his head and stared hopefully at the lettering on the windows. Even back-to-front he could tell that it wasn't in English. The first letter was a Z.

He groaned again and propped his chin up with his hands, carefully, so as not to slosh. He tried to stay that way, not moving, not looking, not noticing, but eventually an insistent thought brought him upright again.

How long?

How long was this going to last? How long could it last before the whole world went to hell in a hand basket? Not very long.

Without language, how could you buy anything, sell anything, order anything? And if you could, what would you use for money—four-dollar bills marked YVA PYNNIT?

. . . Or, he amended bitterly, something equally outlandish. Because that was the point he had overlooked a few drunken hours ago—everybody's alphabet was different. To Cavanaugh, YVA PYNNIT. To somebody else, AGU MATTEK, or ENY ZEBBAL, or . . .

Twenty-six letters in the alphabet. Possible combinations, 26 x 25 x 24 x 23 x 22 and so on down to x 1 . . . figure roughly one decimal place for each operation . . .

Something in the *septillions*.

Not as many if vowels were traded for vowels, consonants for consonants, as seemed to have happened in his case, but still plenty. More than the number of people alive in the world.

That was for the written word. For speech, he realized suddenly, it would be just about twenty-five decimal places worse. Not letters, phonemes—forty of them in ordinary spoken English.

A swizzle stick that stirred up your brains—that switched the reflex arcs around at random, connecting the receptor pattern for K with the response pattern for H, or D or anything. . . .

Cavanaugh traced a letter with his forefinger on the tabletop, frowning at it. Hadn't he always made an A like that—a vertical stroke and three horizontal ones?

But, damn it, that was the fiendish thing about it—memory didn't mean a thing, because all the memories were still there but they were scrambled. As if you had ripped out all the connections in a telephone switchboard and put them back differently.

Of course; it *had* to be that way—nobody had gone around repainting all the signs or reprinting all the newspapers or forging a phony signature on Cavanaugh's social-security card. That half-circle first letter of his name, even though it looked like a Z to him, was still a C.

Or was it? If a tree falls with nobody to hear it, is there a sound? And if beauty is in the eye of the beholder, then which way is up? Or, rather, thought Cavanaugh, repressing a tendency toward hysteria, *which way is out?*

First things first.

The Hooligan.

He came from some place that wasn't exactly a place, across a distance that wasn't exactly a distance. But it must be a difficult journey, because there was no record of any previous appearances of little cockatoo-crested art collectors. . . .

He bought the local handicrafts with stones that were priceless on this planet, and very likely dirt-common where he came from. Pretty beads for the natives. In politeness, you offered him a drink. And being polite right back at you, he gave you a shot of swizzle-sticks-in-the-head.

Firewater. A mild stimulant to the Hooligan, hell on wheels to the aborigines. Instead of getting two people mildly confused, it turned a whole planet pole over equator . . . and, communicating by pictures as he did, it was probable that the Hooligan *still* didn't know what damage he had done. He would finish his tour and go happily back home with his prizes, and then a few thousand years from now, maybe, when the human race had put itself together again into half-acre nations and two-for-a-nickel empires, another Hooligan would come along. . . .

Cavanaugh upset his chair.

Icicles were forming along his spine.

This wasn't the first time. It had happened at least once before, a few thousand years ago, in the valley of the Euphrates.

Not Bedlam—Babel.

III

The sun was quartering down toward the west, gilding a deserted Forty-second Street with the heartbreaking false promise of spring in New York. Leaning dizzily against the door frame, Cavanaugh saw broken display windows and dark interiors. He heard a confused roaring from somewhere uptown, but the few people who passed him were silent, bewildered.

There was a nasty wreck at the corner of Seventh Avenue, and another at Eighth; that accounted, he saw with relief, for the lack of traffic in this block. Holding the top of his head down with one hand, he scuttled across the street and dived into the black maw of the IRT subway.

The arcade and the station itself were empty, echoing. Nobody behind the newsstands, nobody playing the pinball machines, nobody in the change booth. Swallowing hard, Cavanaugh went through the open gate and clattered down the stairs to the downtown platform.

A train was standing in the express lane, doors open, lights burning, motor chuffing quietly. Cavanaugh ran down to the first car and went across the vestibule to the motorman's cubicle.

The control lever was missing.

Cursing, Cavanaugh climbed back to the street. He had to find the Hooligan; he had one chance in a million of doing it, and one wasted minute now might be the one minute that mattered.

The little man could be anywhere on the planet by now. But he'd expressed interest in objects in Cavanaugh's apartment that came variously from the Philippines, Mexico, Malaya, Sweden, India—and Greenwich Village. If, improbably, he hadn't got around to the Village yet, then Cavanaugh might be able to catch him there; it was the only hope he had.

On Eighth Avenue south of Forty-first, he came upon a yellow cab parked at the curb. The driver was leaning against the wall under a Zyzi-Zyni sign, talking to himself, with gestures.

Cavanaugh clutched him by the sleeve and made urgent motions southward. The driver looked at him vaguely, cleared his throat, moved two feet farther down the wall and resumed his interrupted discourse.

Fuming, Cavanaugh hesitated for a moment, then fumbled in his pockets for pen and paper. He found the envelope with his world-saving alphabet on it, tore it open to get a blank space, and sketched rapidly:

The driver looked at it boredly, then with a faint gleam of intelligence. Cavanaugh pointed to the first picture and looked at him interrogatively.

"Oweh?" said the driver.

"That's right," said Cavanaugh, nodding violently. "Now the next—" The driver hesitated. "Mtshell?"

That couldn't be right, with a consonant at the end of it. Cavanaugh shook his head and pointed to the blacked-in circle.

"Vcode," said the driver.

Cavanaugh moved his finger to the white circle.

"Mah."

"Right!" said Cavanaugh. "Oweh mah—" He pointed to the third picture.

That was the tough one; the driver couldn't get it. "Vnakjaw?" he hazarded.

Not enough syllables. Cavanaugh shook his head and passed on to the fourth picture.

"Vbzyetch."

Cavanaugh nodded, and they started through the sequence again. "Oweh—mah—vbzyetch." A look of enlightenment spread over the driver's face. "Jickagl! Jickagl! Vbzyetch!"

"You've got it," Cavanaugh told him: "Sheridan Square. Jickagl Vbzyetch."

Halfway to the cab, the driver stopped short, with a remembering look on his face, and held out his hand insinuatingly.

Cavanaugh took the bills out of his wallet and fanned them at him. The driver shook his head. "Ngup-joke," he said sadly, and turned back toward his wall.

Twenty minutes later Cavanaugh was poorer by one thirty-carat diamond, and the cab driver, with a smile on his honest face, was opening the door for him at the western corner of Sheridan Square (which is triangular), a few yards from the bullet-colored statue of the General.

Cavanaugh made signs to him to wait, got a happy grin and a nod in reply, and ran down the block.

He passed Janigian's shop once without recognizing it, and for an excellent reason: there was not a shoe or a slipper visible anywhere in the big, bare work- and sales-room.

The door was ajar. Cavanaugh went in, stared suspiciously at the empty shelves and then at the door to the back room, which was closed by a hasp and the largest, heaviest padlock he had ever seen in his life. This was odd (a) because Janigian did not believe in locking his doors, and this one, in fact, had never even had a latch, and (b) because Janigian never went anywhere—having been permanently startled, some years ago, by E. B. White's commentary on the way the pavement comes up to meet your foot when you lift it.

Cavanaugh stepped forward, got his fingernails into the crack between the door and the jamb, and pulled.

The hasp, being attached to the jamb only by the sawed-off heads of two screws, came free; the door swung open.

Inside was Janigian.

He was sitting cross-legged on a small wooden chest, looking moderately wild-eyed. He had a rusty shotgun across his thighs, and two ten-inch butcher knives were stuck into the floor in front of him.

When he saw Cavanaugh he raised the gun, then lowered it a trifle. "Odeh!" he said. Cavanaugh translated this as "Aha!" which was Janigian's standard greeting.

"Odeh yourself," he said. He took out his wallet, removed his other diamond—the big one—and held it up.

Janigian nodded solemnly. He stood up, holding the shotgun carefully under one arm, and with the other, without looking down, opened the lid of the chest. He pulled aside a half-dozen dirty shirts, probed deeper, and scrabbled up a handful of something.

He showed it to Cavanaugh.

Diamonds.

He let them pour back into the chest, dropped the shirts back on top, closed the lid and sat down again. "Odeh!" he said.

This time it meant "Good-by." Cavanaugh went away.

His headache, which had left him imperceptibly somewhere on Forty-second Street, was making itself felt again. Cursing without inspiration, Cavanaugh walked back up to the corner.

Now what? Was he supposed to pursue the Hooligan to the Philippines, or Sweden, or Mexico?

Well, why not?

If I don't get him, Cavanaugh told himself, I'll be living in a cave a year from now. I'll make a lousy caveman. Grubs for dinner *again* . . .

The cabman was still waiting on the corner. Cavanaugh snarled at him and went into the cigar store across the street. From an ankle-deep layer of neckties, pocketbooks and mashed candy bars he picked out a five-borough map. He trudged back across the street and got into the cab.

The driver looked at him expectantly. "Your mother has hairy ears," Cavanaugh told him.

"Zee kwa?" said the driver.

"Three of them," Cavanaugh said. He opened the map to the Queens-Long Island section, managed to locate Flushing Bay, and drew an X —which, on second thought, he scribbled into a dot—where La Guardia Field ought to be.

The driver looked at it, nodded—and held out his meaty hand.

Cavanaugh controlled an impulse to spit. Indignantly, he drew a picture of the diamond he had already given the man, pointed to it, then to the cabman, then to the map.

The driver shrugged and gestured outside with his thumb.

Cavanaugh gritted his teeth, shut his eyes tight, and counted to twenty. Eventually, when he thought he could trust himself to hold anything with a sharp point, he picked up the pen, found the Manhattan section of the map, and made a dot at Fiftieth and Second Avenue. He drew another picture of a diamond, with an arrow pointing to the dot.

The driver studied it. He leaned farther over the seat and put a stubby finger on the dot. "Fa mack alaha gur'l hih?" he demanded suspiciously.

"Your father comes from a long line of orangutans with loathsome diseases," said Cavanaugh, crossing his heart.

Reassured by the polysyllables, the driver put his machine into motion.

At the apartment, while the driver lurked heavily in the living room, Cavanaugh picked out the very smallest diamond to pay his fare, and twelve others, from middling to big, for further emergencies. He also took two cans of hash, a can of tamales, an opener, a spoon, and a bottle of tomato juice in a paper bag; the thought of food revolted him at the moment, but he would have to eat sometime. Better than grubs, anyway. . . .

All the main arteries out of New York, Cavanaugh discovered, were choked—everybody who was on the island was apparently trying to get off, and vice versa. Nobody was paying much attention to traffic signals, and the battered results were visible at nearly every intersection.

It took them two hours to get to La Guardia.

Some sort of a struggle was going on around a car parked in front of the terminal building. As Cavanaugh's cab pulled up, the crowd broke and surged toward them; Cavanaugh had barely time to open the door and leap out. When he had bounced off the hood, tripped over somebody's feet, butted someone else in the stomach, and finally regained his balance a few seconds later, he saw the cab turning on two wheels, with one rear door hanging open, and a packed mass of passengers bulging out like a bee swarm. The cab's taillights wavered off down the road, a few stragglers running frantically after it.

Cavanaugh walked carefully around the diminished mob, still focused on the remaining car, and went into the building. He fought his way through the waiting room, losing his paper bag, several buttons from his shirt and nine tenths of his temper, and found an open gate onto the field.

The huge, floodlighted area was one inextricable confusion of people, dogs and airplanes—more planes than Cavanaugh had ever seen in one place before; forests of them—liners, transports, private planes of every size and shape.

The dogs were harder to account for. There seemed to be several dozen of them in his immediate vicinity, all large and vociferous. One especially active Dalmatian, about the size of a cougar, circled Cavanaugh twice and then reared up to put two tremendous forepaws on his chest. Cavanaugh fell like a tree. Man and dog stared at each other, eye to eye, for one poignant moment; then the beast whirled, thumping Cavanaugh soundly in the ribs, and was gone.

Raging, Cavanaugh arose and stalked forth onto the field. Somebody grabbed his sleeve and shouted in his ear; Cavanaugh swung at him, whirled completely around, and cannoned into somebody else, who hit him with a valise. Some time later, confused in mind and bruised of body, he found himself approaching a small, fragile-looking monoplane on whose wing sat an expressionless man in a leather jacket.

Cavanaugh climbed up beside him, panting. The other looked at him thoughtfully and raised his left hand, previously concealed by his body. There was a spanner in it.

Cavanaugh sighed. Raising one hand for attention, he opened his wallet and took out one of the larger gems.

The other man lowered the spanner a trifle.

Cavanaugh felt for his fountain pen; it was gone. Dipping one finger in the blood that was trickling from his nose, he drew a wobbly outline map of North America on the surface of the wing.

The other winced slightly, but watched with interest.

Cavanaugh drew the United States–Mexico border, and put a large dot, or blob, south of it. He pointed to the plane, to the dot, and held up the diamond.

The man shook his head.

Cavanaugh added a second.

The man shook his head again. He pointed to the plane, made motions as if putting earphones on his head, cocked his head in a listening attitude, and shook his head once more. *No radio.*

With one flattened hand, he made a zooming motion upward; with the other, he drew a swift line across his throat. *Suicide.*

Then he sketched an unmilitary salute. *Thanks just the same.*

Cavanaugh climbed down from the wing. The next pilot he found gave him the same answer; and the next; and the next. There wasn't any fifth, because, in taking a shortcut under a low wing, he tripped over two silently struggling gentlemen who promptly transferred their quarrel to him. When he recovered from a momentary inattention, they were gone, and so was the wallet with the diamonds.

Cavanaugh walked back to Manhattan.

Counting the time he spent asleep under a trestle somewhere in Queens, it took him twelve hours. Even an Oregonian can find his way around in Manhattan, but a Manhattanite gets lost anywhere away from his island. Cavanaugh missed the Queensborough Bridge somehow, wandered south into Brooklyn without realizing it (he would rather have died), and wound up some sixty blocks off his course at the Williamsburg Bridge; this led him via Delancey Street into the Lower East Side, which was not much improvement.

Following the line of least resistance, and yearning for civilization (i.e., midtown New York), Cavanaugh moved northwestward along that erstwhile cowpath variously named the Bowery, Fourth Avenue and Broadway. Pausing only to rummage in a Union Square fruit-drink stand for cold frankfurters, he reached Forty-second Street at half-past ten, twenty-three and one half hours after his introduction to the Hooligan.

Times Square, never a very inspiring sight in the morning, was very sad and strange. Traffic, a thin trickle, was moving spasmodically. Every car had its windows closed tight, and Cavanaugh saw more than one passenger holding a rifle. The crowds on the littered sidewalks did not seem to be going anywhere, or even thinking about going anywhere. They were huddling.

Bookstores were empty and their contents scattered over the pavement; novelty shops, cafeterias, drugstores . . . the astonishing thing was that, here and there, trade was still going on. Money would still buy you a bottle of liquor, or a pack of cigarettes, or a can of food—the necessities. Pricing was a problem, but it was being solved in a forthright manner: above each counter, the main items of the store's stock in trade were displayed, each with one or two bills pasted to it. Cigarettes—George Washington. A fifth of whisky—Alexander Hamilton and Abraham Lincoln. A can of ersatzized meat—Andrew Jackson.

There was even one movie house open for business. It was showing a Charlie Chaplin Festival.

Cavanaugh was feeling extremely lightheaded and unsubstantial. Babylon, that great city! he thought; and Somewhere, apparently, in the ginnandgo gap between antediluvious and annodominant the copyist must have fled with his scroll. . . .

The human race had now, in effect, Had It. New York was no longer a city; it was simply the raw material for an archeologist's puzzle—a midden heap. And thinking of *Finnegan* again, he remembered, What a mnice old mness it all mnakes!

He looked at the faces around him, blank with a new misery, the misery of silence. That's what hits them the hardest, he thought. The speechlessness. They don't care about not being able to read—it's a minor annoyance. But they like to talk.

And yet, the human race could have survived if only the spoken word had been bollixed up, not the written word. It would have been easy enough to work out universal sound symbols for the few situations where speech was really vital. Nothing could replace the textbooks, the records, the libraries, the business letters.

By now, Cavanaugh thought bitterly, the Hooligan was trading shiny beads for grass skirts in Honolulu, or carved walrus tusks in Alaska, or . . .

Or was he? Cavanaugh stopped short. He had, he realized, been thinking of the Hooligan popping into view all over the globe the way he had appeared in his apartment—and, when he was through, popping back to where he belonged from wherever he happened to be.

But, if he could travel that way, *why had he left Cavanaugh's place on a Second Avenue bus?*

Cavanaugh scrabbled frantically through his memory. His knees sagged.

The Hooligan had showed him in the disk, that the two—universes, call them—came together rarely, and when they did, touched at one point only. Last time, the plain of Shinar. This time, Cavanaugh's living room.

And that one flicker, light-dark-light, before the pictured Hooligan moved back to its own sphere . . .

Twenty-four hours.

Cavanaugh looked at his watch. It was 10:37.

He ran.

Lead-footed, three quarters dead, and cursing himself, the Hooligan, the human race, God the Creator and the entire imaginable cosmos with the last breath in his body, Cavanaugh reached the corner of Forty-ninth and Second just in time to see the Hooligan pedaling briskly up the avenue on a bicycle.

He shouted, or tried to; nothing but a wheeze came out.

Whistling with agony, he lurched around the corner and ran to keep from falling on his face. He almost caught up with the Hooligan at the entrance to the building, but he couldn't stop to get the breath to make a noise. The Hooligan darted inside and up the stairs; Cavanaugh followed.

He can't open the door, he thought, halfway up. But when he reached the third-floor landing, the door was open.

Cavanaugh made one last effort, leaped like a salmon, tripped over the doorsill, and spread-eagled himself on the floor in the middle of the room.

The Hooligan, one step away from the drawing table, turned with a startled "Chaya-dnih?"

Seeing Cavanaugh, he came forward with an expression of pop-eyed concern. Cavanaugh couldn't move.

Muttering excitedly to himself, the Hooligan produced the green-and-white doodad from somewhere—much, presumably, as a human being might have gone for the medicinal brandy—and set it on the floor near Cavanaugh's head.

"Urgh!" said Cavanaugh. With one hand, he clutched the Hooligan's disk.

The pictures formed without any conscious planning: the doodad, the lights flashing off and on in a skull—dozens, hundreds of skulls—then buildings falling, trains crashing, volcanoes erupting. . . .

The Hooligan's eyes bulged half out of their sockets. "Hakdaz!" he said, clapping his hands to his ears. He seized the disk and made conciliatory pictures—the doodad and a glass of wine melting into each other.

"I know that," said Cavanaugh hoarsely, struggling up to one elbow. "But *can you fix it?*" He made a picture of the Hooligan gesturing at the flashing lights, which promptly vanished.

"Deech, deech," said the Hooligan, nodding violently. He picked up the doodad and somehow broke the green base of it into dozens of tiny cubes, which he began to reassemble, apparently in a different order, with great care.

Cavanaugh hauled himself up into an armchair and let himself go limp as a glove. He watched the Hooligan, telling himself drowsily that if he wasn't careful, he'd be asleep in another minute. There was something odd about the room, something extraordinarily soothing. . . . After a moment he realized what it was.

The silence.

The two fishwives who infested the floor below were not screaming pleasantries across the courtyard at each other. Nobody was playing moron music on a radio tuned six times too loud for normal hearing.

The landlady was not shouting instructions from the top floor to the janitor in the basement.

Silence. Peace.

For some reason, Cavanaugh's mind turned to the subject of silent films: Chaplin, the Keystone Cops, Douglas Fairbanks, Garbo . . . they would have to bring them out of the cans again, he thought, for everybody, not just the patrons of the Museum of Modern Art Film Library. . . .

Congress would have to rig up some sort of Telautograph system, with a screen above the Speaker's desk, perhaps.

Television. Television, thought Cavanaugh dreamily, would have to shut up and put up.

No more campaign oratory.

No more banquet speeches.

No more singing commercials.

Cavanaugh sat up. "Listen," he said tensely. "Could you fix just the writing—not the speech?"

The Hooligan goggled at him and held out the disk.

Cavanaugh took it and slowly began putting the idea into careful pictures. . . .

The Hooligan was gone—vanished like a burst soap bubble at the end of a headfirst dive across Cavanaugh's drawing table.

Cavanaugh sat where he was, listening. From outside, after a moment, came a confused, distance-muted roar. All over the city—all over the world, Cavanaugh supposed—people were discovering that they could read again; that the signs meant what they said; that each man's sudden island had been rejoined to the main.

It lasted twenty minutes and then faded slowly. In his mind's eye, Cavanaugh saw the orgy of scribbling that must be beginning now. He sat, and listened to the blessed silence.

In a little while a growing twinge forced itself upon his attention, like a forgotten toothache. After a moment, Cavanaugh identified it as his conscience. Just who are you, conscience was saying, to take away the gift of speech—the thing that once was all that distinguished man from the apes?

Cavanaugh dutifully tried to feel repentant, but it didn't work. Who said it was a gift? he asked his conscience. What did we use it for?

I'll tell you, he said. In the cigar store: Hey, waddaya think of them Yankees? Yeah, that was som'n, wasn't it? Sure was! I tell you . . .

At home: So, how was the office t'day? Aa. Same goddamn madhouse. How'd it go with you? Awright. I can't complain. Kids okay? Yaa. Uh-huh. What's f-dinner?

At a party: Hello, Harry! Whattaya say, boy! How are ya? That's good. How's the . . . so I said to him, you can't tell me what I'm gonna . . . like to, but it don't agree with me. It's my stummick; th' doctor says . . . organdy, with little gold buttons . . . Oh, yeah? Well, how would you like a poke in the snoot?

On the street corners: Lebensraum . . . Nordische Blut . . .

I, said Cavanaugh, rest my case.

Conscience did not reply.

In the silence, Cavanaugh walked across the room to the record cabinet and pulled out an album. He could read the lettering on its spine: MAHLER, *The Song of the Earth*.

He picked out one of the disks and put it on the machine—the "Drunkard's Song" in the fifth movement.

Cavanaugh smiled beatifically, listening. It was an artificial remedy, he was thinking; from the Hooligan's point of view, the human race was now permanently a little tipsy. And so what?

The words the tenor was singing were gibberish to Cavanaugh—but then they always had been; Cavanaugh spoke no German. He knew what the words meant.

Was geht mich denn der Frühling an!?
Lasst mich betrunken sein!
"What then is the spring to me?
. . . Let me be drunk!"

ANACHRON

The body was never found. And for that reason alone, there was no body to find.

It sounds like inverted logic—which, in a sense, it is—but there's no paradox involved. It was a perfectly orderly and explicable event, even though it could only have happened to a Castellare.

Odd fish, the Castellare brothers. Sons of a Scots-Englishwoman and an expatriate Italian, born in England, educated on the Continent, they were at ease anywhere in the world and at home nowhere.

Nevertheless, in their middle years, they had become settled men. Expatriates like their father, they lived on the island of Ischia, off the Neapolitan coast, in a palace—*quattrocento*, very fine, with peeling cupids on the walls, a multitude of rats, no central heating and no neighbors.

They went nowhere; no one except their agents and their lawyers came to them. Neither had ever married. Each, at about the age of thirty, had given up the world of people for an inner world of more precise and more enduring pleasures. Each was an amateur—a fanatical, compulsive amateur.

They had been born out of their time.

Peter's passion was virtu. He collected relentlessly, it would not be too much to say savagely; he collected as some men hunt big game. His taste was catholic, and his acquisitions filled the huge rooms of the palace and half the vaults under them—paintings, statuary, enamels, porcelain, glass, crystal, metalwork. At fifty, he was a round little man with small, sardonic eyes and a careless patch of pinkish goatee.

Harold Castellare, Peter's talented brother, was a scientist. An amateur scientist. He belonged in the nineteenth century, as Peter was a throwback to a still earlier epoch. Modern science is largely a matter of teamwork and drudgery, both impossible concepts to a Castellare. But Harold's intelligence was in its own way as penetrating and original as a

Newton's or a Franklin's. He had done respectable work in physics and electronics, and had even, at his lawyer's instance, taken out a few patents. The income from these, when his own purchases of instruments and equipment did not consume it, he gave to his brother, who accepted it without gratitude or rancor.

Harold, at fifty-three, was spare and shrunken, sallow and spotted, with a bloodless, melancholy countenance; on his upper lip grew a neat hedge of pink-and-salt mustache, the companion piece and antithesis of his brother's goatee.

On a certain May morning, Harold had an accident.

Goodyear dropped rubber on a hot stove; Archimedes took a bath; Curie left a piece of uranium ore in a drawer with a photographic plate. Harold Castellare, working patiently with an apparatus which had so far consumed a great deal of current without producing anything more spectacular than some rather unusual corona effects, sneezed convulsively and dropped an ordinary bar magnet across two charged terminals.

Above the apparatus a huge, cloudy bubble sprang into being.

Harold, getting up from his instinctive crouch, blinked at it in profound astonishment. As he watched, the cloudiness abruptly disappeared and he was looking *through* the bubble at a section of tesselated flooring that seemed to be about three feet above the real floor. He could also see the corner of a carved wooden bench, and on the bench a small, oddly shaped stringed instrument.

Harold swore fervently to himself, made agitated notes, and then began to experiment. He tested the sphere cautiously with an electroscope, with a magnet, with a Geiger counter. Negative. He tore a tiny bit of paper from his notepad and dropped it toward the sphere. The paper disappeared; he couldn't see where it went.

Speechless, Harold picked up a meter stick and thrust it delicately forward. There was no feeling of contact; the rule went into and through the bubble as if the latter did not exist. Then it touched the stringed instrument, with a solid click. Harold pushed. The instrument slid over the edge of the bench and struck the floor with a hollow thump and jangle.

Staring at it, Harold suddenly recognized its tantalizingly familiar shape.

Recklessly he let go the meter stick, reached in and picked the fragile thing out of the bubble. It was solid and cool in his fingers. The varnish was clear, the color of the wood glowing through it. It looked as if it might have been made yesterday.

Peter owned one almost exactly like it, except for preservation— a viola d'amore of the seventeenth century.

Harold stooped to look through the bubble horizontally. Gold and rust tapestries hid the wall, fifty feet away, except for an ornate door in the center. The door began to open; Harold saw a flicker of umber.

Then the sphere went cloudy again. His hands were empty; the viola d'amore was gone. And the meter stick, which he had dropped inside the sphere, lay on the floor at his feet.

"Look at that," said Harold simply.

Peter's eyebrows went up slightly. "What is it, a new kind of television?"

"No, no. Look here." The viola d'amore lay on the bench, precisely where it had been before. Harold reached into the sphere and drew it out.

Peter started. "Give me that." He took it in his hands, rubbed the smoothly finished wood. He stared at his brother. "By God and all the saints," he said. "Time travel."

Harold snorted impatiently. "My dear Peter, 'time' is a meaningless word taken by itself, just as 'space' is."

"But, barring that, time travel."

"If you like, yes."

"You'll be quite famous."

"I expect so."

Peter looked down at the instrument in his hands. "I'd like to keep this, if I may."

"I'd be very happy to let you, but you can't."

As he spoke, the bubble went cloudy; the viola d'amore was gone like smoke.

"There, you see?"

"What sort of devil's trick is that?"

"It goes back. . . . Later you'll see. I had that thing out once before, and this happened. When the sphere became transparent again, the viol was where I had found it."

"And your explanation for this?"

Harold hesitated. "None. Until I can work out the appropriate mathematics—"

"Which may take you some time. Meanwhile, in layman's language—"

Harold's face creased with the effort and interest of translation. "Very roughly, then—I should say it means that events are conserved. Two or three centuries ago—"

"Three. Notice the sound holes."

"Three centuries ago, then, at this particular time of day, someone was in that room. If the viola were gone, he or she would have noticed the fact. That would constitute an alteration of events already fixed; therefore it doesn't happen. For the same reason, I conjecture, we can't see into the sphere, or"—he probed at it with a fountain pen—"I thought not—or reach into it to touch anything; that would also constitute an alteration. And anything we put into the sphere while it is transparent comes out again when it becomes opaque. To put it very crudely, we cannot alter the past."

"But it seems to me that we did alter it. Just now, when you took the viol out, even if no one of that time saw it happen."

"This," said Harold, "is the difficulty of using language as a means of exact communication. If you had not forgotten all your calculus . . . However. It may be postulated (remembering of course that everything I say is a lie, because I say it in English) than an event which doesn't influence other events is not an event. In other words—"

"That, since no one saw you take it, it doesn't matter whether you took it or not. A rather dangerous precept, Harold; you would have been burned at the stake for that at one time."

"Very likely. But it can be stated in another way or, indeed, in an infinity of ways which only seem to be different. If someone, let us say God, were to remove the moon as I am talking to you, using zero duration, and substitute an exact replica made of concrete and plaster of Paris, with the same mass, albedo and so on as the genuine moon, it would make no measurable difference in the universe as we perceive it —and therefore we cannot certainly say that it hasn't happened. Nor, I may add, does it make any difference whether it has or not."

" 'When there's no one about on the quad,' " said Peter.

"Yes. A basic and, as a natural consequence, a meaningless problem of philosophy. Except," he added, "in this one particular manifestation."

He stared at the cloudy sphere. "You'll excuse me, won't you, Peter? I've got to work on this."

"When will you publish, do you suppose?"

"Immediately. That's to say, in a week or two."

"Don't do it till you've talked it over with me, will you? I have a notion about it."

Harold looked at him sharply. "Commercial?"

"In a way."

"No," said Harold. "This is not the sort of thing one patents or keeps secret, Peter."

"Of course. I'll see you at dinner, I hope?"

"I think so. If I forget, knock on the door, will you?"

"Yes. Until then."

"Until then."

At dinner, Peter asked only two questions.

"Have you found any possibility of changing the time your thing reaches—from the seventeenth century to the eighteenth, for example, or from Monday to Tuesday?"

"Yes, as a matter of fact. Amazing. It's lucky that I had a rheostat already in the circuit; I wouldn't dare turn the current off. Varying the amperage varies the time set. I've had it up to what I think was Wednesday of last week—at any rate, my smock was lying over the workbench where I left it, I remember, Wednesday afternoon. I pulled it out. A curious sensation, Peter—I was wearing the same smock at the time. And then the sphere went opaque and of course the smock vanished. That must have been myself, coming into the room."

"And the future?"

"Yes. Another funny thing, I've had it forward to various times in the near future, and the machine itself is still there, but nothing's been done to it—none of the things I'm thinking I might do. That might be because of the conservation of events, again, but I rather think not. Still farther forward there are cloudy areas, blanks; I can't see anything that isn't in existence now, apparently, but here, in the next few days, there's nothing of that.

"It's as if I were going away. Where do you suppose I'm going?"

Harold's abrupt departure took place between midnight and morning. He packed his own grip, it would seem, left unattended, and was seen no more. It was extraordinary, of course, that he should have left at all, but the details were in no way odd. Harold had always detested what he called "the tyranny of the valet." He was, as everyone knew, a most independent man.

On the following day Peter made some trifling experiments with the time-sphere. From the sixteenth century he picked up a scent bottle of Venetian glass; from the eighteenth, a crucifix of carved rosewood;

from the nineteenth, when the palace had been the residence of an Austrian count and his Italian mistress, a hand-illuminated copy of De Sade's *La Nouvelle Justine*, very curiously bound in human skin.

They all vanished, naturally, within minutes or hours—all but the scent bottle. This gave Peter matter for reflection. There had been half a dozen flickers of cloudiness in the sphere just futureward of the bottle; it ought to have vanished, but it hadn't. But then, he had found it on the floor near a wall with quite a large rat hole in it.

When objects disappeared unaccountably, he asked himself, was it because they had rolled into rat holes, or because some time fisher had picked them up when they were in a position to do so?

He did not make any attempt to explore the future. That afternoon he telephoned his lawyers in Naples and gave them instructions for a new will. His estate, including his half of the jointly owned Ischia property, was to go to the Italian government on two conditions: (1) that Harold Castellare should make a similar bequest of the remaining half of the property and (2) that the Italian government should turn the palace into a national museum to house Peter's collection, using the income from his estate for its administration and for further acquisitions. His surviving relatives—two cousins in Scotland—he cut off with a shilling each.

He did nothing more until after the document had been brought out to him, signed and witnessed. Only then did he venture to look into his own future.

Events were conserved, Harold had said—meaning, Peter very well understood, events of the present and future as well as of the past. But was there only one pattern in which the future could be fixed? Could a result exist before its cause had occurred?

The Castellare motto was *Audentes fortuna juvat*—into which Peter, at the age of fourteen, had interpolated the word "*prudentesque*": "Fortune favors the bold—and the prudent."

Tomorrow: no change; the room he was looking at was so exactly like this one that the time sphere seemed to vanish. The next day: a cloudy blur. And the next, and the next . . .

Opacity, straight through to what Peter judged, by the distance he had moved the rheostat handle, to be ten years ahead. Then, suddenly, the room was a long marble hall filled with display cases.

Peter smiled wryly. If you were Harold, obviously you could not look ahead and see Peter working in your laboratory. And if you were Peter, equally obviously, you could not look ahead and know whether the room you saw was an improvement you yourself were going to make, or part of a museum established after your death, eight or nine years from now, or . . .

No. Eight years was little enough, but he could not even be sure of that. It would, after all, be seven years before Harold could be declared legally dead. . . .

Peter turned the vernier knob slowly forward. A flicker, another, a long series. Forward faster. Now the flickering melted into a grayness; objects winked out of existence and were replaced by others in the showcases; the marble darkened and lightened again, darkened and lightened, darkened and remained dark. He was, Peter judged, looking at the hall as it would be some five hundred years in the future. There was a thick film of dust on every exposed surface; rubbish and the carcass of some small animal had been swept carelessly into a corner.

The sphere clouded.

When it cleared, there was an intricate trail of footprints in the dust, and two of the showcases were empty.

The footprints were splayed, trifurcate, and thirty inches long.

After a moment's deliberation Peter walked around the workbench and leaned down to look through the sphere from the opposite direction. Framed in the nearest of the four tall windows was a scene of picture-postcard banality: the sun-silvered bay and the foreshortened arc of the city, with Vesuvio faintly fuming in the background. But there was something wrong about the colors, even grayed as they were by distance.

Peter went and got his binoculars.

The trouble was, of course, that Naples was green. Where the city ought to have been, a rankness had sprouted. Between the clumps of foliage he could catch occasional glimpses of gray-white that might equally well have been boulders or the wreckage of buildings. There was no movement. There was no shipping in the harbor.

But something rather odd was crawling up the side of the volcano. A rust-orange pipe, it appeared to be, supported on hairline struts like the legs of a centipede, and ending without rhyme or reason just short of the top.

While Peter watched, it turned slowly blue.

One day further forward: now all the display cases had been looted; the museum, it would seem, was empty.

Given, that in five centuries the world, or at any rate the department of Campania, has been overrun by a race of Somethings, the human population being killed or driven out in the process; and that the conquerors take an interest in the museum's contents, which they have accordingly removed.

Removed where, and why?

This question, Peter conceded, might have a thousand answers, nine hundred and ninety-nine of which would mean that he had lost his gamble. The remaining answer was: to the vaults, for safety.

With his own hands Peter built a hood to cover the apparatus on the workbench and the sphere above it. It was unaccustomed labor; it took him the better part of two days. Then he called in workmen to break a hole in the stone flooring next to the interior wall, rig a hoist, and cut the power cable that supplied the time-sphere loose from its supports all the way back to the fuse box, leaving him a single flexible length of cable more than a hundred feet long. They unbolted the workbench from the floor, attached casters to its legs, lowered it into the empty vault below, and went away.

Peter unfastened and removed the hood. He looked into the sphere.

Treasure.

Crates, large and small, racked in rows into dimness.

With pudgy fingers that did not tremble, he advanced the rheostat. A cloudy flicker, another, a leaping blur of them as he moved the vernier faster—and then there were no more, to the limit of the time-sphere's range.

Two hundred years, Peter guessed—A.D. 2700 to 2900 or thereabout —in which no one would enter the vault. Two hundred years of "unliquidated time."

He put the rheostat back to the beginning of that uninterrupted period. He drew out a small crate and prized it open.

Chessmen, ivory with gold inlay, Florentine, fourteenth century. Superb.

Another, from the opposite rack.

Tang figurines, horses and men, ten to fourteen inches high. Priceless.

The crates would not burn, Tomaso told him. He went down to the kitchen to see, and it was true. The pieces lay in the roaring stove untouched. He fished one out with a poker; even the feathery splinters of the unplaned wood had not ignited.

It made a certain extraordinary kind of sense. When the moment came for the crates to go back, any physical scrambling that had occurred in the meantime would have no effect; they would simply put themselves together as they had been before, like Thor's goats. But burning was another matter; burning would have released energy which could not be replaced.

That settled one paradox, at any rate. There was another that nagged at Peter's orderly mind. If the things he took out of that vault, seven hundred-odd years in the future, were to become part of the collection bequeathed by him to the museum, preserved by it, and eventually stored in the vault for him to find—then precisely where had they come from in the first place?

It worried him. Peter had learned in life, as his brother had in physics, that one never gets anything for nothing.

Moreover, this riddle was only one of his perplexities, and that not among the greatest. For another example, there was the obstinate opacity of the time-sphere whenever he attempted to examine the immediate future. However often he tried it, the result was always the same: a cloudy blank, all the way forward to the sudden unveiling of the marble gallery.

It was reasonable to expect the sphere to show nothing at times when he himself was going to be in the vault, but this accounted for only five or six hours out of every twenty-four. Again, presumably, it would show him no changes to be made by himself, since foreknowledge would make it possible for him to alter his actions. But he laboriously cleared one end of the vault, put up a screen to hide the rest and made a vow—which he kept—not to alter the clear space or move the screen for a week. Then he tried again—with the same result.

The only remaining explanation was that sometime during the next ten years something was going to happen which he would prevent if he could; and the clue to it was there, buried in that frustrating, unbroken blankness.

As a corollary, it was going to be something which he *could* prevent if only he knew what it was . . . or even when it was supposed to happen.

The event in question, in all probability, was his own death. Peter therefore hired nine men to guard him, three to a shift—because one man alone could not be trusted, two might conspire against him, whereas three, with the very minimum of effort, could be kept in a state of mutual suspicion. He also underwent a thorough medical examination, had new locks installed on every door and window, and took every other precaution ingenuity could suggest. When he had done all these things, the next ten years were as blank as before.

Peter had more than half expected it. He checked through his list of safeguards once more, found it good, and thereafter let the matter rest. He had done all he could; either he would survive the crisis or he would not. In either case, events were conserved; the time-sphere could give him no forewarning.

Another man might have found his pleasure blunted by guilt and fear; Peter's was whetted to a keener edge. If he had been a recluse before, now he was an eremite; he grudged every hour that was not given to his work. Mornings he spent in the vault, unpacking his acquisitions; afternoons and evenings, sorting, cataloguing, examining and—the word is not too strong—gloating. When three weeks had passed in this way, the shelves were bare as far as the power cable would allow him to reach in every direction, except for crates whose contents were undoubtedly too large to pass through the sphere. These, with heroic self-control, Peter had left untouched.

And still he had looted only a hundredth part of that incredible treasure house. With grappling hooks he could have extended his reach by perhaps three or four yards, but at the risk of damaging his prizes; and in any case this would have been no solution but only a postponement of the problem. There was nothing for it but to go through the sphere himself and unpack the crates while on the other "side" of it.

Peter thought about it in a fury of concentration for the rest of the day. So far as he was concerned, there was no question that the gain would be worth any calculated risk; the problem was how to measure the risk and if possible reduce it.

Item: He felt a definite uneasiness at the thought of venturing through that insubstantial bubble. Intuition was supported, if not by logic, at least by a sense of the dramatically appropriate. Now, if ever, would be the time for his crisis.

Item: Common sense did not concur. The uneasiness had two symbols. One was the white face of his brother Harold just before the water closed over it; the other was a phantasm born of those gigantic, splayed footprints in the dust of the gallery. In spite of himself, Peter had often found himself trying to imagine what the creatures that made them must look like, until his visualization was so clear that he could almost swear he had seen them.

Towering monsters they were, with crested ophidian heads and great unwinking eyes; and they moved in a strutting glide, nodding their heads, like fantastic barnyard fowl.

But, taking these premonitory images in turn: first, it was impossible that he should ever be seriously inconvenienced by Harold's death. There were no witnesses, he was sure; he had struck the blow with a stone; stones also were the weights that had dragged the body down, and the rope was an odd length Peter had picked up on the shore. Second, the three-toed Somethings might be as fearful as all the world's bogies put together; it made no difference, he could never meet them.

Nevertheless, the uneasiness persisted. Peter was not satisfied; he wanted a lifeline. When he found it, he wondered that he had not thought of it before.

He would set the time-sphere for a period just before one of the intervals of blankness. That would take care of accidents, sudden illnesses, and other unforeseeable contingencies. It would also insure him against one very real and not at all irrational dread: the fear that the mechanism which generated the time-sphere might fail while he was on the other side. For the conservation of events was not a condition created by the sphere but one which limited its operation. No matter what happened, it was impossible for him to occupy the same place-time as any future or past observer; therefore, when the monster entered that vault, Peter would not be there any more.

There was, of course, the scent bottle to remember. Every rule has its exception; but in this case, Peter thought, the example did not apply. A scent bottle could roll into a rat hole; a man could not.

He turned the rheostat carefully back to the last flicker of grayness; past that to the next, still more carefully. The interval between the two, he judged, was something under an hour: excellent.

His pulse seemed a trifle rapid, but his brain was clear and cool. He thrust his head into the sphere and sniffed cautiously. The air was stale and had a faint, unpleasant odor, but it was breathable.

Using a crate as a stepping stool, he climbed to the top of the workbench. He arranged another crate close to the sphere to make a platform level with its equator. And seven and a half centuries in the future, a third crate stood on the floor directly under the sphere.

Peter stepped into the sphere, dropped, and landed easily, legs bending to take the shock. When he straightened, he was standing in what to all appearances was a large circular hole in the workbench; his chin was just above the top of the sphere.

He lowered himself, half squatting, until he had drawn his head through and stepped down from the crate.

He was in the future vault. The sphere was a brightly luminous thing that hung unsupported in the air behind him, its midpoint just higher than his head. The shadows it cast spread black and wedge-shaped in every direction, melting into obscurity.

Peter's heart was pounding miserably. He had an illusory stifling sensation, coupled with the idiotic notion that he ought to be wearing a diver's helmet. The silence was like the pause before a shout.

But down the aisles marched the crated treasures in their hundreds.

Peter set to work. It was difficult, exacting labor, opening the crates where they lay, removing the contents and nailing the crates up again, all without disturbing the positions of the crates themselves, but it was the price he had to pay for his lifeline. Each crate was in a sense a microcosm, like the vault itself—a capsule of unliquidated time. But the vault's term would end some fifty minutes from now, when crested heads nodded down these aisles; those of the crates' interiors, for all that Peter knew to the contrary, went on forever.

The first crate contained lacework porcelain; the second, shakudô sword hilts; the third, an exquisite fourth-century Greek ornament in *repoussé* bronze, the equal in every way of the Siris bronzes.

Peter found it almost physically difficult to set the thing down, but he did so; standing on his platform crate in the future with his head projecting above the sphere in the present—like (again the absurd thought!) a diver rising from the ocean—he laid it carefully beside the others on the workbench.

Then down again, into the fragile silence and the gloom. The next crates were too large, and those just beyond were doubtful. Peter followed his shadow down the aisle. He had almost twenty minutes left: enough for one more crate, chosen with care, and an ample margin.

Glancing to his right at the end of the row, he saw a door. It was a heavy door, rivet-studded, with a single iron step below it. There had been no door there in Peter's time; the whole plan of the building must have been altered. *Of course!* he realized suddenly. If it had not, if so much as a single tile or lintel had remained of the palace as he knew it, then the sphere could never have let him see or enter this particular here-and-now, this—what would Harold have called it?—this nexus in space-time.

For if you saw any now-existing thing as it was going to appear in the future, you could alter it in the present—carve your initials in it, break it apart, chop it down—which was manifestly impossible, and therefore . . .

And therefore the first ten years were necessarily blank when he looked into the sphere, not because anything unpleasant was going to happen to him, but because in that time the last traces of the old palace had not yet been eradicated.

There was no crisis.

Wait a moment, though! Harold had been able to look into the near future. . . . But—of course—Harold had been about to die.

In the dimness between himself and the door he saw a rack of crates that looked promising. The way was uneven; one of the untidy accumulations of refuse that seemed to be characteristic of the Somethings lay in windrows across the floor. Peter stepped forward carefully—but not carefully enough.

Harold Castellare had had another accident—and again, if you choose to look at it in that way, a lucky one. The blow stunned him; the old rope slipped from the stones; flaccid, he floated where a struggling man might have drowned. A fishing boat nearly ran him down, and picked him up instead. He was suffering from a concussion, shock, exposure, asphyxiation and was more than three quarters dead. But he was still alive when he was delivered, an hour later, to a hospital in Naples.

There were, of course, no identifying papers, labels or monograms in his clothing—Peter had seen to that—and for the first week after his rescue Harold was quite genuinely unable to give any account of himself. During the second week he was mending but uncommunicative, and at the end of the third, finding that there was some difficulty about gaining his release in spite of his physical recovery, he affected to regain his memory, gave a circumstantial but entirely fictitious identification and was discharged.

To understand this as well as all his subsequent actions, it is only necessary to remember that Harold was a Castellare. In Naples, not wishing to give Peter any unnecessary anxiety, he did not approach his bank for funds but cashed a check with an incurious acquaintance, and predated it by four weeks. With part of the money so acquired he paid his hospital bill and rewarded his rescuers. Another part went for new clothing and for four days' residence in an inconspicuous hotel, while he grew used to walking and dressing himself again. The rest, on his last day, he spent in the purchase of a discreetly small revolver and a box of cartridges.

He took the last boat to Ischia and arrived at his own front door a few minutes before eleven. It was a cool evening, and a most cheerful fire was burning in the central hall.

"Signor Peter is well, I suppose," said Harold, removing his coat.
"Yes, Signor Harold. He is very well, very busy with his collection."
"Where is he? I should like to speak to him."
"He is in the vaults, Signor Harold. But . . ."
"Yes?"
"Signor Peter sees no one when he is in the vaults. He has given strict orders that no one is to bother him, Signor Harold, when he is in the vaults."
"Oh, well," said Harold. "I daresay he'll see me."

It was a thing something like a bear trap, apparently, except that instead of two semicircular jaws it had four segments that snapped together in the middle, each with a shallow, sharp tooth. The pain was quite unendurable.

Each segment moved at the end of a thin arm, cunningly hinged so that the ghastly thing would close over whichever of the four triggers you stepped on. Each arm had a spring too powerful for Peter's muscles. The whole affair was connected by a chain to a staple solidly embedded in the concrete floor; it left Peter free to move some ten inches in any direction. Short of gnawing off his own leg, he thought sickly, there was very little he could do about it.

The riddle was, what could the thing possibly be doing here? There were rats in the vaults, no doubt, now as in his own time, but surely nothing larger. Was it conceivable that even the three-toed Somethings would set an engine like this to catch a rat?

Lost inventions, Peter thought irrelevantly, had a way of being rediscovered. Even if he suppressed the time-sphere during his lifetime and it did not happen to survive him, still there might be other time-fishers in the remote future—not here, perhaps, but in other treasure houses of the world. And that might account for the existence of this metal-jawed horror. Indeed, it might account for the vault itself—a better man-trap—except that it was all nonsense; the trap could only be full until the trapper came to look at it. Events, and the lives of prudent time-travelers, were conserved.

And he had been in the vault for almost forty minutes. Twenty minutes to go, twenty-five, thirty at the most, then the Somethings would enter and their entrance would free him. He had his lifeline; the knowledge was the only thing that made it possible to live with the pain that was the center of his universe just now. It was like going to the dentist, in the bad old days before procaine; it was very bad, sometimes, but you knew that it would end.

He cocked his head toward the door, holding his breath. A distant thud, another, then a curiously unpleasant squeaking, then silence.

But he had heard them. He knew they were there. It couldn't be much longer now.

Three men, two stocky, one lean, were playing cards in the passageway in front of the closed door that led to the vault staircase. They got up slowly.

"Who is he?" demanded the shortest one.

Tomaso clattered at him in furious Sicilian; the man's face darkened, but he looked at Harold with respect.

"I am now," stated Harold, "going down to see my brother."

"No, Signor," said the shortest one positively.

"You are impertinent," Harold told him.

"Yes, Signor."

Harold frowned. "You will not let me pass?"

"No, Signor."

"Then go and tell my brother I am here."

The shortest one said apologetically but firmly that there were strict orders against this also; it would have astonished Harold very much if he had said anything else.

"Well, at least I suppose you can tell me how long it will be before he comes out?"

"Not long, Signor. One hour, no more."

"Oh, very well, then," said Harold pettishly, turning half away. He paused. "One thing more," he said, taking the gun out of his pocket as he turned, "put your hands up and stand against the wall there, will you?"

The first two complied slowly. The third, the lean one, fired through his coat pocket, just like the gangsters in the American movies.

It was not a sharp sensation at all, Harold was surprised to find; it was more as if someone had hit him in the side with a cricket bat. The racket seemed to bounce interminably from the walls. He felt the gun jolt in his hand as he fired back, but couldn't tell if he had hit anybody. Everything seemed to be happening very slowly, and yet it was astonishingly hard to keep his balance. As he swung around he saw the two stocky ones with their hands half inside their jackets, and the lean one with his mouth open, and Tomaso with bulging eyes. Then the wall came at him and he began to swim along it, paying particular attention to the problem of not dropping one's gun.

As he weathered the first turn in the passageway the roar broke out afresh. A fountain of plaster stung his eyes; then he was running clumsily, and there was a bedlam of shouting behind him.

Without thinking about it he seemed to have selected the laboratory as his destination; it was an instinctive choice, without much to recommend it logically. In any case, he realized halfway across the central hall, he was not going to get there.

He turned and squinted at the passageway entrance; saw a blur move and fired at it. It disappeared. He turned again awkwardly, and had taken two steps nearer an armchair which offered the nearest shelter, when something clubbed him between the shoulderblades. One step more, knees buckling, and the wall struck him a second, softer blow. He toppled, clutching at the tapestry that hung near the fireplace.

When the three guards, whose names were Enrico, Alberto and Luca, emerged cautiously from the passage and approached Harold's body, it was already flaming like a Viking's in its impromptu shroud; the dim horses and men and falcons of the tapestry were writhing and crisping into brilliance. A moment later an uncertain ring of fire wavered toward them across the carpet.

Although the servants came with fire extinguishers and with buckets of water from the kitchen, and although the fire department was called, it was all quite useless. In five minutes the whole room was ablaze; in ten, as windows burst and walls buckled, the fire engulfed the second story. In twenty a mass of flaming timbers dropped into the vault through the hole Peter had made in the floor of the laboratory, utterly destroying the time-sphere apparatus and reaching shortly thereafter, as the authorities concerned were later to agree, an intensity of heat entirely sufficient to consume a human body without leaving any identifiable trace. For that reason alone, there was no trace of Peter's body to be found.

The sounds had just begun again when Peter saw the light from the time-sphere turn ruddy and then wink out like a snuffed candle.

In the darkness, he heard the door open.

SPECIAL DELIVERY

Len and Moira Connington lived in a rented cottage with a small yard, a smaller garden and too many fir trees. The lawn, which Len seldom had time to mow, was full of weeds, and the garden was overgrown with blackberry brambles. The house itself was clean and smelled better than most city apartments, and Moira kept geraniums in the windows; however, it was dark on account of the firs and on the wrong side of town. Approaching the door one late spring afternoon, Len tripped on a flagstone and scattered examination papers all the way to the porch.

When he picked himself up, Moira was giggling in the doorway. "That was funny."

"The hell it was," said Len. "I banged my nose." He picked up his Chemistry B papers in a stiff silence; a red drop fell on the last one. "God *damn* it!"

Moira held the screen door for him, looking contrite and faintly surprised. She followed him into the bathroom. "Len, I didn't mean to laugh. Does it hurt much?"

"No," said Len, staring fiercely at his scraped nose in the mirror, although in point of fact it was throbbing like a gong.

"That's good. It was the funniest thing—I mean, funny-peculiar," she said hastily.

Len stared at her; the whites of her eyes were showing. "Is there anything the matter with you?" he demanded.

"I don't know," she said on a rising note. "Nothing like that ever happened to me before. I didn't think it was funny at all, I was worried about you, and I didn't know I was going to laugh—" She laughed again, a trifle nervously. "Maybe I'm cracking up?"

Moira was a dark-haired young woman with a placid, friendly disposition; Len had met her in his senior year at Columbia, with—looking at it impartially, which Len seldom did—regrettable results. At present, in her seventh month, she was shaped like a rather bosomy kewpie doll.

Emotional upsets, he remembered, may occur frequently during this period. He leaned to get past her belly and kissed her forgivingly. "You're probably tired. Go sit down and I'll get you some coffee."

. . . Except that Moira had never had any hysterics till now, or morning sickness, either—she burped instead—and anyhow, was there anything in the literature about fits of giggling?

After supper he marked seventeen sets of papers desultorily in red pencil, then got up to look for the baby book. There were four dog-eared paperbound volumes with smiling infants' faces on the covers, but the one he wanted wasn't there. He looked behind the bookcase and on the wicker table beside it. "Moira!"

"Hm?"

"Where the bloody hell is the other baby book?"

"I've got it."

Len went and looked over her shoulder. She was staring at a mildly obscene drawing of a fetus lying in a sort of upside-down Yoga position inside a cutaway woman's body.

"That's what he looks like," she said. "Mama."

The diagram was of a fetus at term. "What was that about your mother?" Len asked, puzzled.

"Don't be silly," she said abstractedly.

He waited, but she didn't look up or turn the page. After a while he went back to his work.

He watched her. Eventually she leafed through to the back of the book, read a few pages, and put it down. She lighted a cigarette and immediately put it out again. She fetched up a resounding belch.

"That was a good one," said Len admiringly. Moira's belches surpassed anything ever heard in the men's locker rooms at Columbia; they shook doors and rattled windows.

Moira sighed.

Feeling tense, Len picked up his coffee cup and started toward the kitchen. He halted beside Moira's chair. On the side table was her after-dinner cup, still full of coffee: black, scummed with oil droplets, stone-cold.

"Didn't you want your coffee?"

She looked at the cup. "I did, but . . ." She paused and shook her head, looking perplexed. "I don't know."

"Well, do you want another cup now?"

"Yes, please. No."

Len, who had begun a step, rocked back on his heels. "Which, damn it?"

Her face got all swollen. "Oh, Len, I'm so mixed up," she said, and began to tremble.

Len felt part of his irritation spilling over into protectiveness. "What you need," he said firmly, "is a drink."

He climbed a stepladder to get at the top cabinet shelf which housed their liquor when they had any; small upstate towns and their school boards being what they were, this was one of many necessary precautions.

Inspecting the doleful three fingers of whisky in the bottle, Len swore under his breath. They couldn't afford a decent supply of booze, or new clothes for Moira, or— The original idea had been for Len to teach for a year while they saved enough money so that he could go back for his master's; more lately, this proving unlikely, they had merely been trying to put aside enough for summer school, and even that was beginning to look like the wildest optimism.

High-school teachers without seniority weren't supposed to be married. Or graduate physics students, for that matter.

He mixed two stiff highballs and carried them back into the living room. "Here you are. Skoal."

"Ah," she said appreciatively. "That tastes— Ugh." She set the glass down and stared at it with her mouth half open.

"What's the matter now?"

She turned her head carefully, as if she were afraid it would come off. "Len, *I don't know.* Mama."

"That's the second time you've said that. What is this all—"

"Said what?"

"Mama. Look, kid, if you're—"

"I didn't." She looked a little feverish.

"Sure you did," said Len reasonably. "Once when you were looking at the baby book, and then again just now, after you said ugh to the highball. Speaking of which—"

"Mama drink milk," said Moira, speaking with exaggerated clarity.

Moira hated milk. Len swallowed half his highball, turned and went silently into the kitchen.

When he came back with the milk, Moira looked at it as if it contained a snake. "Len, I didn't say that."

"Okay."

"I didn't. I didn't say mama and I didn't say that about the milk." Her voice quavered. "And I didn't laugh at you when you fell down."

"It was somebody else."

"It *was*." She looked down at her gingham-covered bulge. "You won't believe me. Put your hand there. A little lower."

Under the cloth her flesh was warm and solid against his palm. "Kicks?" he inquired.

"Not yet. Now," she said in a strained voice. "You in there. If you want your milk, kick three times."

Len opened his mouth and shut it again. Under his hand there were three squirming thrusts, one after the other.

Moira closed her eyes, held her breath and drank the milk down in one long horrid gulp.

"Once in a great while," Moira read, "cell cleavage will not have followed the orderly pattern that produces a normal baby. In these rare cases some parts of the body will develop excessively, while others do not develop at all. This disorderly cell growth, which is strikingly similar to the wild cell growth that we know as cancer—" Her shoulders moved convulsively. "Bluh."

"Why do you keep reading that stuff if it makes you feel that way?"

"I have to," she said absently. She picked up another book from the stack. "There's a page missing."

Len attacked the last of his egg in a noncommittal manner. "Wonder it's held together this long," he said. This was perfectly just; the book had had something spilled on it, partially dissolving the glue, and was in an advanced state of anarchy; however the fact was that Len had torn out the page in question four nights ago, after reading it carefully: the topic was "Psychoses in Pregnancy."

Moira had now decided that the baby was male, that his name was Leonardo (not referring to Len but to da Vinci), that he had informed her of these things along with a good many others, that he was keeping her from her favorite foods and making her eat things she detested, like liver and tripe, and that she had to read books of his choice all day long in order to keep him from kicking her in the bladder.

It was miserably hot; Commencement was only two weeks away, Len's students were fish-eyed and galvanic by turns. Then there was the matter of his contract for next year, and the possible opening at Oster High, which would mean more money, and the Parent-Teacher's thing tonight at which Superintendent Greer and his wife would be regally present. . . .

Moira was knee-deep in Volume I of *Der Untergang des Abendlandes,* moving her lips; an occasional guttural escaped her.

Len cleared his throat. "Moy?"

. . . *und also des tragischen*—what in God's name he means by that— What, Len?"

He made an irritated noise. "Why not try the English edition?"

"Leo wants to learn German. What were you going to say?"

Len closed his eyes for a moment. "About this PTA business—you sure you want to go?"

"Well, of *course.* It's pretty important, isn't it? Unless you think I look too sloppy—"

"No. No, damn it. But are you feeling up to it?"

There were faint violet crescents under Moira's eyes; she had been sleeping badly. "Sure," she said.

"All right. And you'll go see the sawbones tomorrow."

"I said I would."

"And you won't say anything about Leo to Mrs. Greer or anybody—"

She looked slightly embarrassed. "No. Not till he's born, I think, don't you? It would be an awful hard thing to prove—you wouldn't even have believed me if you hadn't felt him kick."

This experiment had not been repeated, though Len had asked often enough; all little Leo had wanted, Moira said, was to establish communication with his mother—he didn't seem to be really interested in Len at all. "Too young," she explained.

And still . . . Len recalled the frogs his biology class had dissected last semester. One of them had had two hearts. This disorderly cell growth . . . like a cancer. Unpredictable: extra fingers or toes—or a double helping of cortex?

"And I'll burp like a lady, if at all," Moira said cheerfully.

When the Conningtons arrived, the room was empty except for the ladies of the committee, two nervously smiling male teachers and the impressive bulk of Superintendent Greer. Card-table legs *skreeked* on the bare floor; the air was heavy with wood polish and musk.

Greer advanced, beaming fixedly. "Well, isn't this nice. How are you young folks this warm evening?"

"Oh, we thought we'd be *earlier,* Mr. Greer," said Moira with pretty vexation. She looked surprisingly schoolgirlish and chic; the lump that was Leo was hardly noticeable unless you caught her in profile. "I'll go right now and help the ladies. There must be *something* I can still do."

"No, now, we won't hear of it. But I'll tell you what you can do—you can go right over there and say hello to Mrs. Greer. I know she's dying to sit down and have a good chat with you. Go ahead now—don't worry about this husband of yours; I'll take care of him."

Moira receded into a scattering of small shrieks of pleasure, at least half of them arcing across a gap of mutual dislike.

Greer, exhibiting perfect dentures, exhaled Listerine. His pink skin looked not only scrubbed but disinfected; his gold-rimmed glasses belonged in an optometrist's window, and his tropical suit had obviously come straight from the cleaner's. It was impossible to think of Greer unshaven, Greer smoking a cigar, Greer with a smudge of axle grease on his forehead, or Greer making love to his wife.

"Well, sir, this weather . . ."

"When I think of what this valley was like twenty years ago . . ."

"At today's prices . . ."

Len listened with growing admiration, putting in comments where required; he had never realized before that there were so many absolutely neutral topics of conversation.

A few more people straggled in, raising the room temperature about half a degree per capita. Greer did not perspire, he merely glowed.

Across the room Moira was now seated chummily with Mrs. Greer, a large-bosomed woman in an outrageously unfashionable hat. Moira appeared to be telling a joke; Len knew perfectly well that it was a clean one, but he listened tensely, all the same, until he heard Mrs. Greer yelp with laughter. Her voice carried well. "Oh, that's *priceless!* Oh, dear, I *only* hope I can remember it!"

Len, who had resolutely not been thinking of ways to turn the conversation toward the Oster vacancy, stiffened again when he realized that Greer had abruptly begun to talk shop. His heart began pounding absurdly; Greer was asking highly pertinent questions in a good-humored but businesslike way—drawing Len out, and not even bothering to be Machiavellian about it.

Len answered candidly, except when he was certain he knew what the superintendent wanted to hear; then he lied like a Trojan.

Mrs. Greer had conjured up a premature pot of tea; and oblivious to the stares of the thirstier teachers present, she and Moira were hogging it, heads together, as if they were plotting the overthrow of the Republic or exchanging recipes.

Greer listened attentively to Len's final reply, which was delivered with as pious an air as if Len had been a Boy Scout swearing on the *Manual;* but since the question had been "Do you plan to make teaching your career?" there was not a word of truth in it.

He then inspected his paunch and assumed a mild theatrical frown. Len, with that social sixth sense which is unmistakable when it operates, knew that his next words were going to be: "You may have heard that Oster High will be needing a new science teacher next fall. . . ."

At this point Moira barked like a seal.

The ensuing silence was broken a moment later by a hearty scream, followed instantly by a clatter and a bone-shaking thud.

Mrs. Greer was sitting on the floor; legs sprawled, hat over her eye, she appeared to be attempting to perform some sort of orgiastic dance.

"It was Leo," Moira said incoherently. "You know she's English—and said of course a cup of tea wouldn't hurt me, and she kept telling me to go ahead and drink it while it was hot, and I couldn't—"

"No. No. Wait," said Len in a controlled fury. "What—"

"So I *drank* some. And Leo kicked up and made me burp the burp I was saving. And—"

"Oh, Christ."

"Then he kicked the teacup out of my hand into her lap, and I wish I was *dead.*"

On the following day, Len took Moira to the doctor's office, where they read dog-eared copies of *The Rotarian* and *Field and Stream* for an hour.

Dr. Berry was a round little man with soulful eyes and a twenty-four-hour bedside manner. On the walls of his office, where it is customary for doctors to hang at least seventeen diplomas and certificates of membership, Berry had three; the rest of the space was filled with enlarged, colored photographs of beautiful, beautiful children.

When Len followed Moira determinedly into the consulting room, Berry looked mildly shocked for a moment, then apparently decided to carry on as if nothing *outré* had happened. You could not say that he spoke, or even whispered; he rustled.

"Now, Mrs. Connington, we're looking just fine today. How have we been feeling?"

"Just fine. My husband thinks I'm insane."

"That's g—— Well, that's a funny thing for him to think, isn't it?"

Berry glanced at the wall midway between himself and Len, then shuffled some file cards rather nervously. "Now. Have we had any burning sensations in our urine?"

"No. Not as far as I'm— No."

"Any soreness in our stomach?"

"Yes. He's been kicking me black and blue."

Berry misinterpreted Moira's brooding glance at Len, and his eyebrows twitched involuntarily.

"The baby," said Len. "The baby kicks her."

Berry coughed. "Any headaches? Dizziness? Vomiting? Swelling in our legs or ankles?"

"No."

"All rightie. Now let's just find out how much we've gained, and then we'll get up on the examining table."

Berry drew the sheet down over Moira's abdomen as if it were an exceptionally fragile egg. He probed delicately with his fat fingertips, then used the stethoscope.

"Those X rays," said Len. "Have they come back yet?"

"Mm-hm," said Berry. "Yes, they have." He moved the stethoscope and listened again.

"Did they show anything unusual?"

Berry's eyebrows twitched a polite question.

"We've been having a little argument," Moira said in a strained voice, "about whether this is an ordinary baby or not."

Berry took the stethoscope tubes out of his ears. He gazed at Moira like an anxious spaniel. "Now let's not worry about *that*. We're going to have a perfectly healthy, wonderful baby, and if anybody tells us differently, why, we'll just tell them to jump in the lake, won't we?"

"The baby is absolutely normal?" Len said in a marked manner.

"Absolutely." Berry applied the stethoscope again. His face blanched.

"What's the matter?" Len asked after a moment. The doctor's gaze was fixed and glassy.

"*Vagitus uterinus*," Berry muttered. He pulled the stethoscope off abruptly and stared at it. "No, of course it couldn't be. Now isn't that a nuisance: we seem to be picking up a radio broadcast with our little stethoscope here. I'll just go and get another instrument."

Moira and Len exchanged glances. Moira's was almost excessively bland.

Berry came confidently in with a new stethoscope, put the diaphragm against Moira's belly, listened for an instant and twitched once all over, as if his mainspring had broken. Visibly jangling, he stepped away from the table. His jaw worked several times before any sound came out.

"Excuse me," he said, and walked out in an uneven line.

Len snatched up the instrument he had dropped.

Like a bell ringing under water, muffled but clear, a tiny voice was shouting: "*You bladder-headed pill-pusher! You bedside vacuum! You fifth-rate tree surgeon! You inflated enema bag!*" A pause. "*Is that you, Connington? Get off the line; I haven't finished with Dr. Bedpan yet.*"

Moira smiled, like a Buddha-shaped bomb. "Well?" she said.

"We've got to think," Len kept saying over and over.

"*You've* got to think." Moira was combing her hair, snapping the comb smartly at the end of each stroke. "I've had plenty of time to think, ever since it happened. When you catch up—"

Len flung his tie at the carved wooden pineapple on the corner of the footboard. "Moy, be *reasonable*. The chances against the kid kicking three times in any one-minute period are only about one in a hundred. The chances against anything like—"

Moira grunted and stiffened for a moment. Then she cocked her head to one side with a listening expression, a new mannerism of hers that was beginning to send intangible snakes crawling up Len's spine.

"What?" he asked sharply.

"He says to keep our voices down, he's thinking."

Len's fingers clenched convulsively, and a button flew off his shirt. Shaking, he pulled his arms out of the sleeves and dropped the shirt on the floor. "Look. I just want to get this straight. When he talks to you, you don't hear him shouting all the way up past your liver and lights. What—"

"You know perfectly well. He reads my mind."

"That isn't the same as—" Len took a deep breath. "Let's not get off on that. What I want to know is what is it like, do you seem to hear a real voice, or do you just know what he's telling you, without knowing how you know, or—"

Moira put the comb down in order to think better. "It isn't like hearing a voice. You'd never confuse one with the other. It's more— The nearest I can come to it, it's like remembering a voice. Except that you don't know what's coming."

"My God." Len picked his tie off the floor and abstractedly began knotting it on his bare chest. "And he sees what you see, he knows what you're thinking, he can hear when people talk to you?"

"Of course."

"But damn it, this is tremendous!" Len began to blunder around the bedroom, not looking where he was going. "They thought Macaulay was a genius. This kid isn't even *born*. Quints, schmints. I *heard* him. He was cussing Berry out like Monty Woolley."

"He had me reading *The Man Who Came to Dinner* two days ago."

Len made his way around a small bedside table by trial and error. "That's another thing. How much could you say about his . . . his personality? I mean, does he seem to know what he's doing, or is he just striking out wildly in all directions?" He paused. "Are you sure he's really conscious at all?"

Moira began. "That's a silly—" and stopped. "Define consciousness," she said doubtfully.

"All right, what I really mean is— Why am I wearing this necktie?" He ripped it off and threw it over a lampshade. "What I mean—"

"Are you sure you're really conscious?"

"Okay. You make joke, I laugh, ha. What I'm trying to ask you is, have you seen any evidence of creative thought, organized thought, or is he just . . . integrating, along the lines of, of instinctive responses. Do you—"

"I know what you mean. Shut up a minute. . . . I don't know."

"I mean, is he awake, or asleep and dreaming about us, like the Red King?"

"I don't *know*."

"And if that's it, what'll happen when he wakes up?"

Moira took off her robe, folded it neatly, and maneuvered herself between the sheets. "Come to bed."

Len got one sock off before another thought struck him. "He reads your mind. Can he read other people's?" He looked appalled. "Can he read mine?"

"He doesn't. Whether it's because he can't, I don't know. I think he just doesn't care."

Len pulled the other sock halfway down and left it there. In another tone he said, "One of the things he doesn't care about is whether I have a job."

"No . . . He thought it was funny. I wanted to sink through the floor, but I had all I could do to keep from laughing when she fell down. . . . Len, what are we going to do?"

He swiveled around and looked at her. "Look," he said, "I didn't mean to sound that gloomy. We'll do something. We'll fix it. Really."

"All right."

Careful of his elbows and knees, Len climbed into the bed beside her. "Okay now?"

"Mm . . . Ugh." Moria tried to sit up suddenly and almost made it. She wound up propped on one elbow and said indignantly, "Oh, no."

Len stared at her in the dimness. "What?"

She grunted again. "Len, get up. All *right*. Len, *hurry!*"

Len fought his way convulsively past a treacherous sheet and staggered up, goose-pimpled and tense. "Now what?"

"You'll have to sleep on the couch. The sheets are in the bottom—"

"On that couch? Are you crazy?"

"I can't help it," she said in a thin voice. "Please don't let's argue, you'll just have to—"

"*Why?*"

"We can't sleep in the same bed," she wailed. "He says it's—oh!—unhygienic!"

Len's contract was not renewed. He got a job waiting on tables in a resort hotel, an occupation which pays more money than teaching future citizens the rudiments of three basic sciences, but for which Len had no aptitude. He lasted three days at it; he was then idle for a week and a half, until his four years of college physics earned him employment as a clerk in an electrical shop. His employer was a cheerfully aggressive man who assured Len that there were great opportunities in radio-TV, and firmly believed that atom-bomb tests were causing all the bad weather.

Moira, in her eighth month, walked to the county library every day and trundled a load of books home in the perambulator. Little Leo, it appeared, was working his way simultaneously through biology, astrophysics, phrenology, chemical engineering, architecture, Christian Science, psychosomatic medicine, marine law, business management, Yoga, crystallography, metaphysics and modern literature.

His domination of Moira's life remained absolute, and his experiments with her regimen continued. One week, she ate nothing but nuts and fruit washed down with distilled water; the next, she was on a diet of porterhouse steak, dandelion greens and Hadacol.

With the coming of full summer, fortunately, few of the high-school staff were in evidence. Len met Dr. Berry once on the street. Berry started, twitched, and walked off rapidly in an entirely new direction.

The diabolical event was due on or about July 29. Len crossed off each day on their wall calendar with an emphatic black grease pencil. It would, he supposed, be an uncomfortable thing at best to be the parent of a super-prodigy—Leo would no doubt be dictator of the world by the time he was fifteen, unless he was assassinated first—but almost anything would be a fair price for getting Leo out of his maternal fortress.

Then there was the day when Len came home to find Moira weeping over the typewriter, with a half-inch stack of manuscript beside her.

"It isn't anything, I'm just tired. He started this after lunch. Look."

Len turned the face-down sheaf the right way up.

> Droning. Abrasing
> the demiurge.
> Hier begrimms the tale:
> Eyes undotted, grewling
> and looking, turns off
> a larm, seizes cloes.
> Stewed! Bierly a wretch!
> Pence, therefore jews we. Pons!
> Let the pants take air of themsulves.
> Searches in the bottom of a hole
> for soap; hawks up a good gob.
> Flayed on fable, a
> round cut of cat's meat . . .

The first three sheets were all like that. The fourth was a perfectly good Petrarchan sonnet reviling the current administration and the party of which Len was an assenting member.

The fifth was hand-lettered in the Cyrillic alphabet and illustrated with geometric diagrams. Len put it down and stared shakily at Moira.

"No, go on," she said. "Read the rest."

The sixth and seventh were dirty limericks, and the eight, ninth and so on to the end of the stack were what looked like the first chapters of a rattling good historical adventure novel.

Its chief characters were Cyrus the Great, his gallon-bosomed daughter Lygea, of whom Len had never previously heard, and a one-armed Graeco-Mede adventurer named Xanthes; there were also courtesans, spies, apparitions, scullery slaves, oracles, cutthroats, lepers, priests, whoremasters and men-at-arms in magnificent profusion.

"He's decided," said Moira, "what he wants to be when he's born."

Leo refused to be bothered with mundane details. When there were eighty pages of the manuscript, Moira invented a title and by-line for it—*The Virgin of Persepolis*, by Leon Lenn—and mailed it off to a literary agent in New York. His response, a week later, was cautiously enthusiastic and a trifle plaintive. He asked for an outline of the remainder of the novel.

Moira replied that this was impossible, trying to sound as unworldly and impenetrably artistic as she could. She enclosed the thirty-odd pages Leo had turned out in the meantime.

Nothing was heard from the agent for two weeks. At the end of this time Moira received an astonishing document, exquisitely printed and bound in imitation leather, thirty-two pages including the index, containing three times as many clauses as a lease.

This turned out to be a book contract. With it came the agent's check for nine hundred dollars.

Len tilted his mop handle against the wall and straightened carefully, conscious of every individual gritty muscle in his back. How did women do housework every day, seven days a week, fifty-two bloody weeks a year? It was a little cooler now that the sun was down, and he was working stripped to shorts and bath slippers, but he might as well have been wearing an overcoat in a Turkish bath.

The clatter of Moira's monstrous new typewriter stopped, leaving a faint hum. Len went into the living room and sagged on the arm of a chair. Moira, gleaming sweatily in a flowered housecoat, was lighting a cigarette.

"How's it going?"

She switched off the machine wearily. "Page two-eighty-nine. Xanthes killed Anaxander."

"Thought he would. How about Ganesh and Zeuxias?"

"I don't know." She frowned. "I can't figure it out. You know who it was that raped Miriam in the garden?"

"No, who?"

"*Ganesh.*"

"You're kidding."

"Nope." She pointed to the stack of typescript. "See for yourself."

Len didn't move. "But Ganesh was in Lydia, buying back the sapphire. He didn't get back till—"

"I know, I know. But he *wasn't*. That was Zeuxias in a putty nose and his beard dyed. It's all perfectly logical, the way he explains it. Zeuxias overheard Ganesh talking to the three Mongols—you remember, Ganesh thought there was somebody behind the curtain, only that was when they heard Lygea scream, and while their backs were turned—"

"All right, but for God's sake this fouls everything up. If Ganesh never went to Lydia, then he *couldn't* have had anything to do with distempering Cyrus's armor. And Zeuxias couldn't, either, because—"

"I *know*. It's exasperating. I know he's going to pull another rabbit out of the hat and clear everything up, but I don't see how."

Len brooded. "It beats me. It had to be either Ganesh or Zeuxias. Or Philomenes. But look, damn it, if Zeuxias knew about the sapphire all the time, that rules out Philomenes once and for all. Unless . . . No. I forgot about that business in the temple. Whuff. Do you think he really knows what he's doing?"

"I'm certain. Lately I've been able to tell what he's thinking even when he isn't talking to me—I mean just generally, like when he's puzzling over something, or when he's feeling mean. It's going to be something brilliant, and he knows what it is, but he won't tell me. We'll just have to wait."

"I guess." Len stood up, grunting. "You want me to see if there's anything in the pot?"

"Please."

Len wandered into the kitchen, turned the flame on under the Silex, stared briefly at the dishes waiting in the sink, and wandered out again. Since the onslaught of The Novel, Leo had relinquished his interest in Moira's diet, and she had been living on coffee. Small blessings . . .

Moira was leaning back with her eyes closed, looking very tired. "How's the money?" she asked without moving.

"Lousy. We're down to twenty-one bucks."

She raised her head and opened her eyes wide. "We couldn't be. Len, how could anybody go through nine hundred dollars that fast?"

"Typewriter. And the dictaphone that Leo thought he wanted, till about half an hour after it was paid for. We spent about fifty on ourselves, I guess. Rent. Groceries. It goes, when there isn't any coming in."

She sighed. "I thought it would last longer."

"So did I. . . . If he doesn't finish this thing in a few days, I'll have to go look for work again."

"Oh. That isn't so good."

"I know it, but—"

"All right, if it works out, fine, if it doesn't . . . He must be near the end by now." She stubbed out her cigarette abruptly and sat up, hands poised over the keyboard. "He's getting ready again. See about that coffee, will you?"

Len poured two cups and carried them in. Moira was still sitting in front of the typewriter, with a curious half-formed expression on her face.

Abruptly the carriage whipped over, muttered to itself briefly and thumped the paper up twice. Then it stopped. Moira's eyes got bigger and rounder.

"What's the matter?" said Len. He went and looked over her shoulder.

The last line on the page read:

(TO BE CONTINUED IN OUR NEXT)

Moira's hands curled into small, helpless fists. After a moment she turned off the machine.

"What?" said Len incredulously. "To be continued— What kind of talk is that?"

"He says he's bored with the novel," Moira replied dully. "He says he knows the ending, so it's artistically complete; it doesn't matter whether anybody else thinks so or not." She paused. "But he says that isn't the real reason."

"Well?"

"He's got two. One is that he doesn't want to finish the book till he's certain he'll have complete control of the money it earns."

"Well," said Len, swallowing a lump of anger, "that makes a certain amount of sense. It's his book. If he wants guarantees . . ."

"You haven't heard the other one."

"All right, let's have it."

"He wants to teach us, so we'll never forget, who the boss is in this family."

"Len, I'm awfully tried."

"Let's just go over it once more; there has to be some way— He still isn't talking to you?"

"I haven't felt anything from him for the last twenty minutes. I think he's asleep."

"All right, let's suppose he *isn't* going to listen to reason—"

"We might as well."

Len made an incoherent noise. "Okay. I still don't see why we can't write the last chapter ourselves—a few pages—"

"*Who* can?"

"Well, not me, but you've done a little writing—damned good, too. And if you're so sure all the clues are there— Look, if you say you can't do it, okay, we'll hire somebody. A professional writer. It happens all the time. Thorne Smith's last novel—"

"Ugh."

"Well, it *sold*. What one writer starts, another can finish."

"Nobody ever finished *The Mystery of Edwin Drood*."

"Oh, hell."

"Len, it's impossible. It *is*. Let me finish. If you're thinking we could have somebody rewrite the last part Leo did—"

"Yeah, I just thought of that."

"Even that wouldn't do any good, you'd have to go all the way back, almost to page one, it would be another story when you got through. Let's go to bed."

"Moy, do you remember when we used to worry about the law of opposites?"

"Mm?"

"The law of *opposites*. When we used to be afraid the kid would turn out to be a pick-and-shovel man with a pointy head."

"Uh. Mm."

He turned. Moira was standing with one hand on her belly and the other behind her back. She looked as if she were about to start practicing a low bow but doubted she could make it.

"What's the matter now?" he asked.

"Pain in the small of my back."

"Bad one?"

"No . . ."

"Belly hurt, too?"

She frowned. "Don't be foolish. I'm feeling for the contraction. There it comes."

"The . . . but you just said the small of your back."

"Where do you think labor pains usually start?"

The pains were coming at twenty-minute intervals, and the taxi had not arrived. Moira was packed and ready. Len was trying to set her a good example by remaining calm. He strolled over to the wall calendar, gazed at it in an offhand manner, and turned away.

"Len, I know it's only the fifteenth of July."

"Huh? I didn't say that aloud."

"You said it seven times. Sit down; you're making me nervous."

Len perched on the corner of the table, folded his arms, and immediately got up to look out the window. On the way back he circled the table in an aimless way, picked up a bottle of ink and shook it to see if the cap was on tight, stumbled over a wastebasket, carefully upended it and sat down with an air of *J'y suis, j'y reste.* "Nothing to worry about," he said firmly. "Women do this all the time."

"True."

"What for?" he demanded violently.

Moira grinned at him, then winced slightly and looked at the clock. "Eighteen minutes. This is a good one."

When she relaxed, Len put a cigarette in his mouth and lighted it in only two tries. "How's Leo taking it?"

"Isn't saying. He feels—" She concentrated. "Apprehensive. He's feeling strange and he doesn't like it. . . . I don't think he's entirely awake. Funny."

"I'm glad this is happening now," Len announced.

"So am I, but . . ."

"Look," said Len, moving energetically to the arm of her chair, "we've always had it pretty good, haven't we? Not that it hasn't been tough at times, but—you know."

"I know."

"Well, that's the way it'll be again, once this is over. I don't care how much of a superbrain he is, once he's born—you know what I mean? The only reason he's had the bulge on us all the time is he could get at us and we couldn't get at him. He's got the mind of an adult, he can learn to act like one. It's that simple."

Moira hesitated. "You can't take him out to the woodshed. He's going to be a helpless baby, physically, like anybody else's. He has to be taken care of. You can't—"

"No, all right, but there are plenty of other ways. If he behaves, he gets read to. Like that."

"That's right, but—there's one other thing I thought of. You remember when you said suppose he's asleep and dreaming . . . and what happens if he wakes up?"

"Yeah."

"Well, that reminded me of something else, or maybe it's the same thing. Did you know that a fetus in the womb gets only about half the amount of oxygen in his blood that he'll have when he starts to breathe?"

Len looked thoughtful. "Forgot. Well, that's just one more thing Leo does that babies aren't supposed to do."

"Use as much energy as he does, you mean. All right, but what I'm getting at is, it can't be because he's getting more than the normal amount of oxygen, can it? I mean, he's the prodigy, not me. He must be using it more efficiently. . . . And if that's it, what happens when he's getting twice as much?"

They had soaped and shaved and disinfected her, along with other indignities, and now she could see herself in the reflector of the big delivery-table light—the image clear and bright, like everything else, but very haloed and swimmy, and looking like a statue of Sita. She had no idea how long she had been here—there was the scopolamine, probably—but she was getting pretty tired.

"Bear down," said the staff doctor kindly, and before she could answer, the pain came up like violins and she had to gulp at the tingly coldness of laughing gas. When the mask lifted she said, "I *am* bearing down," but the doctor had gone back to the other end of her and wasn't listening.

Anyhow, she had Leo. *How are you feeling?*

His answer was muddled—because of the anesthetic?—but she didn't really need it; her perception of him was clear: darkness and pressure, impatience, a slow Satanic anger . . . and something else. Uncertainty? Apprehension?

"Two or three more ought to do it. Bear down."

Fear. Unmistakable now. And a desperate determination.

"Doctor, he doesn't want to be born!"

"Seems that way sometimes, doesn't it? Now bear down good and hard."

Tell him stop blurrrrrr too dangerrrrrrr stop I feel wowrrrrr stop I tellrrrr stop.

"What, Leo, what?"

"Bear down."

Faintly, like a voice far under water: *Hurry I hate you tell him . . . sealed incubator . . . tenth oxygen, nine tenths inert gases . . . Hurry.*

The pressure abruptly relaxed.

Leo was born.

The doctor was holding him up by the heels, red, bloody, wrinkled, trailing a lumpy soft snake. The voice was still there, very small, very far away: *Too late. The same as death.* Then a hint of the old cold arrogance: *Now you'll never know . . . who killed Cyrus.*

The doctor slapped him smartly on the minuscule buttocks. The wizened, malevolent face writhed open; but it was only the angry squall of an ordinary infant that came out. Leo was gone, like a light turned off under the measureless ocean.

Moira raised her head weakly. "Give him one for me," she said.

YOU'RE ANOTHER

It was a warm spring Saturday, and Johnny Bornish spent the morning in Central Park. He drew sailors lying on the grass with their girls; he drew old men in straw hats, and Good Humor men pushing their carts. He got two quick studies of children at the toy-boat pond, and would have had another, a beauty, except that somebody's damned big Dalmatian, romping, blundered into him and made him sit down hard in the water.

A bright-eyed old gentleman solemnly helped him arise. Johnny thought it over, then wrung out his wet pants in the men's rest room, put them back on and spread himself like a starfish in the sun. He dried before his sketchbook did, so he took the bus back downtown, got off at Fourteenth Street and went into Mayer's.

The only clerk in sight was showing an intricate folding easel to a tweedy woman who didn't seem to know which end was which. Johnny picked up the sketchbook he wanted from a pile on the table and pottered around looking at lay figures, paper palettes and other traps for the amateur. He glimpsed some interesting textured papers displayed in the other aisle and tried to cross over to them, but misjudged his knobby-kneed turning circle, as usual, and brought down a cascade of little paint cans. Dancing for balance, somehow he managed to put one heel down at an unheard-of angle, buckle the lid of one of the cans and splash red enamel all over hell.

He paid for the paint, speechless, and got out. He had dropped the sketchbook somewhere, he discovered. Evidently God did not care for him to do any sketching today.

Also, he was leaving the red heel prints across the pavement. He wiped off his shoe as well as he could with some newspaper from the trash basket at the corner, and walked down to the Automat for coffee.

The cashier scooped in his dollar and spread two rows of magical dimes on the marble counter, all rattling at once like angry metal insects. They were alive in Johnny's palm; one of them got away, but he lunged for it and caught it before it hit the floor.

Flushed with victory, he worked his way through the crowd to the coffee dispenser, put a china cup under the spigot and dropped his dime in the slot. Coffee streamed out, filled his cup and went on flowing.

Johnny watched it for a minute. Coffee went on pouring over the lip and handle of the cup, too hot to touch, splashing through the grilled metal and gurgling away somewhere below.

A white-haired man shouldered him aside, took a cup from the rack and calmly filled it at the spigot. Somebody else followed his example, and in a moment there was a crowd.

After all, it was his dime. Johnny got another cup and waited his turn. An angry man in a white jacket disappeared violently into the crowd, and Johnny heard him shouting something. A moment later the crowd began to disperse.

The jet had stopped. The man in the white jacket picked up Johnny's original cup, emptied it, set it down on a busboy's cart, and went away.

Evidently God did not care for him to drink any coffee, either. Johnny whistled a few reflective bars of "Dixie" and left, keeping a wary eye out for trouble.

At the curb a big pushcart was standing in the sunshine, flaming with banana yellows, apple reds. Johnny stopped himself. "Oh, no," he said, and turned himself sternly around, and started carefully down the avenue, hands in pockets, elbows at his sides. On a day like what this one was shaping up to be, he shuddered to think what he could do with a pushcart full of fruit.

How about a painting of that? Semi-abstract—"Still Life in Motion." Flying tangerines, green bananas, dusty Concord grapes, stopped by the fast shutter of the artist's eye. By Cézanne, out of Stuart Davis. By heaven, it wasn't bad.

He could see it, big and vulgar, about a 36 by 30 (stretchers: he'd have to stop at Mayer's again, or on second thought somewhere else, for stretchers), the colors grayed on a violent ground, but screaming at each other all the same like a gaggle of parakeets. Black outlines here and there, weaving a kind of cockeyed carpet pattern through it. No depth, no light-and-dark—flat Easter-egg colors, glowing as enigmatically as a Parrish cut up into jigsaw pieces. Frame it in oyster-white molding —wham! The Museum of Modern Art!

The bananas, he thought, would have to go around this way, distorted, curved like boomerangs up in the foreground. Make the old ladies from Oshkosh duck. That saturated buttery yellow, transmuted to a poisonous green . . . He put out a forefinger absently to stroke one of the nearest, feeling how the chalky smoothness curved up and around into the dry hard stem.

"How many, Mac?"

For an instant Johnny thought he had circled the block, back to the same pushcart; then he saw that this one had only bananas on it. He was at the corner of Eleventh Street; he had walked three blocks, blind and deaf.

"No bananas," he said hurriedly, backing away. There was a shriek in his ear. He turned it; it was a glitter-eyed tweedy woman, brandishing an enormous handbag.

"Can't you watch where you're—"

"Sorry, ma'am," he said, desperately trying to keep his balance. He toppled off the curb, grabbing at the pushcart. Something slithery went out from under his foot. He was falling, sliding like a bowling ball, feet first toward the one upright shaft that supported the end of the pushcart. . . .

The first thing that he noticed, as he sat there up to his chest in bananas, with the swearing huckster holding the cart by main force, was that an alert, white-haired old gentleman was in the front rank of the crowd, looking at him.

The same one who—?

And come to think of it, that tweedy woman—

Ridiculous.

All the same, something began to twitch in his memory. Ten confused minutes later he was kneeling asthmatically on the floor in front of his closet, hauling out stacks of unframed paintings, shoeboxes full of letters and squeezed paint tubes, a Scout ax (for kindling), old sweaters and mildewed magazines, until he found a battered suitcase.

In the suitcase, under untidy piles of sketches and water colors, was a small cardboard portfolio. In the portfolio were two newspaper clippings.

One was from the *Post*, dated three years back: it showed Johnny, poised on one heel in a violent adagio pose, being whirled around by the stream of water from a hydrant some Third Avenue urchins had just opened. The other was two years older, from the *Journal*: in this one Johnny seemed to be walking dreamily up a wall—actually, he had just slipped on an icy street in the upper Forties.

He blinked incredulously. In the background of the first picture there were half a dozen figures, mostly kids.

Among them was the tweedy woman.

In the background of the second, there was only one. It was the white-haired old man.

Thinking it over, Johnny discovered that he was scared. He had never actually enjoyed being the kind of buffoon who gets his shirttail caught in zippers, is trapped by elevators and revolving doors, and trips on pebbles; he had accepted it humbly as his portion, and in between catastrophes he'd had a lot of fun.

But suppose somebody was *doing* it to him?

A lot of it was not funny, look at it any way you like. There was the time the bus driver had closed the door on Johnny's foot and dragged him for three yards, bouncing on the pavement. He had got up with nothing worse than bruises—but what if that passenger hadn't seen him in time?

He looked at the clippings again. There they were, the same faces— the same clothing, even, except that the old man was wearing an over-coat. Even in the faded half-tones, there was a predatory sparkle from his rimless eyeglasses; and the tweedy woman's sharp beak was as threatening as a hawk's.

Johnny felt a stifling sense of panic. He felt like a man waiting helplessly for the punchline of a long bad joke; or like a mouse being played with by a cat.

Something bad was going to happen next.

The door opened; somebody walked in. Johnny started, but it was only the Duke, brawny in a paint-smeared undershirt, with a limp cigarette in the corner of his mouth. The Duke had a rakish Errol Flynn mustache, blending furrily now into his day-old beard, and a pair of black, who-are-you-varlet brows. He was treacherous, clever, plausible, quarrelsome, ingenious, a great brawler and seducer of women —in short, exactly like Cellini, except he had no talent.

"*Hiding?*" said Duke, showing his big teeth.

Johnny became aware that, crouched in front of the closet that way, he looked a little as if he were about to dive into it and pull overcoats over his head. He got up stiffly, tried to put his hands in his pockets, and discovered he still had the clippings. Then it was too late. Duke took them gently, inspected them with a judicial eye, and stared gravely at Johnny. "Not flattering," he said. "Is that blood on your forehead?"

Johnny investigated; his fingers came away a little red, not much. "I fell down," he said uncomfortably.

"My boy," Duke told him, "you are troubled. Confide in your old Uncle."

"I'm just— Look, Duke, I'm busy. Did you want something?"

"Only to be your faithful counselor and guide," said Duke, pressing Johnny firmly into a chair. "Just lean back, loosen the sphincters and say the first thing that comes into your mind." He looked expectant.

"Ugh," said Johnny.

Duke nodded sagely. "A visceral reaction. Existentialist. You wish to rid yourself of yourself—get away from it all. Tell me, when you walk down the street, do you feel the buildings are about to close in on you? Are you being persecuted by little green men who come out of the woodwork? Do you feel an overpowering urge to leave town?"

"Yes," said Johnny truthfully.

Duke looked mildly surprised. "Well?" he asked, spreading his hands. "Where would I go?"

"I recommend sunny New Jersey. All the towns have different names —fascinating. Millions of them. Pick one at random. Hackensack, Perth Amboy, Passaic, Teaneck, Newark? No? You're quite right—too suggestive. Let me see. Something farther north? Provincetown. Martha's Vineyard—lovely this time of the year. Or Florida—yes, I can really see you, Johnny, sitting on a rotten wharf in the sunshine, fishing with a bent pin for pompano. Peaceful, relaxed, carefree . . ."

Johnny's fingers stirred the change in his pocket. He didn't know what was in his wallet—he never did—but he was sure it wasn't enough. "Duke, have you seen Ted Edwards this week?" he asked hopefully.

"No. Why?"

"Oh. He owes me a little money, is all. He said he'd pay me today or tomorrow."

"If it's a question of money . . ." said the Duke after a moment. Johnny looked at him incredulously.

Duke was pulling a greasy wallet out of his hip pocket. He paused with his thumb in it. "Do you really want to get out of town, Johnny?"

"Well, sure, but . . ."

"Johnny, what are friends *for*? Really, I'm wounded. Will fifty help?"

He counted out the money and stuffed it into Johnny's paralyzed palm. "Don't say a word. Let me remember you just as you are." He made a frame of his hands and squinted through it. He sighed, then picked up the battered suitcase and went to work with great energy throwing things out of the dresser into it. "Shirts, socks, underwear. Necktie. Clean handkerchief. There you are." He closed the lid. He pumped Johnny's hand. pulling him toward the door. "Don't think it hasn't been great, because it hasn't. So on the ocean of life we pass and speak to each other. Only a look and a voice; then darkness and silence."

Johnny dug in his heels and stopped. "What's the matter?" Duke inquired.

"I just realized—I can't go now. I'll go tonight. I'll take the late train."

Duke arched an eyebrow. "But why wait, Johnny? When the sunne shineth, make hay. When the iron is hot, strike. The tide tarrieth for no man."

"They'll see me leave," said Johnny, embarrassed.

Duke frowned. "You mean the little green men actually are after you?" His features worked; he composed them with difficulty. "Well, this is— Pardon me. A momentary aberration. But now don't you see, Johnny, you haven't got any time to lose. If they're following you, they must know where you live. How do you know they won't come here?"

Johnny, flushing, could think of no adequate reply. He had wanted to get away under cover of darkness, but that would mean another five hours at least. . . .

"Look here," said Duke suddenly, "I know the very thing. Biff Feldstein—works at the Cherry Lane. Your own mother won't admit she knows you. Wait here."

He was back in fifteen minutes, with a bundle of old clothes and an object which turned out, on closer examination, to be a small brown beard.

Johnny put it on unwillingly, using gunk from a tube Duke had brought along. Duke helped him into a cast-off jacket, color indistinguishable, shiny with grease, and clapped a beret on his head. The result, to Johnny's horrified gaze, looked like an old-time Village phony or a peddler of French postcards. Duke inspected him judicially. "It's magnificent, but it isn't war," he said. "However, we can always plant vines. *Allons!* I am the grass; I cover all!"

Walking toward Sixth at a brisk pace, a hand firmly on Johnny's elbow, Duke suddenly paused. "Ho!" he said. He sprang forward, bent, and picked something up.

Johnny stared at it glassily. It was a five-dollar bill.

Duke was calmly putting it away. "Does that happen to you often?" Johnny asked.

"Now and again," said Duke. "Merely a matter of keeping the eyes in focus."

"Luck," said Johnny faintly.

"Never think it," Duke told him. "Take the word of an older and wiser man. You make your own luck in this world. Think of Newton. Think of O'Dwyer. Hand stuck in the jam jar? You asked for it. Now the trouble with you—"

Johnny, who had heard this theory before, was no longer listening. Look, he thought, at all the different things that had had to happen so that Duke could pick up that fiver. Somebody had to lose it, to begin with—say because he met a friend just as he was about to put the bill away, and stuffed it in his pocket instead so he could shake hands, and then forgot it, reached for his handkerchief— All right. Then it just had to happen that everybody who passed this spot between then and now was looking the other way, or thinking about something else. And Duke, finally, had to glance down at just the right moment. It was all extremely improbable, but it happened, somewhere, every day.

And also every day, somewhere, people were being hit by flowerpots knocked off tenth-story window ledges, and falling down manholes, and walking into stray bullets fired by law enforcement officers in pursuit of malefactors. Johnny shuddered.

"Oh-oh," said Duke suddenly. "Where's a cab? Ah— Cabby!" He sprang forward to the curb, whistling and waving.

Looking around curiously, Johnny saw a clumsy figure hurrying toward them down the street. "There's Mary Finigan," he said, pointing her out.

"I know," said Duke irascibly. The cab was just pulling in toward them, the driver reaching back to open the door. "Now here we go, Johnny—"

"But I think she wants to talk to you," said Johnny. "Hadn't we—"

"No time now," said Duke, helping him in with a shove. "She's taken to running off at the mouth—that's why I had to give her up. Get moving!" he said to the driver, and added to Johnny, "Among other things, that is . . . Here will be an old abusing of God's patience, and the King's English."

As they pulled away into traffic, Johnny had a last glimpse of the girl standing on the curb watching them. Her dark hair was straggling down off her forehead; she looked as if she had been crying.

Duke said comfortably, "Every man, as the saying is, can tame a shrew but he that hath her. Now there, John boy, you have just had an instructive object lesson. Was it luck that we got away from the draggle-tailed ear-bender? It was not. . . ."

But, thought Johnny, it was. What if the cab hadn't come along at just the right time?

". . . in a nutshell, boy. Only reason you have bad luck, you go hunting for it."

"That isn't the reason," said Johnny.

He let Duke's hearty voice fade once more into a kind of primitive background music, like the muttering of the extras in a Tarzan picture when the Kalawumbas are about to feed the pretty girl to the lions. It had just dawned on him, with the dazzling glow of revelation, that the whole course of anybody's life was determined by improbable accidents. Here he stood, all five feet ten and a hundred thirty pounds of him—a billion-to-one shot from the word go. (What were the chances against any given sperm's uniting with any given ovum? *More* than a billion to one—unimaginable.) What if the apple hadn't fallen on Newton's head? What if O'Dwyer had never left Ireland? And what did free will have to do with the decision not to become, say, a Kurdish herdsman, if you happened to be born in Ohio?

. . . It meant, Johnny thought, that if you could control the random factors—the way the dice fall in a bar in Sacramento, the temper of a rich uncle in Keokuk, the moisture content of the clouds over Sioux Falls at 3:03 CST, the shape of a pebble in a Wall Street newsboy's sock—you could do anything. You could make an obscure painter named Johnny Bornish fall into the toy-boat pond in Central Park and get red paint all over his shoe and knock down a pushcart . . .

But why would you want to?

The airport waiting room was a little like a scene out of *Things to Come*, except that the people were neither white-robed, leisurely nor cool.

Every place on every bench was taken. Duke found a couple of square feet of floor space behind a pillar and settled Johnny there, seated on his upended suitcase.

"Now you're all set. Got your ticket. Got your magazine. Okay."

Duke made an abrupt menacing gesture in order to look at his wrist-watch.

"Got to run. Now, remember, boy, send me your address as soon as you get one, so I can forward your mail and so on. Oh, almost forgot." He scribbled on a piece of paper, handed it over. "Mere formality. Payable at any time. Sign here."

He had written, "I O U $50." Johnny signed, feeling a little more at home with Duke.

"Right. Oll korrect."

"Duke," said Johnny suddenly. "Mary's pregnant, isn't she?" His expression was thoughtful.

"It has been known to happen," said Duke good-humoredly.

"Why don't you give her a break?" Johnny asked with difficulty.

Duke was not offended. "How? Speak the truth to me, Johnny—do you see me as a happy bridegroom? Well . . ." He pumped Johnny's hand. "The word must be spoken that bids you depart—though the effort to speak it should shatter my heart—though in silence, with something I pine—yet the lips that touch liquor must never touch mine!" With a grin that seemed to linger, like the Cheshire cat's, he disappeared into the crowd.

II

Uncomfortably astride his suitcase, solitary among multitudes, Johnny found himself thinking in words harder and longer at a time than he used to. The kind of thinking he did when he was painting, or had painted, or was about to paint was another process altogether, and there were days on end when he did nothing else. He had a talent, Johnny Bornish. A talent is sometimes defined as a gift of the gods, a thing that most people, who have not had one, confuse with a present under a Christmas tree.

It was not like that at all. It tortured and delighted him, and took up so much room in his skull that a lot of practical details couldn't get in. Without exaggeration, it obsessed him, and when occasionally, as now, its grip relaxed, Johnny had the comical expression of a man who has just waked up to find his pocket picked and a row of hotfoot scars around his shoes.

He was thinking about luck. It was all right to talk about everybody making his own, and to a certain extent he supposed it was true, but Duke *was* the kind of guy who found money on the street. Such a thing had happened to Johnny only once in his life, and then it wasn't legal tender, but a Japanese coin—brass, heavy, about the size of a half dollar, with a chrysanthemum symbol on one side and a character on the other. He thought of it as his lucky piece; he had found it on the street, his last year in high school, and here—he took it out of his pocket—it still was.

. . . Which, when you came to think of it, was odd. He was not superstitious about the coin, or especially fond of it. He called it a lucky piece for want of a better name, because the word *keepsake* had gone out of fashion; and in fact he believed that his luck in the last ten years had been lousy. The coin was the only thing he owned that was anywhere near that old. He had lost three wristwatches, numberless fountain pens, two hats, three or four cigarette lighters and genuine U.S. nickels and dimes by the handful. But here was the Japanese coin.

Now, how could you figure a thing like that, unless it was luck . . . or *interference?*

Johnny sat up straighter. It was a foolish notion, probably born of the fact that he hadn't had any lunch; but he was in a mood to read sinister significance into almost anything.

He already knew that the old man and the tweedy woman had been interfering in his life for at least five years, probably longer. Somehow, they were responsible for the "accidents" that kept happening to him —and *there* was a foolish and sinister notion for you, if you liked. Believing that, how could he help wondering about other odd things that had happened to him, no matter how small—like finding and keeping a Japanese coin?

With that kind of logic, you could prove anything. And yet, he couldn't rid himself of the idea.

Idly, he got up holding the coin and dropped it into a nearby waste can. He sat down on his suitcase again with a feeling of neurosis well quelled. If the coin somehow found its way back to him, he'd have evidence for thinking the worst of it; if it didn't, as of course it wouldn't, small loss.

"Excuse me," said a thinnish prim-faced little man in almost clerical clothes. "I believe you dropped this. A Japanese coin. Quite nice."

Johnny found his tongue." "Uh, thank you. But I don't want it; you keep it."

"Oh, *no*," said the little man, and walked stiffly away.

Johnny stared after him, then at the coin. It was lumpishly solid, a dirty-looking brown, nicked and rounded at the edges. Ridiculous!

His mistake, no doubt, had been in being too obvious. He palmed the coin, trying to look nonchalant. After a while he lighted a cigarette, dropped it, and as he fumbled for it, managed to shove the coin under the leg of the adjoining bench.

He had taken one puff on the retrieved cigarette when a large hulk in a gray suit, all muscles and narrowed eyes, knelt beside him and extracted the coin. The hulk looked at it carefully, front and back; weighed it in his palm, rang it on the floor, and finally handed it over to Johnny. "This yours?" he asked in a gravelly voice.

Johnny nodded. The hulk said nothing more but watched grimly until Johnny put the coin away in his pocket. Then he got up, dusted off his knees, and went away into the crowd.

Johnny felt a cold lump gather at the pit of his stomach. The fact that he had seen this same routine in at least half a dozen bad movies gave him no comfort; he did not believe in the series of natural coincidences that made it impossible to get rid of the neatly wrapped garbage, or the incriminating nylon stocking, or whatever.

He stood up. It was already twenty minutes after his plane's scheduled departure time. He *had* to get rid of the thing. It was intolerable to suppose that he couldn't get rid of it. Of course he could get rid of it.

The low false roof of the baggage counter looked promising. He picked up his suitcase and worked his way toward it, and got there just as the p. a. system burst forth with *"Flight number mnglang for Buzzclickville, now loading at Gate Lumber Lide."* Under cover of this clamor, Johnny swiftly took the coin out of his pocket and tossed it out of sight on the roof.

Now what? Was somebody going to fetch a ladder and climb up there after the coin, and come down and hand it to him?

Nothing at all happened, except that the voice on the p. a. emitted its thunderous mutter again, and this time Johnny caught the name of his destination, Jacksonville.

Feeling better, he stopped at the newsstand for cigarettes. He paid for them with a half dollar, which was promptly slapped back into his palm.

"Flight mumble sixteen for Jagznbull, now loading at Gate Number Nine," said the p. a.

After a moment Johnny handed back the cigarettes, still staring at the Japanese coin that lay, infuriatingly solid, on his palm. . . . He had had a fifty-cent piece in his pocket; it didn't seem to be there now; ergo, he had thrown it up on top of the baggage counter. A natural mistake. Only in ten years of carrying the coin around with him, he had never once mistaken it for a half buck, or vice versa, until now.

"Flight number sixteen . . ."

The tweedy woman, Johnny realized with a slow chill crawling down his back, had been ahead of him in the art store, talking to a clerk. She couldn't have been following him—on the bus, in a cab, or any other way; there wouldn't have been time. She had known where he was going, and when he was going to get there.

It was as if, he thought, while the coin seemed to turn fishily cold and smooth in his fingers, it was just as if the two of them, the tweedy woman and the old man, had planted a sort of beacon on him ten years ago, so that wherever and whenever he went, he was a belled cat. It was as if they might be looking in a kind of radarscope, when it pleased them, and seeing the track of his life like a twisted strand of copper wire coiling and turning. . . .

But of course there was no escape, if that was true. His track went winding through the waiting room and onto a particular aircraft and down again, where that plane landed, and into a particular room and then a particular restaurant, so that a day from now, a month, a year, ten years from now, they could reach out and touch him wherever he might be.

There was no escape, because there was a peculiarity built into this brown Japanese coin, a combination of random events that added up to the mirth-provoking result that he simply couldn't lose it.

He looked around wildly, thinking, Blowtorch. Monkey wrench. Sledge hammer. But there wasn't anything. It was a great big phony Things-to-Comeish wildcat-airline waiting room, without a tool in it anywhere.

A pretty girl came out from behind the counter to his right, swinging up the hinged section of counter and letting it down again behind her. Johnny stared after her stupidly, then at the way she had come out. His scalp twitched. He stepped to the counter, raised the hinged section.

A bald man a few feet away stopped talking to wave a telephone handset at Johnny. "No admittance here, sir! No admittance!"

Johnny put the Japanese coin down at an angle on the place that supported the end of the hinged section. He made sure it was the Japanese coin. He wedged it firmly.

The bald man dropped his telephone and came toward him, hand outstretched.

Johnny slammed the hinged section down as hard as he could. There was a dull *bonk*, and an odd feeling of tension; the lights seemed to blur. He turned and ran. Nobody followed him.

The plane was a two-engined relic that looked faintly Victorian from the outside, inside, it was a slanting dark cavern with an astonishing number of seats crammed into it. It smelled like a locker room. Johnny stumbled down the narrow aisle to what seemed to be the only remaining place, next to a large dark gentleman in an awning-striped tie.

He sat down, a little awkwardly. He had had a peculiar feeling ever since he had bashed the coin with the counter section, and the worst of it was that he couldn't pin it down. It was a physical something-wrong feeling, like an upset stomach or too little sleep or a fever coming on, but it wasn't exactly any of those things. He was hungry, but not that hungry. He thought the trouble might be with his eyes, but whenever he picked out anything as a test, it looked perfectly normal and he could see it fine. It was in his skin, perhaps? A kind of not-quite-prickling that . . . No, it wasn't his skin.

It was a little like being drunk, at the fraction of an instant when you realize how drunk you are and regret it—it was like that, but not very much. And it was partly like the foreboding, stronger and more oppressive than before— *Something bad was going to happen.*

The pilot and copilot walked up the aisle and disappeared into the forward compartment. The door was shut; the stewardess, back in the tail, was poring over the papers on her clipboard. After a while the starters whined and the engines came to life; Johnny, who had flown only once before, and on a scheduled airline at that, was startled to find what a devil of a racket they made. There was another interminable wait, and then the plane was crawling forward, swinging its nose around, crawling a little faster, while an endless blank expanse of concrete slipped by—lumbering along, then, like some huge, preposterous and, above all, flightless bird—and lifting incredibly, a few inches up, air-borne, the runway falling back, tilted, dwindling until they were up, high above the mist of the water, steady as a hammock in the rasping monotone drone of the engines.

Something went *flip* at the corner of Johnny's vision. He turned his head.

Flop.

It was a little metallic disk that went *flip* up the carpet like a tiddly-wink or a Mexican jumping bean, and paused for an instant while his jaw began to come loose at the hinge, and went *flop.* It lay on the carpet next to his seat, and went *hop.*

It landed on his knee, a little brown metallic disk with a chrysanthemum design, bent across the middle. He brushed at it. It hopped, and clung to his hand like a magnet to steel.

"Good heavens!" said an explosive voice in his ear.

Johnny had no attention to spare. He had taken hold of the coin with his other hand—a horrid feeling; it clung clammily to his fingers, and pulled away from his palm with reluctance—and now he was trying to scrape it off against the fabric of the seat. It was like trying to scrape off his own skin. He gave up and furiously began shaking his hand.

"Here, friend, don't do that!" The dark man in the next seat half rose, and there was a moment of confusion; Johnny heard a sharp click and thought he saw something leap from the dark man's vest pocket. Then, for an instant, he had clinging to his fingers a brown Japanese coin *and* a pair of glittering pince-nez. And then the two had somehow twisted together in a nasty, writhing way that hurt his eyes to watch, and uncurled again—no coin, no pince-nez, but an impossible little leather change purse.

Had the coin even been a coin at all? Was the change purse a change purse?

"Now look what you've done! *Ugh!*" The dark man, his face contorted with passion, reached gingerly fingers toward the purse. "Don't move, friend. Let me—"

Johnny pulled away a trifle. "Who are you?"

"F.B.I.," said the man impatiently. He flapped a bill fold at Johnny; there was some kind of official-looking shield inside. "Now you have torn it, my God! Hold that still—just like that. Don't move." He pulled back his sleeves like a conjurer, and began to reach very cautiously for the little brown bit of leather that clung to Johnny's hand.

The thing twitched slightly in his fingers. The next moment, people all around them began getting up and crowding into the aisle, heading for the single washroom back in the tail of the plane.

Palpably, the plane tilted. Johnny heard the stewardess shrieking, "One at a time! One at a time! Take your seats, everyone—you're making the airplane tail-heavy!"

"Steady, steady," moaned the dark man. "Hold it absolutely still!"

Johnny couldn't. His fingers twitched again, and abruptly all the passengers in the aisle were tumbling the other way, fighting to get away from the dangerous tail. The stewardess came helplessly after them, squalling futile orders.

"Am I doing that?" Johnny gasped, staring in horror at the thing in his palm.

"The gadget is. Hold it steady, friend—"

But his hand twitched again, and abruptly all the passengers were back in their seats, quietly sitting as if nothing had happened. Then a chorus of shrieks arose. Looking out the window, Johnny saw a terrifying sea of treetops just below, where nothing but empty air had been the moment before. As the plane nosed up sharply, his hand moved again—

And the shrieks grew louder. Up ahead loomed a blue-violet wall of mountain, topless, gigantic.

His fingers twitched still again: and once more the plane was droning peaceably along between earth and heaven. The passengers were bored or sleeping. There was no mountain, and no trees.

Sweat was beaded on the dark man's forehead. "Now . . ." he said, gritting his teeth and reaching again.

"Wait a minute," said Johnny, pulling away again. "Wait— This is some kind of top secret thing, is it, that I'm not supposed to have?"

"Yes," said the dark man, agonized. "I tell you, friend, don't move it!"

The purse was slowly changing color, turning a watery violet around the edges.

"And you're from the F.B.I.?" Johnny asked, staring hard at the dark man.

"Yes. Hold it steady—"

"No," said Johnny. His voice had a disposition to tremble, but Johnny held it firmly in check. "You forgot about your ears," he said. "Or are they too hard to change?"

The dark man showed his teeth. "What are you talking about?"

"The *ears,*" Johnny said, "and the jawbone. No two people have ears alike. And before, when you were the old man, your neck was too thick. It bothered me, only I was too busy to think about it." He swallowed hard. "I'm thinking about it now. You don't want me to move this thing?"

"Right, friend, right."

"Then tell me what this is all about."

The dark man made placating gestures. "I can't do that, friend.

I really can't. Look—" the tiny weight shifted in Johnny's hand—"out!" shouted the dark man.

Tiny flickerings gathered in the air around them. In the plane window, the clear blue of the sky abruptly vanished. Instead, Johnny saw a tumbling waste of gray cloud. Rain drummed against the window, and the plane heeled suddenly as if a gust had caught it.

Scattered shrieks arose from up forward. Johnny swallowed a large lump, and his fingers twitched. The flickering came again.

The cloud and rain were gone; the sky was an innocent blue again. "*Don't* do that," said the dark man. "Listen, look. You want to know something? Watch me try to tell you." He moistened his lips and began, "When you have trouble . . ." But on the fourth word his throat seemed to tighten and lock. His lips went on moving, his eyes bulged with effort, but nothing came out.

After a moment he relaxed, breathing heavily. "You see?" he said.

"You can't talk," said Johnny. "About that. Literally."

"Right! Now, friend, if you'll just allow me—"

"Easy. Tell me the truth: is there any way you can get around this, whatever it is, this block or whatever?" He let his fingers twitch, deliberately, as he spoke. "Any gadget, or anything you can take?"

The dark man glanced nervously out the window, where blue sky had given way to purple twilight and a large sickle moon. "Yes, but—"

"There is? What?"

The man's throat tightened again as he tried to speak.

"Well, whatever it is, you'd better use it," said Johnny. He saw the dark man's face harden with resolution, and jerked his hand away just in time as the dark man grabbed—

III

There was a whirling moment, then the universe steadied. Johnny clutched at the seat with his free hand. The plane and all the passengers were gone. He and the dark man were sitting on a park bench in the sunshine. Two pigeons took alarm and flapped heavily away.

The dark man's face was twisted unhappily. "Now you have done it! Oh, what time is it, anyway?" He plucked two watches out of his vest and consulted them in turn. "Wednesday, friend, at the latest! Oh, oh, they'll . . ." His mouth worked soundlessly.

"Wednesday?" Johnny managed. He looked around. They were sitting in Union Square Park, the only ones there. There were plenty of people on the streets, all hurrying, most of them women. It looked like a Wednesday, all right.

He opened his mouth and shut it again carefully. He looked down at the limp bit of leather and metal in his hand. Start from the beginning. What did he know?

The coin, which had evidently been some kind of telltale or beacon, had in some way joined itself, after Johnny had damaged it, to some other instrument of the dark man's—apparently the gadget that enabled him to control probability, and move from one time to another, and small chores like that.

In their present fused state, the two gadgets were ungovernable—dangerous, the dark man seemed to think—and no good to anybody.

And that was absolutely all he knew.

He didn't know where the dark man and his companion had come from, what they were up to, anything that would be useful to know, and he wasn't getting any nearer finding out. Except that there was some way of loosening the dark man's tongue. Drugs, which were out of the question . . . liquor . . .

Well, he thought, sitting up a trifle straighter, there was no harm in trying, anyhow. It might not work, but it was the pleasantest thought he had had all afternoon.

He said, "Come on," and stood up carefully; but his motion must have been too abrupt, because the scene around them melted and ran down into the pavement, and they were standing, not in the park, but on the traffic island at Sheridan Square.

It looked to be a little after noon, and the papers on the stand at Johnny's elbow bore today's date.

He felt a little dizzy. Say it was about one o'clock: then he hadn't got out to the airport yet; he was on his way there now, with Duke, and if he could hop a fast cab, he might catch himself and tell himself not to go. . . .

Johnny steadied his mind by a strenuous effort. He had, he told himself, one single, simple problem now in hand, and that was how to get to a bar. He took a careful step toward the edge of the island. The thing in his hand bobbled; the world reeled and steadied.

With the dark man beside him, Johnny was standing on the gallery of the Reptile Room of the Museum of Natural History. Down below, the poised shapes of various giant lizards looked extremely extinct and very dry.

Johnny felt the rising rudiments of a vast impatience. At this rate, it was clear enough, he would never get anywhere he wanted to go, because every step changed the rules. All right, then; if Mohammed couldn't go to the mountain . . .

The dark man, who had been watching him, made a strangled sound of protest.

Johnny ignored him. He swung his hand sharply down. And up. And down.

The world swung around them like a pendulum, twisting and turning. Too far! They were on a street corner in Paris. They were in a dark place listening to the sound of machinery. They were in the middle of a sandstorm, choking, blinding . . .

They were sitting in a rowboat on a quiet river. The dark man was wearing flannels and a straw hat.

Johnny tried to move the thing in his hand more gently: it was as if it had a life of its own; he had to hold it back.

Zip!

They were seated on stools at a marble-topped counter. Johnny saw a banana split with a fly on it.

Zip!

A library, a huge low-ceilinged place that Johnny had never seen before.

Zip!

The lobby of the Art Theatre; a patron bumped into Johnny, slopping his demitasse.

Zip!

They were sitting opposite each other, the dark man and he, at a table in the rear of Dorrie's Bar. Dust motes sparkled in the late-afternoon sun. There was a highball in front of each of them.

Gritting his teeth, Johnny held his hand perfectly upright while he lowered it, so slowly that it hardly seemed to move, until it touched the worn surface of the table. He sighed. "Drink up," he said.

With a wary eye on the thing in Johnny's hand, the dark man drank. Johnny signaled the bartender, who came over with a faintly puzzled expression. "How long you guys been here?"

"I was just going to ask you," said Johnny at random. "Two more."

The bartender retired and came back, looking hostile, with the drinks, after which he went down to the farthermost end of the bar, turned his back on them and polished glasses.

Johnny sipped his highball. "Drink up," he told the dark man. The dark man drank.

After the third swift highball, the dark man looked slightly wall-eyed. "How you feeling?" Johnny asked.

"Fine," said the dark man carefully. "Jus' fine." He dipped two fingers into his vest pocket, drew out a tiny flat pillbox and extracted from it an even tinier pill, which he popped into his mouth and swallowed.

"What was that?" said Johnny suspiciously.

"Just a little pill."

Johnny looked closely at him. His eyes were clear and steady; he looked exactly as if he had not drunk any highballs at all. "Let me hear you say 'The Leith police dismisseth us,' " said Johnny.

The dark man said it.

"Can you say that when you're drunk?" Johnny demanded.

"Don't know, friend. I never tried."

Johnny sighed. Look at it any way you like, the man had been high, at least, before he swallowed that one tiny pill. And now he was cold sober. After a moment, glowering, he pounded on his glass with a swizzle stick until the bartender came and took his order for two more drinks. "Doubles," said Johnny as an afterthought. When they arrived, the dark man drank one down and began to look faintly glassy-eyed. He took out his pillbox.

Johnny leaned forward. "Who's that standing outside?" he whispered hoarsely.

The dark man swiveled around. "Where?"

"They ducked back," said Johnny. "Keep watching." He brought his free hand out of his trousers pocket, where it had been busy extracting the contents of a little bottle of anti-histamine tablets he had been carrying around since February. They were six times the size of the dark man's pills, but they were the best he could do. He slid the pillbox out from under the dark man's fingers, swiftly emptied it onto his own lap, dumped the cold tablets into it and put it back.

"I don't see anybody, friend," said the dark man anxiously. "Was it a man or—" He picked out one of the bogus tablets, swallowed it, and looked surprised.

"Have another drink," said Johnny hopefully. The dark man, still looking surprised, swilled it down. His eyes closed slowly and opened again. They were definitely glassy.

"How do you feel now?" Johnny asked.

"Dandy, thanks. *Vad heter denna ort?*" The dark man's face spread and collapsed astonishingly into a large, loose, foolish smile.

It occurred to Johnny that he might have overdone it. "How was that again?" Swedish, it had sounded like, or some other Scandinavian language . . .

"*Voss hot ir gezugt?*" asked the dark man wonderingly. He batted his head with the heel of his hand several times. "*Favor de desconectar la radio.*"

"The radio isn't—" began Johnny, but the dark man interrupted him. Springing up suddenly, he climbed onto the bench, spread his arms and began singing in a loud operatic baritone. The melody was that of the "Toreador Song" from *Carmen*, but the dark man was singing his own words to it, over and over: "*Dove è il gabinetto?*"

The bartender was coming over with an unpleasant expression. "Cut that out!" Johnny whispered urgently. "You hear? Sit down, or I'll move this thing again!"

The dark man glanced at the object in Johnny's hand. "You don't scare me, bud. Go ahead and move it. *Me cago en su* highball." He began singing again.

Johnny fumbled three five-dollar bills out of his wallet—all he had —and shoved them at the bartender as he came up. The bartender went away.

"Well, why were you scared before, then?" Johnny asked, furiously.

"Simple," said the dark man. "*Vänta ett ögenblick*, it'll come back to me. Sure." He clapped a hand to his brow. "*Herr Gott im Himmel!*" he said, and sat down abruptly. "Don't move it," he said. He was pale and sweat-beaded.

"*Why not?*"

"No control," whispered the dark man. "The instrument is tuned to you—sooner or later you're going to meet yourself. Two bodies can't occupy the same space-time, friend." He shuddered. "*Boom!*"

Johnny's hand and wrist, already overtired, were showing a disposition to tremble. He had the hand propped against a bowl of pretzels, and that helped some, but not enough. Johnny was close to despair. The chief effect of the drinks seemed to have been to make the dark man babble in six or seven foreign tongues. The anti-drink pills were safely in his pocket; there was a fortune in those, no doubt, just as a by-product of this thing if he ever got out of it alive—but that seemed doubtful.

All the same, he checked with a glare the dark man's tentative move toward the object in his hand. His voice shook. "Tell me now, or I'll wave this thing until something happens. I haven't got any more patience! What are you after? What's it all about?"

"*Un autre plat des pets de nonne, s'il vous plaît, garçon,*" murmured the dark man.

"And cut that out," said Johnny. "I mean it!" Intentionally or not, his hand slipped, and he felt the table shudder under them.

Zip!

They were sitting at a narrow table in a Sixth Avenue cafeteria, full of the echoing clatter of inch-thick crockery.

"Well?" said Johnny, close to hysteria. The glasses on the table between them were full of milk, not whisky. Now he was in for it. Unless he could break the dark man's nerve before he sobered up—or unless, which was unlikely in the extreme, they happened to hit another bar . . .

"It's like this, friend," said the dark man. "I'm the last surviving remnant of a race of Lemurians, see, and I like to persecute people. I'm bitter, because you upstarts have taken over the world. You can't—"

"Who's the lady I saw you with?" Johnny asked sourly.

"Her? She's the last surviving remnant of the Atlanteans. We have a working agreement, but we hate each other even more than—"

Johnny's fingers were clammy with sweat around the limp leather that clung to them. He let his hand twitch, not too much.

Zip!

They were sitting facing each other on the hard cane seats of an almost empty subway train, rackety-clacking headlong down its dark tunnel like a consignment to hell. "Try again," said Johnny through his teeth.

"It's like this," said the dark man. "I'll tell you the truth. This whole universe isn't real, get me? It's just a figment of your imagination, but you got powers you don't know how to control, and we been trying to keep you confused, see, because otherwise—"

"Then you don't care if I do this!" said Johnny, and he made a fist around the leather purse and slammed it on his knee.

Zip!

A wind thundered in his ears, snatched the breath from his mouth. He could barely see the dark man, through a cloud of flying sleet, hunkered like himself on a ledge next to nowhere. "We're observers from the Galactic Union," the dark man shouted. "We're stationed here to keep an eye on you people on account of all them A-bomb explosions, because—"

"Or this!" Johnny howled, and jerked his fist again.

Zip!

They were sprawled on a freezing plain, staring at each other in the icy glitter of starlight. "I'll tell you!" said the dark man. "We're time travelers, and we got to make sure you never marry Piper Laurie, because—"

Gently, Johnny told himself.

Zip!

They were sliding side by side down the giant chute in the fun house at Jantzen's Beach in Portland, Oregon. "Listen!" said the dark man. "You're a mutant superman, see? Don't get sore—we had to test you before we could lead you into your glorious heritage of—"

As Johnny started to get to his feet, the movement jarred the thing in his hand, and . . .

Zip!

They were standing on the observation platform on top of the Empire State. It was a cold, raw day. The dark man was shivering—cold, or frightened enough to talk, or too frightened to stay drunk? His voice trembled. "Okay, this is it, friend. You aren't human; you're an android, but such a good imitation, you don't even know it. But we're your inventors, see—"

Gently: it was the little jumps that were dangerous, Johnny reminded himself.

Zip! They were in a revolving door, and *zip!* Johnny was on the staircase of his own rooming house, looking down at the dark man who was goggling up at him, trying to say something, and *zip!* they were standing beside a disordered banana cart while a cold chill ran up Johnny's spine, and . . .

"All right!" the dark man shouted. There was raw sincerity in his voice. "I'll tell you the truth, but *please—*"

Johnny's hand tilted in spite of himself.

Zip!

They were on the top deck of a Fifth Avenue bus parked at the curb, waiting for a load. Johnny lowered his hand with infinite care to the shiny rail top of the seat ahead. "Tell," he said.

The dark man swallowed. "Give me a chance," he said in an undertone. "I can't tell you. If I do, they'll break me, I'll never get a post again—"

"Last chance," said Johnny, looking straight ahead. "*One . . . Two . . .*"

"It's a livie," the dark man said, pronouncing the first *i* long. His voice was resigned and dull.

"A what?"

"Livie. Like movies. You know. You're an actor."

"What is this now?" said Johnny uneasily. "I'm a painter. What do you mean, I'm an ac—"

"You're an *actor, playing* a painter!" said the dark man. "You actors! Dumb cows! You're an actor! Understand? It's a *livie.*"

"What is the livie about?" Johnny asked carefully.

"It's a musical tragedy. All about poor people in the slums."

"I don't live in the slums," said Johnny indignantly.

"*In* the *slums.* You want to tell me, or should I tell you? It's a big dramatic show. You're the comic *relief.* Later on you *die.*" The dark man stopped short, and looked as if he wished he had stopped shorter. "A detail," he said. "Not important. We'll fix it up, next script conference." He put his hands to his temples suddenly. "Oh, why was I decanted?" he muttered. "Glorm will split me up the middle. He'll pulverize me. He'll shove me back into the—"

"You're serious?" said Johnny. His voice cracked. "What is this, I die? I die how?" He twitched uncontrollably.

Zip!

The Fifth Avenue bus was gone. They were sitting in the second row of a movie theater. The house lights had just gone up; the audience was shuffling out. Johnny seized the dark man by the shirt front.

"I forget," said the dark man sullenly. "You fall off something, I think. Right before the end of the livie, when the hero gets to bed with the girl. You want to know who's the hero? Somebody you know. Duke—"

"Fall off what?" said Johnny, tightening his grip.

"Off a building. Into a trash can. Half."

"Comic relief?" said Johnny with an effort.

"Sure. Pratfalls! You'll steal the livie! The lookers'll have heart attacks laughing!"

The sounds of the departing audience abruptly stopped. The walls and ceiling flickered alarmingly; when they steadied, Johnny saw with total bewilderment that they were in a different room altogether. It was nowhere he had ever been before—nowhere, he realized abruptly, with his heart racing, that he ever *could* have been before.

Out across the great silvery bowl, under a cloud-high ceiling, men were floating in the air like gnats, some drifting, some moving quickly around a bulbous metal shape that hung over the center of the huge room. Down below, twenty feet lower than the balcony on which they sat, there was a little puff of light and exploding shape—a brilliant unfolding that lasted only an instant, leaving a crazy memory of moving trees and buildings. After a moment, it happened again.

Johnny was aware that the dark man beside him had stiffened and somehow shrunk into himself.

He turned. Behind them, in the eerie stillness, a silvery man came striding through a doorway.

"*Glorm,*" said the dark man, gasping, "*ne estis mia kulpo. Li—*"

Glorm said, "*Fermu vian truon.*" He was slender and sinewy, dressed in something that looked like tinfoil. He had bulging eyes under a broad shelf of brow. He turned them on Johnny. "Now you vill give me d'in*stru*ment," he said.

Johnny found his breath. The bit of leather in his hand, he discovered, was now as rigid as if it were part of an invisible pillar in the air; but he tightened his grip on it, anyhow. "Why should I give it to you?" he demanded.

Glorm gestured impatiently. "Vait." He turned to look out over the enormous sunken bowl, and his voice suddenly echoed everywhere, somehow a hundred times magnified: "*Gi spinu!*"

Again came that flowering of color and movement under the hanging bulge of metal, but this time it sprang into full life and didn't collapse again.

Fascinated, Johnny stared down over the balcony rim. The floor of the bowl was gone now, buried by a glittering marble street. On either side were white buildings, all porticoes and pillars, and down at the end loomed something that looked like the Parthenon, only as big as the main UN building in New York.

The street was aboil with people, dwarfed by distance. They scattered as a four-horse chariot came hurtling past, then flowed together again. Johnny could hear them muttering angrily, like so many bees. There was a curious acrid scent in the air.

Puzzled, he glanced at Glorm and the dark man. "What's that?" he asked, pointing.

Glorm made a gesture. "Rome," said the dark man, shaking as if with a chill. "They're making a spectacle, back in 44 B.C. This here's the scene where Julius Caesar burns the place down because they won't make him emperor."

Sure enough, the acrid scent was stronger; down below, a thin veil of gray-black smoke was beginning to rise. . . .

"But he didn't," Johnny protested, stung. "That isn't even Rome— the Parthenon's in Athens."

"It used to be," said the dark man. His teeth were chattering. "We changed it. The last outfit that made livies there, they were okay on the little scenes, but they didn't understand spectacle. Glorm—" he cast a furtive glance at the silver man and raised his voice slightly— "he understands spectacle."

"Let me get this straight now," said Johnny with a thick tongue. "You went to all the trouble of building that phony set, with that crazy Parthenon and all, when you could just go back in time and shoot the real thing?"

"*Bona!*" shouted Glorm's amplified voice. "*Gi estu presata!*" The scene down below whirled in upon itself and winked out.

Glorm turned impatiently to Johnny. "Now," he said. "You not understand. Dat vich you see dere *is* vat you call d'real ding. Ve not built set—built not set—not set—*Kiel oni gi diras?*"

"'We din't build no set,'" said the dark man.

"*Putra lingvo!* Ve din build no set. Ve made dat Romans build it. Dey din build no set—dey build Rome, *different*. Understand? Nobody din build no set! Real Rome! Real fire! Real dead! Real history!"

Johnny gaped at him. "You mean you're changing history, just to make movies?"

"Livies," the dark man muttered.

"Livies, then. You must all be loopies. Where does that leave the people up in the future? Look—where are we now? What time?"

"Your calendar, uh, 4400-something. About twenty-five hundred years from your time."

"Twenty-five hundred— Well, what does it do to you, when you change the Romans all around?"

"Noddin'," said Glorm emphatically.

"Noddin'?" said Johnny obtusely.

"Noddin' at all. Vat happens to dog ven you cut off his modder's tail?"

Johnny thought about it. "Noddin'."

"*Korekti.* You dink it is big job?"

Johnny nodded.

"It *is* big job. But ve do it tventy, forty times *every* year. You know how many people live on d'planet now?" Without pausing, he answered himself. "Tirty billion. You know how many go to livies? Half. Fifteen billion. Seven times more people dan live on d'planet in your time. Old, young. Stupid, smart. Livies got to en*ter*tain dem all. Not like your Holl*y*vood. Dat vas not art, not spect*a*cle. Ven d'people tink, deep down—" he tapped his head—"someting is true, den I make it true, and it *is* true! Dat is art! Dat is spect*a*cle!"

"You haven't changed New York much, anyway," said Johnny in self-defense.

Glorm's bulging eyes grew bulgier. "Not change!" He snorted, turned. His amplified voice rang out again: "*Donu al mi flugantan kvieton de Nov-Jorko natural!*"

There was a stirring of floating figures out around the hanging bulge of metal. Glorm cracked his knuckles impatiently. After a long moment the floor of the bowl blossomed again.

Johnny caught his breath.

The illusion was so perfect that the floor seemed to have dropped away: a thousand feet down, Manhattan Island lay spread in the morning sunlight; he could see ships at anchor in the harbor, and the clear glints of the Hudson and the East River running up northward into the mists over the Bronx.

The first thing he noticed was that the chaotic checkerboard of low buildings spread over the whole island: the cluster of skyscrapers at the southern tip, and the scattering at midtown, were missing.

"Guess vat year," said Glorm's voice.

He frowned. "About 1900?" But that couldn't be right, he thought uneasily—there were too many bridges: more, even, than in his own time.

Glorm laughed heartily. "Dat vich you see is Nov-York, 1956—before ve change it. You dink you *in*vent sky*scrap*ers? Oh, no. Me *in*vent it."

"For *Wage Slaves of Broadway*," said the dark man reverently. "That was his first livie. What a spectacle!"

"Now you un*der*stand?" Glorm asked patronizingly. "Long time I vanted to tell dis to actor, see his face. Good—you un*der*stand now." His lean face was shining. "You are actor; I am producer, director. Producer, director is everything. Actor is dirt! So you vill give me d'in*stru*ment."

"Won't," said Johnny weakly.

"You vill," Glorm said. "In a minute you have to let go."

Johnny discovered with shock that his hand was growing numb. So this was what they had all been stalling for, all this time. And now they'd got it. He *was* about to let go; he could feel it. So . . .

"Listen!" he said desperately. "What about the people in the future— I mean your future? Do they make livies, too? If they do, are you an actor to them?"

Glorm's face tautened with fury. "*Kracajo!*" he said. "Vait *until—*" He stared at the thing in Johnny's hand, and his fingers clenched.

Johnny's grip loosened. He was going to let go, and then what? Back to his own time, and more pratfalls, leading inexorably to . . .

His whole arm was tired. He was going to have to let go.

. . . And there was nothing he could do about it. That endless chain of tinkerers, Glorms standing on each others' shoulders, all the way up into the unguessable future—that was too big to change. It was, he supposed, no more frightening or terrible than other kinds of macrocosmic tyranny the human mind had imagined; it would be possible to live with it, if only his part weren't so unpleasant. . . .

His hand dropped.

Smiling, Glorm reached out to the suspended bit of leather. His fingers did something to it that Johnny couldn't follow, and abruptly it sagged into his palm.

It shuddered and flickered there for a moment like a top running down. All at once it split into a brown coin and a pair of pince-nez. The flickering came again, a blur of bright shapes: fountain pen, notebook, watch, cigarette lighter. Then both objects came to rest, tiny and metallic and dead.

Glorm put them into a fold of his clothing.

"*Bona,*" he said indifferently over his shoulder. "*Resendu tion al Nov-Jorkon.*"

Desperation limbered Johnny's tongue. He started talking before he even knew what he was going to say. "What if I don't stay in New York?"

Glorm paused, looking annoyed. "*Kio?*"

"You've got your gadget back," said Johnny, as the idea took shape in his head. "All right, but what are you going to do if I decide to move to Chicago, or someplace? Or get myself arrested and sent to jail? I mean, you can shuffle the probabilities around, but if I try hard enough,

I can put myself where it's *impossible* to have what you want to have happen, happen." He took a deep breath. "See what I mean?"

"*Plejmalpuro*," said Glorm. From his expression, he saw.

"Listen," Johnny said. "Let me get the picture. This Duke you say is the hero—that's the Duke I know?" He got a nod from Glorm. "And that was part of the script, when he helped me get out of town?"

"Dress rehearsal," said the dark man. "You fall in a swamp in Florida—come up all over mud and leeches. A real boff."

Johnny shuddered and turned his mind resolutely away from leeches and falls from high buildings. . . . "What I want to know is, what was Duke's angle? Why did he think he wanted to get me out of town?"

They told him. The answer was brutally simple, and Johnny had been half afraid that he knew it already.

He waited until his nails unclenched from his palms, and he felt able to talk sensibly again. And even then, he found he had nothing to say. How could you talk to people who would do a thing like that and call it art, or entertainment? It was logical, he supposed, that a culture whose taste demanded Glorm's ruthless spec*ta*cles should have such a concept of a "hero." It was also terrifying.

His time was running out again. But the answer to that one occurred to him too.

If Duke were here, what would he say?

"Okay, look," Johnny said rapidly, "I'm just spitballing, you understand, talking off the top of my head—"

Glorm and the dark man leaned forward with interested, wary expressions.

"—but here's how I see it. Instead of this clown type for your comedy relief, we have this suave man-of-the-world type. It's a switch. A really great, uh, producer-director could put it over. I can really see it. Take for instance—here, show me where it says in the script . . ."

Johnny materialized on the quiet side street a few steps from his door. He felt heavy and tired. The sun was still high over the tops of the old buildings; it was about 2:30—an hour and a half after Duke had left him at the airport.

He leaned against a railing and waited. Sure enough, here came Mary Finigan across the street, her hair uncombed, dark circles under her eyes.

"Go home, Mary," he said.

She was startled. "What's the matter, isn't he there? I mean, Duke called me—he said he was at your place."

"He's got an ax," said Johnny. "I'm telling you the truth. He was going to kill you in my apartment, with my Scout ax that I use for kindling, with my fingerprints on it."

When she was gone, Johnny went on around the corner and into the foyer. Duke was there with his hand in Johnny's mailbox. He turned around and swore, and his hand twitched a long fat envelope out of the box. "What the devil are you doing here, Johnny?"

"I decided not to go."

Duke leaned against the wall, grinning. "Well, every coming together again gives a foretaste of the resurrection. Whew!" He glanced at the envelope he was holding as if he had just noticed it. "Now I wonder what this might be."

"You know what it is," said Johnny without rancor. "Ted Edwards' fifty bucks that he owed me. That was what gave you the idea, when he told you he'd put it in the mail. Then this Mary business came up, and I suppose it just seemed to you like a God-given opportunity."

Duke's eyes were narrow and hard. "You know about that, too, do you? What were you planning to do about it, would you tell an old friend that?"

"Nothing," said Johnny. "Just give me my I O U, and we'll call it square."

Duke fished in his pocket for the folded scrap of paper and handed it over. He peered into Johnny's eyes, looking baffled. "Well, well. You're sure, are you?"

Johnny nodded and turned to go up the stairs.

"I believe you are," said Duke. He was shaking his head, arms akimbo. "Johnny, my boy, you're a character."

Johnny looked down at him for a moment. "You're another," he said.

TIME ENOUGH

The walls and the control panel were gray, but in the viewscreen it was green summer noon.

"That's the place," said the boy's voice in Vogel's ear.

The old man gently touched the controls, and the viewpoint steadied, twenty feet or so above the ground. In the screen, maple leaves swayed in a light breeze. There was just a glimpse of the path below, deep in shadow.

The display, on the tiny screen, was as real as if one could somehow squeeze through the frame and drop into those sunlit leaves. A warm breath of air came into the room.

"Guess I could go there blindfold, I remember it so well," he heard Jimmy say. The boy seemed unable to stop talking; his hands tightened and relaxed on his knees. "I remember, we were all standing around in front of the drugstore in the village, and one of the kids said let's go swimming. So we all started off across town, and first thing I knew, we weren't going down to the beach; we were going out to the old quarry."

The leaves danced suddenly in a stronger breeze. "Guess we'll see them in about a minute," Jimmy said. "If you got the right time, that is." His weight shifted, and Vogel knew he was staring up at the dials on the control board, even before his high voice read aloud: "May twenty-eight, nineteen sixty. Eleven-nine-thirty-two A.M."

His voice grew higher. "Here they come."

In the screen, a flicker of running bodies passed under the trees. Vogel saw bare brown backs, sports shirts, tee shirts, dark heads and blond. There were eight or nine boys in the pack, all aged about twelve; the last, lagging behind, was a slender brown-haired boy who seemed a little younger. He paused, clearly visible for a moment through the leaves, and looked up with a white face. Then he turned and was gone into the dark flickering green.

"There I go," said Jimmy's raw voice. "Now we're climbing up the slope to the quarry. Dark and kind of clammy up there, so many old spruces you can't even see the sky. That moss was just like cold mud when you stepped on it barefoot."

"Try to relax," said Vogel carefully. "Would you like to do it later?"

"No, now," said Jimmy convulsively. His voice steadied. "I'm a little tensed up, I guess, but I can do it. I wasn't really *scared*; it was the way it happened, so sudden. They never gave me time to get ready."

"Well, that's what the machine is for," said Vogel soothingly. "More time—time enough for everything."

"I know it," said Jimmy in an inattentive voice.

Vogel sighed. These afternoons tired him; he was not a young man any more and he no longer believed in his work. Things did not turn out as you expected. The work had to be done, of course; there was always the chance of helping someone, but it was not the easy, automatic thing that youth in its terrible confidence believed.

There was a rustle in the screen, and Vogel saw Jimmy's hands clench into desperate fists on his knees.

A boy flashed into view, the same boy, running clumsily with one hand over his face. His head rocked back and forth. He blundered past, whipped by undergrowth, and the swaying branches closed behind him.

Jimmy's hands relaxed slowly. "There I go," his voice said, low and bitter. "Running away. Crying like a baby."

After a moment Vogel's spidery fingers reached out to the controls. The viewpoint drifted slowly closer to the ground. Galaxies of green leaves passed through it like bright smoke, and then the viewpoint stopped and tilted, and they were looking up the leaf-shadowed path, as if from a point five feet or so above the ground.

Vogel asked carefully, "Ready now?"

"Sure," said Jimmy, his voice thin again.

The shock of the passage left him stumbling for balance, and he fetched up against a small tree. The reeling world steadied around him; he laughed. The tree trunk was cool and papery under his hand; the leaves were a dancing green glory all around. He was back in Kellogg's Woods again, on that May day when everything had gone wrong, and here it was, just the same as before. The same leaves were on the trees; the air he breathed was the same air.

He started walking up the trail. After a few moments he discovered that his heart was thumping in his chest. He *hated* them, all the big kids with their superior, grinning faces. They were up there right now, waiting for him. But this time he would show them, and then afterward, slowly, it would be possible to stop hating. He knew that. But oh, Christ, how he hated them now!

It was dark under the spruces as he climbed, and the moss was squashy underfoot. For a passing moment he was sorry he had come. But it was costing his family over a thousand dollars to have him sent back. They were giving him this golden chance, and he wouldn't waste it.

Now he could hear the boys' voices, calling hollow, and the cold splash as one of them dived.

Hating and bitter, he climbed to where he could look down across the deep shadowed chasm of the old quarry. The kids were all tiny figures on the other side, where the rock slide was, the only place where you could climb out of the black water. Some of them were sitting on the rocks, wet and shivering. Their voices came up to him small with distance.

Nearer, he saw the dead spruce that lay slanting downward across the edge of the quarry, with its tangled roots in the air. The trunk was silvery gray, perhaps a foot thick at the base. It had fallen straight down along the quarry wall, an old tree with all the stubs of limbs broken off short, and its tip was jammed into a crevice. Below that, there was a series of ledges you could follow all the way down.

But first you had to walk the dead tree.

He climbed up on the thick, twisting roots, trying not to be aware just yet how they overhung the emptiness below. Down across the shadowed quarry, he could see pale blurs of faces turning up one by one to look at him.

Now he vividly remembered the way it had been before, the line of boys tightrope-walking down the tree, arms waving for balance, bare or tennis-shoed feet treading carefully. If only they hadn't left him till last!

He took one step out onto the trunk. Without intending to, he glanced down and saw the yawning space under him—the black water, and the rocks.

The tree swayed under him. He tried to take the next step and found he couldn't. It was just the same as before, and he realized now that it was *impossible* to walk the tree—you would slip and fall, down, down that cliff to the rocks and the cold water. Standing there fixed between the sky and the quarry, he could tell himself that the others had done it, but it didn't help. What good was that, when he could *see*, when anybody could see, it was impossible?

Down there, the boys were waiting, in their cold and silent comradeship.

Jimmy stepped slowly back. Tears of self-hatred burned his lids, but he climbed over the arching roots and left the quarry edge behind him, hearing the clear, distant shouts begin again as he stumbled down the path.

"Don't blame yourself too much," said Vogel in his gray voice. "Maybe you just weren't ready, this time."

Jimmy wiped his eyes angrily with the heel of his hand. "I wasn't ready," he muttered. "I thought I was, but . . . Must have been too nervous, that's all."

"Or, maybe . . ." Vogel hesitated. "Some people think it's better to forget the past and solve our problems in the present."

Jimmy's eyes widened with shock. "I couldn't give up *now!*" he said. He stood up, agitated. "Why, my whole life would be ruined— I mean, I never thought I'd hear a thing like that from you, Mr. Vogel. I mean, the whole *point* of this machine, and everything . . ."

"I know," said Vogel. "The past can be altered. The scholar can take his exam over again, the lover can propose once more, the words that were thought of too late can be spoken. So I always believed." He forced a smile. "It's like a game of cards. If you don't like the hand that is dealt to you, you can take another, and after that, another. . . ."

"That's right," said Jimmy, sounding appeased. "So if you look at it that way, how can I lose?"

Vogel did not reply but stood up courteously to see him to the door.

"So, then, I'll see you tomorrow, Mr. Vogel," Jimmy said.

Vogel glanced at the wall calendar; it read, *April 21, 1978.* "Yes, all right," he answered.

In the doorway, Jimmy looked back at him with pathetic hopefulness—a pale, slender thirty-year-old man, from whose weak eyes a lost boy seemed to be staring, pleading. . . . "There's always tomorrow, isn't there, Mr. Vogel?" he asked.

"Yes," said Vogel wearily. "There's always tomorrow."

EXTEMPORE

Everybody knew; everybody wanted to help Rossi the time-traveler. They came running up the scarlet beach, naked and golden as children, laughing happily.

"Legend is true," they shouted. "He is here, just like great-grandfathers say!"

"What year is this?" Rossi asked, standing incongruously shirt-sleeved and alone in the sunlight—no great machines bulking around him, no devices, nothing but his own spindling body.

"Thairty-five twainty-seex, Mista Rossi!" they chorused.

"Thank you. Goodbye."

"Goodbyee!"

Flick. Flick. Flick. Those were days. *Flicketaflicketaflick*—weeks, months, years. WHIRRR . . . Centuries, millennia streaming past like sleet in a gale!

Now the beach was cold, and the people were buttoned up to their throats in stiff black cloth. Moving stiffly, like jointed stick people, they unfurled a huge banner: "SORI WI DO NOT SPIC YOUR SPICH. THIS IS YIR 5199 OF YOUR CALINDAR. HELLO MR ROSI."

They all bowed, like marionettes, and Mr. Rossi bowed back. *Flick. Flick. Flicketaflicketa*WHIRRR . . .

The beach was gone. He was inside an enormous building, a sky-high vault, like the Empire State turned into one room. Two floating eggs swooped at him and hovered alertly, staring with poached eyes. Behind them reared a tilted neon slab blazing with diagrams and symbols, none of which he could recognize before *flicketa*WHIRRRR . . .

This time it was a wet stony plain, with salt marshes beyond it. Rossi was not interested and spent the time looking at the figures he had scrawled in his notebook. 1956, 1958, 1965 and so on, the intervals getting longer and longer, the curve rising until it was going almost

straight up. If only he'd paid more attention to mathematics in school
. . . *flick*RRR . . .

Now a white desert at night, bitter cold, where the towers of Manhattan should have been. Something mournfully thin flapped by over
*flk*RRRR . . .

Blackness and fog was all he could *fk*RRRR . . .

Now the light and dark blinks in the grayness melted and ran together, flickering faster and faster until Rossi was looking at a bare
leaping landscape as if through soap-smeared glasses—continents expanding and contracting, icecaps slithering down and back again, the
planet charging toward its cold death while only Rossi stood there to
watch, gaunt and stiff, with a disapproving, wistful glint in his eye.

His name was Albert Eustace Rossi. He was from Seattle, a wild
bony young man with a poetic forelock and the stare-you-down eyes
of an animal. He had learned nothing in twelve years of school except
how to get passing marks, and he had a large wistfulness but no talents
at all.

He had come to New York because he thought something wonderful
might happen.

He averaged two months on a job. He worked as a short-order cook
(his eggs were greasy and his hamburgers burned), a platemaker's
helper in an offset shop, a shill in an auction gallery. He spent three
weeks as a literary agent's critic, writing letters over his employer's
signature to tell hapless reading-fee clients that their stories stank. He
wrote bad verse for a while and sent it hopefully to all the best magazines,
but concluded he was being held down by a clique.

He made no friends. The people he met seemed to be interested in
nothing but baseball, or their incredibly boring jobs, or in making
money. He tried hanging around the Village, wearing dungarees and a
flowered shirt, but discovered that nobody noticed him.

It was the wrong century. What he wanted was a villa in Athens;
or an island where the natives were childlike and friendly, and no masts
ever lifted above the blue horizon; or a vast hygienic apartment in
some future underground Utopia.

He bought certain science-fiction magazines and read them defiantly
with the covers showing in cafeterias. Afterward, he took them home
and marked them up with large exclamatory blue and red and green
pencil and filed them away under his bed.

The idea of building a time machine had been growing a long
while in his mind. Sometimes in the morning on his way to work,

looking up at the blue cloud-dotted endlessness of the sky, or staring at the tracery of lines and whorls on his unique fingertips, or trying to see into the cavernous unexplored depths of a brick in a wall, or lying on his narrow bed at night, conscious of all the bewildering sights and sounds and odors that had swirled past him in twenty-odd years, he would say to himself, Why not?

Why not? He found a secondhand copy of J. W. Dunne's *An Experiment with Time* and lost sleep for a week. He copied off the charts from it, Scotch-taped them to his wall; he wrote down his startling dreams every morning as soon as he awoke. There was a time outside time, Dunne said, in which to measure time; and a time outside that, in which to measure the time that measured time, and a time outside that. . . . Why not?

An article in a barbershop about Einstein excited him, and he went to the library and read the encyclopedia articles on relativity and spacetime, frowning fiercely, going back again and again over the paragraphs he never did understand, but filling up all the same with a threshold feeling, an expectancy.

What looked like time to him might look like space to somebody else, said Einstein. A clock ran slower the faster it went. Good, fine. Why not? But it wasn't Einstein, or Minkowski or Wehl who gave him the clue; it was an astronomer named Milne.

There were two ways of looking at time, Milne said. If you measured it by things that moved, like clock hands and the earth turning and going around the sun, that was one kind; Milne called it dynamical time and his symbol for it was τ. But if you measured it by things happening in the atom, like radioactivity and light being emitted, that was another kind; Milne called it kinematic time, or t. And the formula that connected the two showed that it depended on which you used whether the universe had ever had a beginning or would ever have an end—yes in τ time, no in t.

Then it all added together: Dunne saying you didn't really have to travel along the timetrack like a train, you just thought you did, but when you were asleep you forgot, and that was why you could have prophetic dreams. And Eddington: that all the great laws of physics we had been able to discover were just a sort of spidery framework, and that there was room between the strands for an unimaginable complexity of things.

He believed it instantly; he had known it all his life but had never had any words to think it in—that this reality wasn't all there was. Pay checks, grimy window sills, rancid grease, nails in the shoe—how could it be?

It was all in the way you looked at it. That was what the *scientists* were saying—Einstein, Eddington, Milne, Dunne, all in a chorus. So it was a thing anybody could do, if he wanted it badly enough and was lucky. Rossi had always felt obscurely resentful that the day was past when you could discover something by looking at a teakettle or dropping gunk on a hot stove; but here, incredibly, was one more easy road to fame that everybody had missed.

Between the tip of his finger and the edge of the soiled plastic cover that hideously draped the hideous table, the shortest distance was a straight line containing an infinite number of points. His own body, he knew, was mostly empty space. Down there in the shadowy regions of the atom, in t time, you could describe how fast an electron was moving or where it was, but never both; you could never decide whether it was a wave or a particle; you couldn't even prove it existed at all, except as the ghost of its reflection appeared to you.

Why not?

It was summer, and the whole city was gasping for breath. Rossi had two weeks off and nowhere to go; the streets were empty of the Colorado vacationers, the renters of cabins in the mountains, the tailored flyers to Ireland, the Canadian Rockies, Denmark, Nova Scotia. All day long the sweaty subways had inched their loads of suffering out to Coney Island and Far Rockaway and back again, well salted, flayed with heat, shocked into a fishy torpor.

Now the island was still; flat and steaming, like a flounder on a griddle; every window open for an unimagined breath of air; silent as if the city were under glass. In dark rooms the bodies lay sprawled like a cannibal feast, all wakeful, all moveless, waiting for Time's tick.

Rossi had fasted all day, having in mind the impressive results claimed by Yogis, early Christian saints and Amerinds; he had drunk nothing but a glass of water in the morning and another at blazing noon. Standing now in the close darkness of his room, he felt that ocean of Time, heavy and stagnant, stretching away forever. The galaxies hung in it like seaweed, and down at the bottom it was silted unfathomably deep with dead men. (Seashell murmur: I am.)

There it all was, temporal and eternal, t and tau, everything that was and would be. The electron dancing in its imaginary orbit, the May fly's moment, the long drowse of the sequoias, the stretching of continents, the lonely drifting of stars; it canceled them all against each other, and the result was stillness.

The sequoia's truth did not make the May fly false. If a man could only see some other aspect of that totality, feel it, believe it—another relation of tau time to t . . .

He had chalked a diagram on the floor—not a pentacle but the nearest thing he could find, the quadrisected circle of the Michelson apparatus. Around it he had scrawled, "$e = mc^2$," "Z^2/n^2," "$M = M_0 + 3K + 2V$." Pinned up shielding the single bulb was a scrap of paper with some doggerel on it:

$$\frac{t, \tau, t, \tau, t \tau t}{c}$$
$$\frac{}{R \sqrt{3}}$$

Cartesian co-ordinates x, y, z
$$- c^2t^2 = me$$

It was in his head, hypnotically repeating: *t, tau, t, tau, t tau t* . . .

As he stood there, the outlines of the paper swelled and blurred, rhythmically. He felt as if the whole universe were breathing, slowly and gigantically, all one, the smallest atom and the farthest star.

c over R times the square root of three . . .

He had a curious drunken sense that he was standing *outside*, that he could reach in and give himself a push, or a twist—no, that wasn't the word, either. . . . But something was happening; he felt it, half in terror and half in delight.

less c squared, t squared, equals . . .

An intolerable tension squeezed Rossi tight. Across the room the paper, too near the bulb, crisped and burned. And (as the tension twisted him somehow, finding a new direction for release) that was the last thing Rossi saw before *flick*, it was daylight, and the room was clotted with moist char, *flick*, someone was moving across it, too swift to *flick*. *Flick. Flick. Flick, flick, flicketa-flicketa* . . .

And here he was. Most incredibly, what had seemed so true *was* true: by that effort of tranced will, he had transferred himself to another time rate, another relationship of t to τ—a variable relationship, like a huge merry-go-round that whirled, and paused, and whirled again.

He had got on; how was he going to get off?

And—most terrifying question—where was the merry-go-round going? Whirling headlong to extinction and cold death, where the universe ended—or around the wheel again, to give him a second chance?

The blur exploded into white light. Stunned but safe inside his portable anomaly, Rossi watched the flaming earth cool, saw the emerging continents furred over with green, saw a kaleidoscope whirl of rainstorm and volcanic fury, pelting ice, earthquake, tsunami, fire!

Then he was in a forest, watching the branches sway as some great shape passed.

He was in a clearing, watching as a man in leather breeches killed a copper-skinned man with an ax.

He was in a log-walled room, watching a man in a wide collar stand up, toppling table and crockery, his eyes like onions.

He was in a church, and an old man behind the pulpit flung a book at him.

The church again, at evening, and two lonely women saw him and screamed.

He was in a bare, narrow room reeking of pitch. Somewhere outside, a dog set up a frenzied barking. A door opened and a wild, whiskery face popped in; a hand flung a blazing stick and flame leaped up. . . .

He was on a broad green lawn, alone with a small boy and a frantic white duck. "Good morrow, sir. Will you help me catch this pesky . . ."

He was in a little pavilion. A gray-bearded man at a desk turned, snatching up a silver cross, whispering fiercely to the young man at his side, *"Didn't I tell you!"* He pointed the cross, quivering. "Quick, then! Will New York continue to grow?"

Rossi was off guard. "Sure. This is going to be the biggest city . . ."

The pavilion was gone; he was in a little perfumed nook, facing a long room across a railing. A red-haired youth, dozing in front of the fire, sat up with a guilty start. He gulped. "Who . . . who's going to win the election?"

"What election?" said Rossi. "I don't—"

"Who's going to win?" The youth came forward, pale-faced. "Hoover or Roosevelt? Who?"

"Oh, that election. Roosevelt."

"Uh, will the country . . ."

The same room. A bell was ringing; white lights dazzled his eyes.

The bell stopped. An amplified voice said, "When will Germany surrender?"

"Uh, 1945," said Rossi, squinting. "May, 1945. Look, whoever you are—"

"When will Japan surrender?"

"Same year. September. Look, whoever you are . . ."

A tousle-headed man emerged from the glare, blinking, wrapping a robe around his bulging middle. He stared at Rossi while the mechanical voice spoke behind him.

"Please name the largest new industry in the next ten years."

"Uh, television, I guess. Listen, you right there, can't you . . ."

The same room, the same bell ringing. This was all wrong, Rossi realized irritably. Nineteen thirty-two, 1944 (?)—the next ought to be at least close to where he had started. There was supposed to be a row of cheap rooming houses—his room, *here.*

". . . election, Stevenson or Eisenhower?"

"Stevenson. I mean, Eisenhower. Now look, doesn't *anybody*—"

"When will there be an armistice in Korea?"

"Last year. *Next* year. You're mixing me up. Will you turn off that—"

"When and where will atomic bombs next be used in—"

"Listen!" Rossi shouted. "I'm getting mad! If you want me to answer questions, let me ask some! Get me some help! Get me—"

"What place in the United States will be safest when—"

"*Einstein!*" shouted Rossi.

But the little gray man with the bloodhound eyes couldn't help him, nor the bald mustachioed one who was there the next time. The walls were inlaid now with intricate tracings of white metal. The voice began asking him questions he couldn't answer.

The second time it happened, there was a *puff* and a massive rotten stench rolled into his nostrils. Rossi choked. "Stop that!"

"Answer!" blared the voice. "What's the meaning of those signals from space?"

"I don't know!" *Puff.* Furiously: "But there isn't any New York past here! It's all gone—nothing left but . . ."

Puff!

Then he was standing on the lake of glassy obsidian, just like the first time.

And then the jungle, and he said automatically, "My name is Rossi. What year . . ." But it wasn't the jungle, really. It had been cleared back, and there were neat rows of concrete houses, like an enormous tank trap, instead of grass-topped verandas showing through the trees.

Then came the savanna, and that was all different, too—there was a looming piled ugliness of a city rising half a mile away. Where were the nomads, the horsemen?

And next . . .

The beach: but it was dirty gray, not scarlet. One lone dark figure was hunched against the sun glare, staring out to sea; the golden people were gone.

Rossi felt lost. Whatever had happened to New York, back there—to the whole world, probably—something he had said or done had made it come out differently. Somehow they had saved out some of the old grimy, rushing civilization, and it had lasted just long enough to blight all the fresh new things that ought to have come after it.

The stick men were not waiting on their cold beach.

He caught his breath. He was in the enormous building again, the same tilted slab blazing with light, the same floating eggs bulging their eyes at him. That hadn't changed, and perhaps nothing he could do would ever change it; for he knew well enough that that wasn't a human building.

But then came the white desert, and after it the fog, and his glimpses of the night began to blur together, faster and faster. . . .

That was all. There was nothing left now but the swift vertiginous spin to the end-and-beginning, and then the wheel slowing as he came around again.

Rossi began to seethe. This was worse than dishwashing—his nightmare, the worst job he knew. Standing here, like a second hand ticking around the face of Time, while men who flickered and vanished threaded him with questions: a thing, a tool, a gyrating information booth!

Stop, he thought, and pushed—a costive pressure inside his brain—but nothing happened. He was a small boy forgotten on a carousel, a bug trapped between window and screen, a moth circling a lamp. . . .

It came to him what the trouble was. There had to be the yearning, that single candle-cone focus of the spirit: that was the moving force, and all the rest—the fasting, the quiet, the rhymes—was only to channel and guide.

He would have to get off at the one place in the whole endless sweep of time where he wanted to be. And that place, he knew now without surprise, was the scarlet beach.

Which no longer existed, anywhere in the universe.

While he hung suspended on that thought, the flickering stopped at the prehistoric jungle; and the clearing with its copper dead man; and the log room, empty; the church, empty, too.

And the fiery room, now so fiercely ablaze that the hair of his forearms puffed and curled.

And the cool lawn, where the small boy stood agape.

And the pavilion: the graybeard and the young man leaning together like blasted trees, livid-lipped.

There was the trouble: they had believed him, the first time around, and acting on what he told them, they had changed the world.

Only one thing to be done—destroy that belief, fuddle them, talk nonsense, like a ghost called up at a séance!

"Then you tell me to put all I have in land," says graybeard, clutching the crucifix, "and wait for the increase!"

"Of course!" replied Rossi with instant cunning. "New York's to be the biggest city—in the whole state of Maine!"

The pavilion vanished. Rossi saw with pleasure that the room that took its place was high-ceilinged and shabby, the obvious forerunner of his own roach-haunted cubbyhole in 1955. The long paneled room with its fireplace and the youth dozing before it were gone, snuffed out, a might-have-been.

When a motherly looking woman lurched up out of a rocker, staring, he knew what to do.

He put his finger to his lips. "The lost candlestick is under the cellar stairs!" he hissed, and vanished.

The room was a little older, a little shabbier. A new partition had been added, bringing its dimensions down to those of the room Rossi knew, and there was a bed, and an old tin washbasin in the corner. A young woman was sprawled open-mouthed, fleshy and snoring, in the bed; Rossi looked away with faint prim disgust and waited.

The same room: *his* room, almost: a beefy stubbled man smoking in the armchair with his feet in a pan of water. The pipe dropped from his sprung jaw.

"I'm the family banshee," Rossi remarked. "Beware, for a short man with a long knife is dogging your footsteps." He squinted and bared his fangs; the man, standing up hurriedly, tipped the basin and stumbled half across the room before he recovered and whirled to the door, bellowing, leaving fat wet tracks and silence.

Now; *now* . . . It was night, and the sweaty unstirred heat of the city poured in around him. He was standing in the midst of the chalk marks he had scrawled a hundred billion years ago. The bare bulb was still lighted; around it flames were licking tentatively at the edges of the table, cooking the plastic cover up into lumpy hissing puffs.

Rossi the shipping clerk; Rossi the elevator man; Rossi the *dishwasher!*

He let it pass. The room kaleidoscope-flicked from brown to green; a young man at the washbasin was pouring something amber into a glass, gurgling and clinking.

"Boo!" said Rossi, flapping his arms.

The young man whirled in a spasm of limbs, a long arc of brown droplets hanging. The door banged him out, and Rossi was alone, watching the drinking glass roll, counting the seconds until . . .

The walls were brown again; a calendar across the room said 1965 MAY 1965. An old man, spidery on the edge of the bed, was fumbling spectacles over the rank crests of his ears. "You're real," he said.

"I'm not," said Rossi indignantly. He added, "Radishes. Lemons. Grapes. Blahhh!"

"Don't put me off," said the old man. He was ragged and hollow-templed, like a birdskull, colored like earth and milkweed floss, and his mouth was a drum over porcelain, but his oystery eyes were burning bright. "I knew the minute I saw you—you're Rossi, the one that disappeared. If you can do that—" his teeth clacked—"you must know, you've got to tell me. Those ships that have landed on the moon—what are they building there? What do they want?"

"I don't know. Nothing."

"Please," said the old man humbly. "You can't be so cruel. I tried to warn people, but they've forgotten who I am. If you know: if you could just tell me . . ."

Rossi had a qualm, thinking of heat flashing down in that one intolerable blow that would leave the city squashed, glistening, as flat as the thin film of a bug. But remembering that, after all, the old man was not real, he said, "There isn't anything. You made it up. You're dreaming."

And then, while the pure tension gathered and strained inside him, came the lake of obsidian.

And the jungle, just as it ought to be—the brown people caroling, "Hello, Mister Rossi, hello again, hello!"

And the savanna, the tall black-haired people reining in, breeze-blown, flash of teeth: "Hillo, Misser Rossi!"

And the *beach*.

The scarlet beach with its golden, laughing people: "Mista Rossi, Mista Rossi!" Heraldic glory under the clear sky, and out past the breakers the clear heart-stirring glint of sun on the sea: and the tension of the longing breaking free (stop), no need for symbols now (stop), a lifetime's distillation of *I wish* . . . spurting, channeled, done.

There he stands where he longed to be, wearing the same pleased expression, forever caught at the beginning of a hello—Rossi, the first man to travel in Time, and Rossi, the first man to Stop.

He's not to be mocked or mourned. Rossi was born a stranger; there are thousands of him, unconsidered gritty particles in the gears of history: the ne'er-do-wells, the superfluous people, shaped for some world that has never yet been invented. The air-conditioned utopias have no place for them; they would have been bad slaves and worse masters in Athens. As for the tropic isles—the Marquesas of 1800, or the Manhattan of 3526—could Rossi swim a mile, dive six fathoms, climb a fifty-foot palm? If he had stepped alive onto that scarlet shore, would the young men have had him in their canoes, or the maidens in their bowers? But see him now, stonily immortal, the symbol of a wonderful thing that happened. The childlike golden people visit him every day, except when they forget. They drape his rock-hard flesh with garlands and lay little offerings at his feet; and when he lets it rain, they thump him.

CABIN BOY

The cabin boy's name was unspeakable, and even its meaning would be difficult to convey in any human tongue. For convenience, we may as well call him Tommy Loy.

Please bear in mind that all these terms are approximations. Tommy was not exactly a cabin boy, and even the spaceship he served was not exactly a spaceship, nor was the Captain exactly a captain. But if you think of Tommy as a freckled, scowling, red-haired, willful, prank-play-ing, thoroughly abhorrent brat, and of the Captain as a crusty, ponder-ous old man, you may be able to understand their relationship.

A word about Tommy will serve to explain why these approximations have to be made, and just how much they mean. Tommy, to a human being, would have looked like a six-foot egg made of greenish gelatin. Suspended in this were certain dark or radiant shapes which were Tommy's nerve centers and digestive organs, and scattered about its surface were star-shaped and oval markings which were his sensory organs and gripping mechanisms—his "hands." At the lesser end was an orifice which expelled a stream of glowing vapor—Tommy's means of propulsion. It should be clear that if instead of saying, "Tommy ate his lunch," or, "Tommy said to the Captain . . ." we reported what really happened, some pretty complicated explanations would have to be made.

Similarly, the term "cabin boy" is used because it is the closest in human meaning. Some vocations, like seafaring, are so demanding and so complex that they simply cannot be taught in classrooms; they have to be lived. A cabin boy is one who is learning such a vocation and paying for his instruction by performing certain menial, degrading, and unimportant tasks.

That describes Tommy, with one more similarity—the cabin boy of the sailing vessel was traditionally occupied after each whipping with preparing the mischief, or the stupidity, that earned him the next one.

Tommy, at the moment, had a whipping coming to him and was fighting a delaying action. He knew he couldn't escape eventual punishment, but he planned to hold it off as long as he could.

Floating alertly in one of the innumerable corridors of the ship, he watched as a dark wave sprang into being upon the glowing corridor wall and sped toward him. Instantly, Tommy was moving away from it, and at the same rate of speed.

The wave rumbled: "Tommy! Tommy Loy! Where *is* that obscenity boy?"

The wave moved on, rumbling wordlessly, and Tommy moved with it. Ahead of him was another wave, and another beyond that, and it was the same throughout all the corridors of the ship. Abruptly the waves reversed their direction. So did Tommy, barely in time. The waves not only carried the Captain's orders but scanned every corridor and compartment of the ten-mile ship. But as long as Tommy kept between the waves, the Captain could not see him.

The trouble was that Tommy could not keep this up forever, and he was being searched for by other lowly members of the crew. It took a long time to traverse all of those winding, interlaced passages, but it was a mathematical certainty that he would be caught eventually.

Tommy shuddered, and at the same time he squirmed with delight. He had interrupted the Old Man's sleep by a stench of a particularly noisome variety, one of which he had only lately found himself capable. The effect had been beautiful. In human terms, since Tommy's race communicated by odors, it was equivalent to setting off a firecracker beside a sleeper's ear.

Judging by the jerkiness of the scanning waves' motion, the Old Man was still unnerved.

"Tommy!" the waves rumbled. "Come out, you little piece of filth, or I'll smash you into a thousand separate stinks! By Spore, when I get hold of you—"

The corridor intersected another at this point, and Tommy seized his chance to duck into the new one. He had been working his way outward ever since his crime, knowing that the search parties would do the same. When he reached the outermost level of the ship, there would be a slight possibility of slipping back past the hunters—not much of a chance, but better than none.

He kept close to the wall. He was the smallest member of the crew—smaller than any of the other cabin boys, and less than half the size of an Ordinary; it was always possible that when he sighted one of the search party, he could get away before the crewman saw him. He was in a short connecting corridor now, but the scanning waves cycled endlessly, always turning back before he could escape into the next corridor. Tommy followed their movement patiently, while he listened to the torrent of abuse that poured from them. He snickered to himself. When the Old Man was angry, everybody suffered. The ship would be stinking from stem to stern by now.

Eventually the Captain forgot himself and the waves flowed on around the next intersection. Tommy moved on. He was getting close to his goal by now; he could see a faint gleam of starshine up at the end of the corridor.

The next turn took him into it—and what Tommy saw through the semi-transparent skin of the ship nearly made him falter and be caught. Not merely the fiery pinpoints of stars shone there, but a great, furious glow which could only mean that they were passing through a star system. It was the first time this had happened in Tommy's life, but of course it was nothing to the Captain, or even to most of the Ordinaries. Trust them, Tommy thought resentfully, to say nothing to him about it!

Now he knew he was glad he'd tossed that surprise at the Captain. If he hadn't, he wouldn't be here, and if he weren't here . . .

A waste capsule was bumping automatically along the corridor, heading for one of the exit pores in the hull. Tommy let it catch up to him, then englobed it, but it stretched him so tight that he could barely hold it. That was all to the good; the Captain wouldn't be likely to notice that anything had happened.

The hull was sealed, not to keep atmosphere inside, for there was none except by accident, but to prevent loss of liquid by evaporation. Metals and other mineral elements were replaceable; liquids and their constituents, in ordinary circumstances, were not.

Tommy rode the capsule to the exit sphincter, squeezed through, and instantly released it. Being polarized away from the ship's core, it shot into space and was lost. Tommy hugged the outer surface of the hull and gazed at the astonishing panorama that surrounded him.

There was the enormous black half-globe of space—Tommy's sky, the only one he had ever known. It was sprinkled with the familiar yet always changing patterns of the stars. By themselves, these were marvels enough for a child whose normal universe was one of ninety-foot corridors and chambers measuring, at most, three times as much. But Tommy hardly noticed them. Down to his right, reflecting brilliantly from the long, gentle curve of the greenish hull, was a blazing yellow-white glory that he could hardly look at. A star, the first one he had ever seen close at hand. Off to the left was a tiny, milky-blue disk that could only be a planet.

Tommy let go a shout, for the sheer pleasure of its thin, hollow smell. He watched the thin mist of particles spread lazily away from his body, faintly luminous against the jet blackness. He shivered a little, thickening his skin as much as he could. He could not stay long, he knew; he was radiating heat faster than he could absorb it from the sun or the ship's hull.

But he didn't want to go back inside, and not only because it meant being caught and punished. He didn't want to leave that great, dazzling jewel in the sky. For an instant he thought vaguely of the future time when he would be grown, the master of his own vessel, and could see the stars whenever he chose; but the picture was too far away to have any reality. Great Spore, that wouldn't happen for twenty thousand years!

Fifty yards away, an enormous dark spot on the hull, one of the ship's vision devices, swelled and darkened. Tommy looked up with interest. He could see nothing in that direction, but evidently the Captain had spotted something. Tommy watched and waited, growing colder every second, and after a long time he saw a new pinpoint of light spring into being. It grew steadily larger, turned fuzzy at one side, then became two linked dots, one hard and bright, the other misty.

Tommy looked down with sudden understanding, and saw that another wide area of the ship's hull was swollen and protruding. This one showed a pale color under the green and had a dark ring around it: it was a polarizer. The object he had seen must contain metal, and the Captain was bringing it in for fuel. Tommy hoped it was a big one; they had been short of metal ever since he could remember.

When he glanced up again, the object was much larger. He could see now that the bright part was hard and smooth, reflecting the light of the nearby sun. The misty part was a puzzler. It looked like a crewman's voice, seen against space—or the ion trail of a ship in motion. But was it possible for metal to be alive?

II

Leo Roget stared into the rear-view scanner and wiped beads of sweat from his brown, half-bald scalp. Flaming gas from the jets washed up toward him along the hull; he couldn't see much. But the huge dark ovoid they were headed for was still there, and it was getting bigger. He glanced futilely at the control board. The throttle was on full. They were going to crash in a little more than two minutes, and there didn't seem to be a single thing he could do about it.

He looked at Frances McMenamin, strapped into the acceleration harness beside his own. She said, "Try cutting off the jets, why don't you?"

Roget was a short, muscular man with thinning straight black hair and sharp brown eyes. McMenamin was slender and ash-blond, half an inch taller than he was, with one of those pale, exquisitely shaped faces that seem to be distributed equally among the very stupid and the very bright. Roget had never been perfectly sure which she was, although they had been companions for more than three years. That, in a way, was part of the reason they had taken this wild trip: she had made Roget uneasy, and he wanted to break away, and at the same time he didn't. So he had fallen in with her idea of a trip to Mars—"to get off by ourselves and think"—and here, Roget thought, they were, not thinking particularly.

He said, "You want us to crash quicker?"

"How do you know we will?" she countered. "It's the only thing we haven't tried. Anyhow, we'd be able to see where we're going, and that's more than we can do now."

"All right," said Roget, "all *right*." She was perfectly capable of giving him six more reasons, each screwier than the last, and then turning out to be right. He pulled the throttle back to zero, and the half-heard, half-felt roar of the jets died.

The ship jerked backward suddenly, yanking them against the couch straps, and then slowed.

Roget looked into the scanner again. They were approaching the huge object, whatever it was, at about the same rate as before. Maybe, he admitted unwillingly, a little slower. Damn the woman! How could she possibly have figured that one out in advance?

"And," McMenamin added reasonably, "we'll save fuel for the take-off."

Roget scowled at her. "If there is a takeoff," he said. "Whatever is pulling us down there isn't doing it to show off. What do we do—tell them that was a very impressive trick and we enjoyed it, but we've got to be leaving now?"

"We'll find out what's doing it," said McMenamin, "and stop it if we can. If we can't, the fuel won't do us any good anyway."

That was, if not Frances' most exasperating trick, at least high on the list. She had a habit of introducing your own argument as if it were not only a telling point on her side, but something you have been too dense to see. Arguing with her was like swinging at someone who abruptly disappeared and then sandbagged you from behind.

Roget was fuming, but he said nothing. The greenish surface below was approaching more and more slowly, and now he felt a slight but definite tightening of the couch straps that could only mean deceleration. They were being maneuvered in for a landing as carefully and efficiently as if they were doing it themselves.

A few seconds later, a green horizon line appeared in the direct-view ports, and they touched. Roget's and McMenamin's couches swung on their gimbals as the ship tilted slowly, bounced and came to rest.

Frances reached inside the wide collar of her pressure suit to smooth a ruffle that had got crumpled between the volcanic swell of her bosom and the front of the transparent suit. Watching her, Roget felt a sudden irrational flow of affection and—as usually happened—a simultaneous notification that his body disagreed with his mind's opinion of her. This trip, it had been tacitly agreed, was to be a kind of final trial period. At the end of it, either they would split up or decide to make it permanent, and up to now, Roget had been silently determined that it was going to be a split. Now he was just as sure that, providing they ever got to Mars or back to Earth, he was going to nail her for good.

He glanced at her face. She knew, all right, just as she'd known when he'd felt the other way. It should have irritated him, but he felt oddly pleased and comforted. He unstrapped himself, fastened down his helmet, and moved toward the airlock.

He stood on a pale-green, almost featureless surface that curved gently away in every direction. Where he stood, it was brilliantly lighted by the sun, and his shadow was sharp and as black as space. About two thirds of the way to the horizon, looking across the short axis of the ship, the sunlight stopped with knife-edge sharpness, and he could make out the rest only as a ghostly reflection of starlight.

Their ship was lying on its side, with the pointed stern apparently sunk a few inches into the green surface of the alien ship. He took a cautious step in that direction, and nearly floated past it before he could catch himself. His boot magnets had failed to grip. The metal of this hull—if it *was* metal—must be something that contained no iron.

The green hull was shot through with other colors here, and it rose in a curious, almost rectangular mound. At the center, just at the tip of the earth vessel's jets, there was a pale area; around that was a dark ring which lapped up over the side of the ship. He bent to examine it. It was in shadow, and he used his helmet light.

The light shone through the mottled green substance; he could see the skin of his own ship. It was pitted, corroding. As he watched, another pinpoint of corruption appeared on the shiny surface, and slowly grew.

Roget straightened up with an exclamation. His helmet phones asked, "What is it, Leo?"

He said, "Acid or something eating the hull. Wait a minute." He looked again at the pale and dark mottlings under the green surface. The center area was not attacking the ship's metal; that might be the muzzle of whatever instrument had been used to pull them down out of their orbit and hold them there. But if it was turned off now . . . He had to get the ship away from the dark ring that was destroying it. He couldn't fire the jets otherwise, because they were half buried; he'd blow the tubes if he tried.

He said, "You still strapped in?"

"Yes."

"All right, hold on." He stepped back to the center of the little ship, braced his corrugated boot soles against the hard green surface, and shoved.

The ship rolled. But it rolled like a top, around the axis of its pointed end. The dark area gave way before it, as if it were jelly-soft. The jets still pointed to the middle of the pale area, and the dark ring still lapped over them. Roget moved farther down and tried again, with the same result. The ship would move freely in every direction but the right one. The attracting power, clearly enough, was still on.

He straightened dejectedly and looked around. A few hundred yards away, he saw something he had noticed before, without attaching any significance to it; a six-foot egg, of some lighter, more translucent substance than the one on which it lay. He leaped toward it. It moved sluggishly away, trailing a cloud of luminous gas. A few seconds later he had it between his gloved hands. It squirmed, then ejected a thin spurt of vapor from its forward end. It was alive.

McMenamin's head was silhouetted in one of the forward ports. He said, "See this?"

"Yes! What is it?"

"One of the crew, I think. I'm going to bring it in. You work the airlock—it won't hold both of us at once."

". . . All right."

The huge egg crowded the cabin uncomfortably. It was pressed up against the rear wall, where it had rolled as soon as Frances had pulled it into the ship. The two human beings stood at the other side of the room, against the control panel, and watched it.

"No features," said Roget, "unless you count those markings on the surface. This thing isn't from anywhere in the solar system, Frances—it isn't even any order of evolution we ever heard of."

"I know," she said abstractedly. "Leo, is he wearing any protection against space that you can see?"

"No," said Roget. "That's *him*, not a spacesuit. Look, you can see halfway into him. But—"

Frances turned to look at him. "That's it," she said. "It means this is his natural element—space!"

Roget looked thoughtfully at the egg. "It makes sense," he said. "He's adapted for it, anyhow—ovoid, for a high volume-to-surface ratio. Tough outer shell. Moves by jet propulsion. It's hard to believe, because we've never run into a creature like him before, but I don't see why not. On earth there are organisms, plants, that can live and reproduce in boiling water, and others that can stand near-zero temperatures."

"He's a plant, too, you know," Frances put in.

Roget stared at her, then back at the egg. "That color, you mean? Chlorophyll. It could be."

"Must be," she corrected firmly. "How else would he live in a vacuum?" And then, distressedly, "Oh, what a smell!"

They looked at each other. It *had* been something monumental in the way of smells, though it had only lasted a fraction of a second. There had been a series of separate odors, all unfamiliar and all overpoweringly strong. At least a dozen of them, Roget thought; they had gone past too quickly to count.

"He did it before, outside, and I saw the vapor." He closed his helmet abruptly and motioned McMenamin to do the same. She frowned and shook her head. He opened his helmet again. "It might be poisonous!"

"I don't think so," said McMenamin. "Anyway, we've got to try something." She walked toward the green egg. It rolled away from her, and she went past it into the bedroom.

In a minute she reappeared, carrying an armload of plastic boxes and bottles. She came back to Roget and knelt on the floor, lining up the containers with their nipples toward the egg.

"What's this for?" Roget demanded. "Listen, we've got to figure some way of getting out of here. The ship's being eaten up—"

"Wait," said McMenamin. She reached down and squeezed three of the nipples quickly, one after the other. There was a tiny spray of face powder, then one of cologne (*Nuit Jupitérienne*), followed by a jet of good Scotch.

Then she waited. Roget was about to open his mouth when another blast of unfamiliar odors came from the egg. This time there were only three: two sweet ones and one sharp.

McMenamin smiled. "I'm going to name him Stinky," she said. She pressed the nipples again, in a different order. Scotch, face powder, *Nuit Jupitérienne*. The egg replied: sharp, sweet, sweet.

She gave him the remaining combination, and he echoed it; then she put a record cylinder on the floor and squirted the face powder. She added another cylinder and squeezed the cologne. She went along the line that way, releasing a smell for each cylinder until there were ten. The egg had responded, recognizably in some cases, to each one. Then she took away seven of the cylinders and looked expectantly at the egg.

The egg released a sharp odor.

"If ever we tell anybody," said Roget in an awed tone, "that you taught a six-foot Easter egg to count to ten by selectine flatulence—"

"Hush, fool," she said. "This is a tough one."

She lined up three cylinders, waited for the sharp odor, then added six more to make three rows of three. The egg obliged with a penetrating smell which was a good imitation of citron extract, Frances' number nine. He followed it immediately with another of his own rapid, complicated series of smells.

"He gets it," said McMenamin. "I think he just told us that three times three are nine." She stood up. "You go out first, Leo. I'll put him out after you and then follow. There's something more we've got to show him before we let him go."

Roget followed orders. When the egg came out and kept on going, he stepped in its path and held it back. Then he moved away, hoping the thing would get the idea that they weren't trying to force it but wanted it to stay. The egg wobbled indecisively for a moment and then stayed where it was. Frances came out the next minute, carrying one of the plastic boxes and a flashlight.

"My nicest powder," she said regretfully, "but it was the only thing I could find enough of." She clapped her gloved hands together sharply, with the box between them. It burst, and a haze of particles spread around them, glowing faintly in the sunlight.

The egg was still waiting, somehow giving the impression that it was watching them alertly. McMenamin flicked on the flashlight and pointed it at Roget. It made a clear, narrow path in the haze of dispersed particles. Then she turned it on herself, on the ship, and finally upward, toward the tiny blue disk that was Earth. She did it twice more, then stepped back toward the airlock, and Roget followed her.

They stood watching as Tommy scurried off across the hull, squeezed himself into it and disappeared.

"That was impressive," Roget said. "But I wonder just how much good it's going to do us."

"He knows we're alive, intelligent, friendly, and that we come from Earth," said McMenamin thoughtfully. "Or, anyhow, we did our best to tell him. That's all we can do. Maybe he won't want to help us; maybe he can't. But it's up to him now."

III

The mental state of Tommy, as he dived through the hull of the ship and into the nearest radial corridor, would be difficult to describe fully to any human being. He was the equivalent of a very small boy—that approximation still holds good—and he had the obvious reactions to novelty and adventure. But there was a good deal more. He had seen living, intelligent beings of an unfamiliar shape and substance, who lived in metal and had some connection with one of those enormous, enigmatic ships called planets, which no captain of his own race dared approach.

And yet Tommy *knew*, with all the weight of knowledge accumulated, codified and transmitted over a span measured in billions of years, that there was no other intelligent race than his own in the entire universe, that metal, though life-giving, could not itself be alive, and that no living creature, having the ill luck to be spawned aboard a planet, could ever hope to escape so tremendous a gravitational field.

The final result of all this was that Tommy desperately wanted to go somewhere by himself and think. But he couldn't; he had to keep moving, in time with the scanning waves along the corridor, and he had to give all his mental energy to the problem of slipping past the search party.

The question was—how long had he been gone? If they had reached the hull while he was inside the metal thing, they might have looked for him outside and concluded that he had somehow slipped past them, back to the center of the ship. In that case, they would probably be working their way back, and he had only to follow them to the axis and hide in a chamber as soon as they left it. But if they were still working outward, his chances of escape were almost nil. And now it seemed more important to escape than it had before.

There was one possibility which Tommy, who, in most circumstances, would try anything, hated to think about. Fuel lines—tubes carrying the rushing, radiant ion vapor that powered the ship—adjoined many of these corridors, and it was certain that if he dared to enter one, he would be perfectly safe from detection as long as he remained in it. But, for one thing, these lines radiated from the ship's axis and none of them would take him where he wanted to go. For another, they were the most dangerous places aboard ship. Older crew members sometimes entered them to make emergency repairs, but they got out as quickly as they could. Tommy did not know how long he could survive there; he had an unpleasant conviction that it would not be long.

Only a few yards up the corridor was the sealed sphincter which gave entrance to such a tube. Tommy looked at it indecisively as the motion of the scanning waves brought him nearer. He had still not made up his mind when he caught a flicker reflected around the curve of the corridor behind him.

Tommy squeezed himself closer to the wall and watched the other end of the corridor approach with agonizing slowness. If he could only get around that corner . . .

The flicker of motion was repeated, and then he saw a thin rind of green poke into view. There was no more time to consider entering the fuel line, no time to let the scanning waves' movement carry him around the corner. Tommy put on full speed, cutting across the next wave and down the cross-corridor ahead.

Instantly the Captain's voice shouted from the wall, "Ah! Was that him, the dirty scut? After him, lads!"

Tommy glanced behind as he turned another corner, and his heart sank. It was no cabin boy who was behind him, or even an Ordinary, but a Third Mate—so huge that he filled nearly half the width of the corridor, and so powerful that Tommy, in comparison, was like a boy on a bicycle racing an express train.

He turned another corner, realizing in that instant that he was as good as caught: the new corridor ahead of him stretched straight and without a break for three hundred yards. As he flashed down it, the hulk of the Mate appeared around the bend behind.

The Mate was coming up with terrifying speed, and Tommy had time for only one last desperate spurt. Then the other body slammed with stunning force against his, and he was held fast.

As they coasted to a halt, the Captain's voice rumbled from the wall, "*That's* it, Mister. Hold him where I can see him!"

The scanning areas were stationary now. The Mate moved Tommy forward until he was squarely in range of the nearest.

Tommy squirmed futilely. The Captain said, "*There's* our little jokester. It's a pure pleasure to see you again, Tommy. What—no witty remarks? Your humor all dried up?"

Tommy gasped, "Hope you enjoyed your nap, Captain."

"Very good," said the Captain with heavy sarcasm. "Oh, *very* entertaining, Tommy. Now would you have anything more to say, before I put the whips to you?"

Tommy was silent.

The Captain said to the Mate, "Nice work, Mister. You'll get extra rations for this."

The Mate spoke for the first time, and Tommy recognized his high, affected voice. It was George Adkins, who had recently spored and was so proud of the new life inside his body that there was no living with him. George said prissily, "Thank you, sir, I'm sure. Of course, I really shouldn't have exerted myself the way I just did, in my state."

"Well, you'll be compensated for it," the Captain said testily. "Now take the humorist down to Assembly Five. We'll have a little ceremony there."

"Yes, sir," said the Mate distantly. He moved off, shoving Tommy ahead of him, and dived into the first turning that led downward.

They moved along in silence for the better part of a mile, crossing from one lesser passage to another until they reached a main artery that led directly to the center of the ship. The scanning waves were still stationary, and they were moving so swiftly that there was no danger of being overheard. Tommy said politely, "You won't let them be too hard on me, will you, sir?"

The Mate did not reply for a moment. He had been baited by Tommy's mock courtesy before, and he was as wary as his limited intelligence allowed. Finally he said, "You'll get no more than what's coming to you, young Tom."

"Yes, sir. I know that, sir. I'm sorry I made you exert yourself, sir, in your condition and all."

"You should be," said the Mate stiffly, but his voice betrayed his pleasure. It was seldom enough that even a cabin boy showed a decent interest in the Mate's prospective parenthood. "They're moving about, you know," he added, unbending a little.

"Are they, sir? Oh, you must be careful of yourself, sir. How many are there, please, sir?"

"Twenty-eight," said the Mate, as he had on every possible occasion for the past two weeks. "Strong and healthy—so far."

"That's remarkable, sir!" cried Tommy. "Twenty-eight! If I might be so bold, sir, you ought to be careful of what you eat. Is the Captain going to give you your extra rations out of that mass he just brought in topside, sir?"

"I'm sure I don't know."

"Gosh!" exclaimed Tommy. "I wish I could be sure . . ."

He let the pause grow. Finally the Mate said querulously, "What do you mean? Is there anything wrong with the metal?"

"I don't really know, sir, but it isn't like any we ever had before. That is," Tommy added, "since I was spored, sir."

"Naturally," said the Mate. "*I've* eaten all kinds myself, you know."

"Yes, sir. But doesn't it usually come in ragged shapes, sir, and darkish?"

"Of course it does. Everybody knows that. Metal is nonliving, and only living things have regular shapes."

"Yes, sir. But I was topside, sir, while I was trying to get away, and I saw this metal. It's quite regular, except for some knobs at one end, sir, and it's as smooth as you are, sir, and shiny. If you'll forgive me, sir, it didn't look at all appetizing to me."

"Nonsense," said the Mate uncertainly. "Nonsense," he repeated, in a stronger tone. "You must have been mistaken. Metal can't be alive."

"That's just what I thought, sir," said Tommy excitedly. "But there are live things in this metal, sir. I saw them. And the metal wasn't just floating along the way it's supposed to, sir. I saw it when the Captain brought it down, and . . . But I'm afraid you'll think I'm lying, sir, if I tell you what it was doing."

"Well, what was it doing?"

"I swear I saw it, sir," Tommy went on. "The Captain will tell you the same thing, sir, if you ask him—he must have noticed."

"Sterilize it all, what *was* it doing?"

Tommy lowered his voice. "There was an ion trail shooting from it, sir. It was trying to get away!"

While the Mate was trying to absorb that, they reached the bottom of the corridor and entered the vast globular space of Assembly Five, lined with crewmen waiting to witness the punishment of Tommy Loy.

This was not going to be any fun at all, thought Tommy, but at least he had paid back the Third Mate in full measure. The Mate, for the moment, at any rate, was not taking any joy in his promised extra rations.

When it was over, Tommy huddled in a corner of the crew compartment where they had tossed him, bruised and smarting in every nerve, shaken by the beating he had undergone. The pain was still rolling through him in faint, uncontrollable waves, and he winced at each one, in spite of himself, as though it were the original blow.

In the back of his mind, the puzzle of the metal ship was still calling, but the other experience was too fresh, the remembered images too vivid.

The Captain had begun, as always, by reciting the Creed.

In the beginning was the Spore, and the Spore was alone.

(And the crew: *Praised be the Spore!*)

Next there was light, and the light was good. Yea, good for the Spore and the Spore's First Children.

(*Praised be they!*)

But the light grew evil in the days of the Spore's Second Children.

(*Woe unto them!*)

And the light cast them out. Yea, exiled were they, into the darkness and the Great Deep.

(*Pity for the outcasts in the Great Deep!*)

Tommy had mumbled his responses with the rest of them, thinking rebellious thoughts. There was nothing evil about light; they lived by it still. What must have happened—the Captain himself admitted as much when he taught history and natural science classes—was that the earliest ancestors of the race, spawned in the flaming heart of the Galaxy, had grown too efficient for their own good.

They had specialized, more and more, in extracting energy from starlight and the random metal and other elements they encountered in space; and at last they absorbed, willy-nilly, more than they could use. So they had moved, gradually and naturally, over many generations, out from that intensely radiating region into the "Great Deep"—the universe of thinly scattered stars. And the process had continued, inevitably; as the level of available energy fell, their absorption of it grew more and more efficient.

Now, not only could they never return to their birthplace, but they could not even approach a single sun as closely as some planets did. Therefore the planets, and the stars themselves, were objects of fear. That was natural and sensible. But why did they have to continue this silly ritual, invented by some half-evolved, superstitious ancestor, of "outcasts" and "evil"?

The Captain finished:

Save us from the Death that lies in the Great Deep . . .
(*The creeping Death that lies in the Great Deep!*)
And keep our minds pure . . .
(*As pure as the light in the days of the Spore, blessed be He!*)
And our course straight . . .
(*As straight as the light, brothers!*)
That we may meet our lost brothers again in the Day of Reuniting.
(*Speed that day!*)

Then the pause, the silence that grew until it was like the silence of space. At last the Captain spoke again, pronouncing judgment against Tommy, ending, "Let him be whipped!"

Tommy tensed himself, thickening his skin, drawing his body into the smallest possible compass. Two husky Ordinaries seized him and tossed him at a third. As Tommy floated across the room, the crewman pressed himself tightly against the wall, drawing power from it until he could contain no more. And as Tommy neared him, he discharged it in a crackling arc that filled Tommy's body with the pure essence of pain, and sent him hurtling across the chamber to the next shock, and the next, and the next.

Until the Captain had boomed, "Enough!" and they had carried him out and left him here alone.

He heard the voices of crewmen as they drew their rations. One of them was grumbling about the taste, and another, sounding happily bloated, was telling him to shut up and eat, that metal was metal.

That would be the new metal, however much of it had been absorbed by now, mingled with the old in the reservoir. Tommy wondered briefly how much of it there was, and whether the alien ship—if it *was* a ship—could repair even a little damage to itself. But that assumed life in the metal, and in spite of what he had seen, Tommy couldn't believe in it. It seemed beyond question, though, that there were living things inside the metal; and when the metal was gone, how would they live?

Tommy imagined himself set adrift from the ship, alone in space, radiating more heat than his tiny volume could absorb. He shuddered.

He thought again of the problem that had obsessed him ever since he had seen the alien, five-pointed creatures in the metal ship. Intelligent life was supposed to be sacred. That was part of the Creed, and it was stated in a sloppy, poetic way like the rest of it, but it made a certain kind of sense. No crewman or captain had the right to destroy another for his benefit, because the same heredity was in them all. They were all potentially the same, none better than another.

And you ate metal, because metal was nonliving and certainly not intelligent. But if that stopped being true . . .

Tommy felt he was missing something. Then he had it: In the alien ship, trying to talk to the creatures that lived in metal, he had been scared almost scentless—but underneath the fright and the excitement, he had felt wonderful. It had been, he realized suddenly, like the mystic completion that was supposed to come when all the straight lines met, in the "Day of Reuniting"—when all the far-flung ships, parted for all the billions of years of their flight, came together at last. It was talking to someone different from yourself.

He wanted to talk again to the aliens, teach them to form their uncouth sounds into words, learn from them . . . Vague images swirled in his mind. They were products of an utterly different line of evolution. Who knew what they might be able to teach him?

And now the dilemma took shape. If his own ship absorbed the metal of theirs, they would die; therefore he would have to make the Captain let them go. But if he somehow managed to set them free, they would leave and he would never see them again.

A petty officer looked into the cubicle and said, "All right, Loy, out of it. You're on garbage detail. You eat after you work, if there's anything left. Lively, now!"

Tommy moved thoughtfully out into the corridor, his pain almost forgotten. The philosophical problems presented by the alien ship, too, having no apparent solution, were receding from his mind. A new thought was taking their place, one that made him glow inside with the pure rapture of the devoted practical jokester.

The whipping he was certainly going to get—and, so soon after the last offense, it would be a beauty—scarcely entered his mind.

IV

Roget climbed in, opening his helmet, and sat down warily in the acceleration couch. He didn't look at the woman.

McMenamin said quietly, "Bad?"

"Not good. The outer skin's gone all across that area, and it's eating into the lead sheathing. The tubes are holding up pretty well, but they'll be next."

"We've done as much as we can, by rolling the ship around?"

"Just about. I'll keep at it, but I don't see how it can be more than a few hours before the tubes go. Then we're cooked, whatever your fragrant little friend does."

He stood up abruptly and climbed over the slanting wall which was now their floor, to peer out the direct-view port. He swore, slowly and bitterly. "You try the radio again while I was out?" he asked.

"Yes." She did not bother to add that there had been no response. Here, almost halfway between the orbits of Earth and Mars, they were hopelessly out of touch. A ship as small as theirs couldn't carry equipment enough to bridge the distance.

Roget turned around, said, "By God—" and then clenched his jaw and strode out of the room. McMenamin heard him walk through the bedroom and clatter around in the storage compartment behind.

In a few moments he was back with a welding torch in his hand. "Should have thought of this before," he said. "I don't know what'll happen if I cut into that hull—damn thing may explode, for all I know—but it's better than sitting doing nothing." He put his helmet down with a bang and his voice came tinnily in her helmet receiver. "Be back in a minute."

"Be careful," McMenamin said again.

Roget closed the outer lock door behind him and looked at the ravished hull of the ship. The metal had been eaten away in a broad band all around the ship, just above the tail, as if a child had bitten around the small end of a pear. In places the clustered rocket tubes showed through. He felt a renewed surge of anger, with fear deep under it.

A hundred years ago, he reminded himself, the earliest space voyagers had encountered situations as bad as this one, maybe worse. But Roget was a city man, bred for city virtues. He didn't, he decided, know quite how to feel or act. What were you supposed to do when you were about to die, fifteen million miles from home? Try to calm McMenamin —who was dangerously calm already—or show your true nobility by making one of those deathbed speeches you read in the popular histories? What about suggesting a little suicide pact? There was nothing in the ship that would give them a cleaner death than the one ahead of them. About all he could do would be to stab Frances, then himself, with a screwdriver.

Her voice said in the earphones, "You all right?"

He said, "Sure. Just going to try it." He lowered himself to the green surface, careful not to let his knees touch the dark, corrosive area. The torch was a small, easily manageable tool. He pointed the snout at the dark area where it lapped up over the hull, turned the switch on and pressed the button. Flame leaped out, washing over the dark surface. Roget felt the heat through his suit. He turned off the torch to see what effect it had had.

There was a deep, charred pit in the dark stuff, and it seemed to him that it had pulled back a little from the area it was attacking. It was more than he had expected. Encouraged, he tried again.

There was a sudden tremor under him and he leaped nervously to his feet, just in time to avoid the corrosive wave as it rolled under him. For a moment he was only conscious of the thick metal of his boot soles and the thinness of the fabric that covered his knees; then, as he was about to step back out of the way, he realized that it was not only the dark ring that had expanded, that was still expanding.

He moved jerkily—too late—as the pale center area swept toward and under him. Then he felt as if he had been struck by a mighty hammer.

His ears rang, and there was a mist in front of his eyes. He blinked, tried to raise an arm. It seemed to be stuck fast at the wrist and elbow. Panicked, he tried to push himself away and couldn't. As his vision cleared, he saw that he was spread-eagled on the pale disk that had spread out under him. The metal collars of his wrist and elbow joints, all the metal parts of his suit, were held immovably. The torch lay a few inches away from his right hand.

For a few moments, incredulously, Roget still tried to move. Then he stopped and lay in the prison of his suit, looking at the greenish-cream surface under his helmet.

Frances' voice said abruptly, "Leo, is anything wrong?"

Roget felt an instant relief that left him shaken and weak. His forehead was cold. He said after a moment, "Pulled a damn fool trick, Frances. Come out and help me if you can."

He heard a click as her helmet went down. He added anxiously, "But don't come near the pale part, or you'll get caught too."

After a while she said, "Darling, I can't think of anything to do."

Roget was feeling calmer, somehow not much afraid any more. He wondered how much oxygen was left in his suit. Not more than an hour, he thought. He said, "I know. I can't, either."

Later he called, "Frances?"

"Yes?"

"Roll the ship once in a while, will you? Might get through to the wiring or something, otherwise."

". . . All right."

After that, they didn't talk. There was a great deal to be said, but it was too late to say it.

V

Tommy was on garbage detail with nine other unfortunates. It was a messy, hard, unpleasant business, fit only for a cabin boy—collecting waste from the compartment and corridor receptacles and pressing it into standard capsule shapes, then hauling it to the nearest polarizer. But Tommy, under the suspicious eye of the petty officer in charge, worked with an apparent total absorption until they had cleaned out their section of the six inmost levels and were well into the seventh.

This was the best strategic place for Tommy's departure, since it was about midway from axis to hull, and the field of operations of any pursuit was correspondingly broadened. Also, the volume in which they labored had expanded wedgewise as they climbed, and the petty officer, though still determined to watch Tommy, could no longer keep him constantly in view.

Tommy saw the officer disappear around the curve of the corridor, and kept on working busily. He was still at it, with every appearance of innocence and industry, when the officer abruptly popped into sight again about three seconds later.

The officer stared at him with baffled disapproval and said unreasonably, "Come on, come on, Loy. Don't slack."

"Right," said Tommy, and scurried faster.

A moment later Third Mate Adkins hove majestically into view. The petty officer turned respectfully to face him.

"Keeping young Tom well occupied, I see," said the Mate.

"Yes, sir," said the officer. "Appears to be a reformed character, now, sir. Must have learned a lesson, one way or another."

"Ha!" said the Mate. "Very good. Oh, Loy, you might be interested in this—the Captain himself has told me that the new metal is perfectly all right. Unusually rich, in fact. I've had my first ration already—very good it was, too—and I'm going to get my extras in half an hour or so. Well, good appetite, all." And, while the lesser crewmen clustered against the walls to give him room, he moved haughtily off down the corridor.

Tommy kept on working as fast as he could. He was draining energy he might need later, but it was necessary to quiet the petty officer's suspicions entirely, in order to give himself a decent start. In addition, his artist's soul demanded it. Tommy, in his own way, was a perfectionist.

Third Mate Adkins was due to get his extras in about half an hour, and if Tommy knew the Captain's habits, the Captain would be taking his first meal from the newly replenished reservoir at about the same time. That set the deadline. Before the half hour was up, Tommy would have to cut off the flow of the new metal, so that stomachs which had been gurgling in anticipation would remain desolately void until the next windfall.

The Mate, in spite of his hypochondria, was a glutton. With any luck, this would make him bitter for a month. And the Old Man—but it was better not to dwell on that.

The petty officer hung around irresolutely for another ten minutes, then dashed off down the corridor to attend to the rest of his detail. Without wasting a moment, Tommy dropped the capsule he had just collected and shot away in the other direction.

The rest of the cabin boys, as fearful of Tommy as they were of constituted authority, would not dare to raise an outcry until they spotted the officer coming back. The officer, because of the time he had wasted in watching Tommy, would have to administer a thorough lecture on slackness to the rest of the detail before he returned.

Tommy had calculated his probable margin to a nicety, and it was enough, barring accidents, to get him safely away. Nevertheless, he turned and twisted from one system of corridors to another, carefully confusing his trail, before he set himself to put as much vertical distance behind him as he could.

This part of the game had to be accomplished in a fury of action, for he was free to move in the corridors only until the Captain was informed that he was loose again. After that, he had to play hounds and hares with the moving strips through which the Captain could see him.

When the time he had estimated was three quarters gone, Tommy slowed and came to a halt. He inspected the corridor wall minutely, and found the almost imperceptible trace that showed where the scanning wave nearest him had stopped. He jockeyed his body clear of it, and then waited. He still had a good distance to cover before he dared play his trump, but it was not safe to move now; he had to wait for the Captain's move.

It came soon enough: the scanning waves erupted into simultaneous motion and anger. "Tommy!" they bellowed. "Tommy Loy! Come back, you unmentionable excrescence, or by Spore you'll regret it! Tommy!"

Moving between waves, Tommy waited patiently until their motion carried him from one corridor to another. The Captain's control over the waves was not complete: in some corridors they moved two steps upward for one down, in others the reverse. When he got into a downward corridor, Tommy scrambled out of it again as soon as he could and started over.

Gradually, with many false starts, he worked his way up to the thirteenth level, one level short of the hull.

Now came the hard part. This time he had to enter the fuel lines, not only for sure escape, but to gather the force he needed. And for the first time in his life, Tommy hesitated before something that he had set himself to do.

Death was a phenomenon that normally touched each member of Tommy's race only once—only captains died, and they died alone. For lesser members of the crew, there was almost no mortal danger; the ship protected them. But Tommy knew what death was, and as the sealed entrance to the fuel line swung into view, he knew that he faced it.

He made himself small, as he had under the lash. He broke the seal.

Quickly, before the following wave could catch him, he thrust himself through the sphincter.

The blast of ions gripped him, flung him forward, hurting him like a hundred whips. Desperately he held himself together, thickening his insulating shell against that deadly flux of energy; but still his body absorbed it, till he felt a horrid fullness.

The walls of the tube fled past him, barely perceptible in the rush of glowing haze. Tommy held in that growing tautness with his last strength, meanwhile looking for an exit. He neither knew nor cared whether he had reached his goal; he had to get out or die.

He saw a dim oval on the wall ahead, hurled himself at it, clung, and forced his body through.

He was in a horizontal corridor, just under the hull. He drank the blessed coolness of it for an instant, before moving to the nearest sphincter. Then he was out, under the velvet-black sky and the diamond blaze of stars.

He looked around. The pain was fading now; he felt only an atrocious bloatedness that tightened his skin and made all his movements halting. Forward of him, up the long shallow curve of the hull, he could see the alien ship, and the two five-pointed creatures beside it. Carefully, keeping a few feet between himself and the hull, he headed toward it.

One of the creatures was sprawled flat on the polarizer that had brought its ship down. The other, standing beside it, turned as Tommy came near, and two of its upper three points moved in an insane fashion that made Tommy feel ill. He looked away quickly and moved past them, till he was directly over the center of the polarizer and only a few inches away.

Then, with a sob of relief, he released the energy his body had stored. In one thick, white bolt, it sparked to the polarizer's center.

Shaken and spent, Tommy floated upward and surveyed what he had done. The muzzle of the polarizer was contracting, puckering at the center, the dark corrosive ring following it in. So much energy, applied in one jolt, must have shorted and paralyzed it all the way back to the ship's nerve center. The Captain, Tommy thought wryly, would be jumping now!

And he wasn't done yet. Tommy took one last look at the aliens and their ship. The sprawled one was up now, and the two of them had their upper points twined around each other in a nauseating fashion. Then they parted suddenly, and, facing Tommy, wiggled their free points. Tommy moved purposefully off across the width of the ship, heading for the three heavy-duty polarizers.

He had to go in again through that hell not once more, but twice. Though his nerves shrank from the necessity, there was no way of avoiding it. For the ship could not alter its course, except by allowing itself to be attracted by a sun or other large body—which was unthinkable—but it could rotate at the Captain's will. The aliens were free now, but the Captain had only to spin ship in order to snare them again.

Four miles away, Tommy found the second polarizer. He backed away a carefully calculated distance before he re-entered the hull. At least he could know in advance how far he had to go—and he knew now, too, that the energy he had stored the first time had been adequate twice over. He rested a few moments; then, like a diver plunging into a torrent, he thrust himself into the fuel line.

He came out again, shuddering with pain, and pushed himself through the exit. He felt as bloated as he had before. The charge of energy was not as great, but Tommy knew that he was weakening. This time, when he discharged over the polarizer and watched it contract into a tiny, puckered mass, he felt as if he could never move again, let alone expose himself once more to that tunnel of flame.

The stars, he realized dully, were moving in slow, ponderous arcs over his head. The Captain was spinning ship. Tommy sank to the hull and lay motionless, watching half attentively for a sight of the alien ship.

There it was, a bright dot haloed by the flame of its exhaust. It swung around slowly, gradually, with the rest of the firmament, growing smaller slowly.

"He'll get them before they're out of range," Tommy thought. He watched as the bright dot climbed overhead, began to fall on the other side.

The Captain had one polarizer left. It would be enough.

Wearily Tommy rose and followed the bright star. It was not a joke any longer. He would willingly have gone inside to the bright, warm, familiar corridors that led downward to safety and deserved punishment. But somehow he could not bear to think of those fascinating creatures—those wonderful playthings—going to fill the Captain's fat belly.

Tommy followed the ship until he could see the pale gleam of the functioning polarizer. Then he crawled through the hull once more, and again he found a sealed entrance to the fuel tube. He did not let himself think about it. His mind was numb already, and he pushed himself through uncaring.

This time it was worse than ever before; he had not dreamed that it could be so bad. His vision dimmed and he could barely see the exit, or feel its pressure, when he dragged himself out. Lurching drunkenly, he passed a scanning wave on his way to the hull sphincter, and heard the Captain's voice explode.

Outside, ragged black patches obscured his vision of the stars. The pressure inside him pressed painfully outward, again and again, and each time he held it back. Then he felt rather than saw that he was over the pale disk, and, as he let go the bolt, he lost consciousness.

When his vision cleared, the alien ship was still above him, alarmingly close. The Captain must have had it almost reeled in again, he thought, when he had let go that last charge.

Flaming, it receded into the Great Deep, and he watched it go until it disappeared.

He felt a great peace and a great weariness. The tiny blue disk that was a planet had moved its apparent position a little nearer its star. The aliens were going back there, to their unimaginable home, and Tommy's ship was forging onward into new depths of darkness—toward the edge of the Galaxy and the greatest Deep.

He moved to the nearest sphincter as the cold bit at him. His spirits lifted suddenly as he thought of those three stabs of energy, equally spaced around the twelve-mile perimeter of the ship. The Captain would be utterly speechless with rage, he thought, like an aged martinet who had had his hands painfully slapped by a small boy.

For, as we warned you, the Captain was not precisely a captain, nor the ship precisely a ship. Ship and captain were one and the same, hive and queen bee, castle and lord.

In effect, Tommy had circumnavigated the skipper.

THE LAST WORD

The first word, I like to think, was "Ouch." Some cave man, trying to knock a stone into better shape with another stone, slipped, hit his thumb—and there you are. Language.

I have an affection for these useless and unverifiable facts. Take the first dog. He, I feel sure, was an unusually clever but cowardly wolf, who managed to terrorize early man into throwing him a scrap. Early man himself was a terrible coward. Man and wolf discovered that they could hunt together, in their cowardly fashion, and there you are again. "Domesticated animals."

I admit that I was lax during the first few thousand years. By the time I realized that Man needed closer supervision, many of the crucial events had already taken place. I was then a young—well, let us say a young fallen angel. Had I been older and more experienced, history would have turned out very differently.

There was that time when I happened across a young Egyptian and his wife sitting on a stone near the bank of the Nile. They looked glum; the water was rising. A hungry jackal was not far away, and it crossed my mind that if I distracted the young people's attention for a few minutes, the jackal might surprise them.

"High enough for you?" I asked agreeably, pointing to the water.

They looked at me rather sharply. I had put on the appearance of a human being, as nearly as possible, but the illusion was no good without a large cloak, which was odd for the time of year.

The man said, "If it never got any higher, it would suit me."

"Why, I'm surprised to hear you say that," I replied. "If the river didn't rise, your fields wouldn't be so fertile—isn't that right?"

"True," said the man, "but also if it didn't rise, my fields would still be my fields." He showed me where the water was carrying away his fences. "Every year we argue over the boundaries, after the flood, and this year my neighbor has a cousin living with him. The cousin is a big, unnecessarily muscular man." Broodingly, he began to draw lines in the dirt with a long stick.

These lines made me a little nervous. The Sumerians, up north, had recently discovered the art of writing, and I was still suffering from the shock.

"Well, life is a struggle," I told the man soothingly. "Eat or be eaten. Let the strong win, and the weak go to the wall."

The man did not seem to be listening. "If there was some way," he said, staring at his marks, "that we could keep tally of the fences, and put them back exactly the way they were before—"

"Nonsense," I interrupted. "You're a wicked boy to suggest such a thing. What would your old dad say? Whatever was good enough for him . . ."

All this time, the woman had not spoken. Now she took the long stick out of the man's hand and examined it curiously. "But why not?" she said, pointing to the lines in the dirt. The man had drawn an outline roughly like that of his fields, with the stone marking one corner.

It was at that moment that the jackal charged. He was gaunt and desperate, and his jaws were full of sharp yellow teeth.

With the stick she was holding, the woman hit him over the snout. The jackal ran away, howling piteously.

"Tut," I said, taken aback. "Life is struggle. . . ."

The woman said a rude word, and the man came at me with a certain light in his eye, so I went away. And do you know, when I came back after the next flood, they were measuring off the fields with ropes and poles?

Cowardice again—that man did not want to argue about the boundaries with his neighbor's muscular cousin. Another lucky accident, and there you are. Geometry.

If only I had had the foresight to send a cave bear after the first man who showed that original, lamentable spark of curiosity . . . Well, it was no use wishing. Not even I could turn the clock back.

Oh, I gained a few points as time went on. Instead of trying to suppress the inventive habit, I learned to direct it along useful lines. I was instrumental in teaching the Chinese how to make gunpowder. (Seventy-five parts saltpeter, thirteen parts brimstone, twelve parts charcoal, if you're interested. But the grinding and mixing are terribly difficult; they never would have worked it out by themselves.) When they used it only for fireworks, I didn't give up; I introduced it again in Europe. Patience was my long suit. I never took offense. When Luther threw an inkwell at me, I was not discouraged. I persevered.

I did not worry about my occasional setbacks; it was my successes that threatened to overthrow me. After each of my wars, there was an impulse that drew men closer together. Little groups fought each other until they formed bigger groups; then the big groups fought each other until there was only one left.

I had played this game out over and over, with the Egyptians, the Persians, the Greeks, and, in the end, I had destroyed every one. But I knew the danger. When the last two groups spanned the world between them, the last war might end in universal peace, because there would be no one left to fight.

My final war would have to be fought with weapons so devastating, so unprecedentedly awful, that man would never recover from it.

It was.

On the fifth day, riding the gale, I could look down on a planet stripped of its forests, its fields, even its topsoil: there was nothing left but the bare, riven rock, cratered like the moon. The sky shed a sickly purple light, full of lightnings that flickered like serpents' tongues. Well, I had paid a heavy price, but Man was gone.

Not quite. There were two left, a man and a woman. I found them alive and healthy, for the time being, on a crag that overhung the radioactive ocean. They were inside a transparent dome, or field of force, that kept out the contaminated air.

You see how near I had come to final defeat? If they had managed to distribute that machine widely before my war started . . . But this was the only one they had made. And there they were inside it, like two white mice in a cage.

They recognized me immediately. The woman was young and comely, as they go.

"This is quite an ingenious device," I told them courteously. In actuality, it was an ugly thing, all wires and tubes and so on, packed layers deep under the floor, with a big semicircular control board and a lot of flashing lights. "It's a pity I didn't know about it earlier; we might have put it to some use."

"Not this one," said the man grimly. "This is a machine for peace. Just incidentally, it generates a field that will keep out an atomic explosion."

"Why do you say, 'just incidentally'?" I asked him.

"It's only the way he talks," the woman said. "If you had held off another six months, we might have beaten you. But now I suppose you think you've won."

"Oh, indeed," I said. "That is, I will have, before long. Meanwhile, we might as well make ourselves comfortable."

They were standing in tense, aggressive attitudes in front of the control board, and took no notice of my suggestion. "Why do you say I 'think' I've won?" I asked.

"It's just the way I talk. Well, at least we gave you a long fight of it."

The man put in, "And now you're brave enough to show yourself." He had a truculent jaw. There had been a good many like him in the assault planes, on the first day of the war.

"Oh," I said, "I've been here all the time."

"From the very beginning?" the woman asked.

I bowed to her. "Almost," I said, to be strictly fair.

There was a little silence, one of those uncomfortable pauses that interrupt the best of talks. A tendril of glowing spray sprang up just outside. After a moment, the floor settled slightly.

The man and woman looked anxiously at their control board. The colored lights were flashing. "Is that the accumulators?" I heard the woman ask in a strained, low voice.

"No," the man answered. "They're all right—still charging. Give them another minute."

The woman turned to me. I was glad of it, because there was something about their talk together that disturbed me. She said, "Why couldn't you let things alone? Heaven knows we weren't perfect, but we weren't that bad. You didn't have to make us do that to each other."

I smiled. The man said slowly, "Peace would have poisoned him. He would have shriveled up like a dried apple." It was the truth, or near enough, and I did not contradict him. The floor lurched again.

"You're waiting to watch us suffer," the woman said. "Aren't you?"

I smiled.

"But that may take a long time. Even if we fall into the ocean, this globe will keep us alive. We might be in here for months before our food gives out."

"I can wait," I said pleasantly.

She turned to her husband. "Then we *must* be the last," she said. "Don't you see? If we weren't, would he be here?"

"That's right," said the man, with a note in his voice that I did not like. He bent over the control board. "There's nothing more to keep us here. Ava, will you . . ." He stepped back, indicating a large red-handled switch.

The woman stepped over and put her hand on it. "One moment," I said uneasily. "What are you doing? What is that thing?"

She smiled at me. "This isn't just a machine to generate a force field," she said.

"No?" I asked. "What else?"

"It's a time machine," the man said.

"We're going back," the woman whispered, "to the beginning."

Back, to the beginning, to start all over.

Without me.

The woman said, "You've won Armageddon, but you've lost Earth."

I knew the answer to that, of course, but she was a woman and had the last word.

I gestured toward the purple darkness outside. "Lost Earth? What do you call this?"

She poised her hand on the switch.

"Hell," she said.

And I have remembered her voice, through ten thousand lonely years.